> **I** always heat up so easily, and I'm always asking myself why because it makes me so vulnerable. Is everyone else this easy? Maybe it's no good to be so easy, no good at all. But of course I want it. I can't possibly tell myself I don't want it. Then, as I'm thinking about this, I feel her hands unbuckling my belt to get my jeans down. "Come on, do it," she says. And she steps back, steps away from me to begin stripping her clothes off.

AFFINITIES

RACHEL PEREZ

MASQUERADE BOOKS, INC.
801 SECOND AVENUE
NEW YORK, N.Y. 10017

Affinities
Copyright © 1993 by Rachel Perez
All Rights Reserved

No part of this book may be reproduced, stored in a retrieval system, or transmitted in any form, by any means, including mechanical, electronic, photocopying, recording or otherwise, without prior written permission of the publishers.

First Masquerade Edition 1993

First printing August 1993

ISBN 1-56333-113-6

Cover Photograph © 1993 by Richard Kern

Cover Design by Julie Miller

Manufactured in the United States of America
Published by Masquerade Books, Inc.
801 Second Avenue
New York, N.Y. 10017

AFFINITIES

ANGELA	7
CHERYL	19
DELORA	31
EVELYN	45
FRANKIE	53
ILENE	65
ISOBEL	97
JAMIE	109
LINDA	121
MARCY	153
MARGOT	165
MEREDITH	175
STEVIE	187
VERNA	203

ANGELA

Kelsy had a liking for cool upper-class blondes, the long-legged girls from Lake Forest and Winnetka who came into the city to cruise the lesbian bars on Halsted looking for breathless ecstasies. Kelsy thought of them as icebergs that needed melting, these girls with a quiet demeanor and so much under the surface; girls who hadn't come out and maybe wouldn't ever come out because they'd settle for a safe marriage to a safe income in a safe suburb.

Angela was from Lake Forest, but when Kelsy met her Angela was living in the city. Angela was twenty-five, with blue eyes and shoulder-length blonde hair and the fine bones that some people called "aristocratic." Kelsy didn't care about aristocratic one way or the other; all she cared about was melting them down to the essentials.

They met at a raucous political meeting organized

by one of the militant lesbian groups, an unlikely place to find women like Angela. At first Kelsy judged Angela to be merely another lipstick dyke; pretty enough as a femme to be intimidating, but maybe not worth the effort because she looked too satisfied with herself. It was no good when they looked too satisfied. There had to be enough uncertainty in their eyes to make the chances of success at least possible. Usually, when they looked too satisfied, it meant they were already with someone, in some kind of relationship no matter how screwed up it might be; and when that was true, a seduction became more work than pleasure.

But Kelsy kept looking at Angela, and Kelsy gradually became more and more interested. They made eye contact a few times, the contact enduring enough to give Kelsy the idea that this cool-looking blonde might not be so difficult. She had the northern suburbs all over her, from the way she had her hair done to the jewelry and clothes. Only her presence at the meeting meant anything; only her presence revealed a dyke-in-the-closet suburban girl. And the way she stared at Kelsy meant that she liked Kelsy's type; the no-nonsense butch look with a mix of denim and black suede that made Kelsy appear risky. Made her appear like she'd call the shots. If they needed a butch who called the shots, Kelsy was definitely what they were looking for.

After a while, Kelsy decided to make an approach. You take no chances in this world, you get nothing back from it. So, after the meeting ended, she walked over to the tall blonde and said, "You must be new—I haven't seen you around."

As if Kelsy knew every dyke in the city. The blonde looked impassive. "I haven't seen you either."

"My name's Kelsy."

"And mine's Angela." They talked casually, but Angela remained as cool as ever.

After a while, Kelsy thought maybe there was nothing here, no chance for anything. "Look, I won't bother you if you don't want to be bothered."

But Angela said it was no bother at all, and when Kelsy suggested that they have coffee somewhere, Angela looked at her a long moment and then nodded. The eyes told it all—the understanding between them in the eyes—and an hour later, Kelsy was in Angela's Lake Shore Drive high-rise apartment.

Angela said, "I just moved in here a few months ago. Would you like some coffee."

"I'd like a kiss instead." The blonde smiled and stepped forward, and Kelsy kissed her.

As the kiss ended, Kelsy slid her hands down Angela's back to stroke Angela's ass.

Angela leaned backward. "What now?"

"Now the bedroom."

"All right." Kelsy walked behind Angela with her eyes on Angela's hips and the sleek lines of Angela's long legs beneath the hem of the short dress.

Angela had a large round bed. Kelsy said, "I'm impressed."

Angela gave her a thin smile. "I thought you'd like it."

"Where are you from? You're not a city girl."

"Lake Forest."

"That figures."

"What does that mean?"

"Nothing at all."

"Anyway, I'm glad you like the bed." Kelsy liked the bed, the room, the building and above all, she liked Angela. She took the blonde in her arms and kissed her, this time closing a hand over one of Angela's breasts and squeezing it gently through her sweater.

"Why don't you get undressed while I watch?" Kelsy said. "I'd like to have a bath first."

"A bath?"

"Just give me ten minutes." Kelsy shrugged. "Is there another bathroom?"

"Down the hall." Then Angela turned and she walked into the bathroom and closed the door.

Ice cold, Kelsy thought. Now she wondered what it would take to melt Angela down. She looked at the round bed and she wondered how it would go on that bed. She ached to have Angela's body in her arms again.

Kelsy was happy to find a shower in the bathroom down the hall. She stripped naked, stepped in, and had ten minutes under a steaming spray without getting much of her hair wet. After she dried her body, she wrapped herself in a huge towel and returned to the bedroom. Angela was still in the bathroom.

Kelsy was about to climb onto the huge round bed, when the bathroom door suddenly opened and Angela came out. The blonde wore a fluffy white robe. She had her hair tied back, revealing her lovely high cheekbones. She smiled softly and said, "How was the bath?"

Kelsy dropped her towel. "I had a shower." Kelsy stood there while Angela looked at her body. "You look very athletic," Angela said finally. "I do body building."

"Oh." Kelsy laughed. "Maybe you don't like it. Here, look at this." And she flexed her biceps, both arms lifted, the muscles bulging.

A flush came to Angela's face. "You must be very strong."

"If you get the robe off, you can come over here and find out."

Angela opened her robe and dropped it. She had a long-boned body, small jutting breasts and sleek hips and thighs. Her love triangle was a wispy blonde tuft that hardly covered anything. Her creamy skin looked as smooth as ivory. When she came forward, Kelsy took her in her arms immediately and kissed her again.

"You excite me," Kelsy whispered. "I may not be any good at this."

"We'll find out, won't we? Come on, let's get on the bed." But first Angela walked over to the wall to touch a switch that changed the lighting to a soft pink. "Is this all right?"

Kelsy chuckled. "I love it." She climbed onto the bed and slipped under the covers. "Dreamland. Come on, hurry and get over here."

Angela came to the bed and leaned forward to lift the covers, her breasts swinging, the perfect pinkish-brown nipples still soft. Kelsy's excitement increased as she looked at her. After Angela slipped under the covers, they lay on their sides facing each other.

"Hello," Kelsy said.

Angela smiled. "Hello."

Kelsy had one of her arms underneath Angela, the other arm outside the cover. The blonde was completely covered, her arms hidden, and then suddenly Kelsy was pleasantly surprised as she felt Angela's hand on her belly, Angela's fingers tentatively sliding into the upper part of Kelsy's pubic triangle.

Angela said, "When I first saw you, I thought you'd be shaved."

Kelsy chuckled. "Why?"

"I don't know. I suppose you look the type—that's all."

"Sorry, if that's what you like."

"No, it doesn't matter." Kelsy deliberately avoided

touching her. Not yet. Then suddenly Kelsy pushed the covers down, all the way down until both their bodies were exposed.

Kelsy gazed down at Angela's blonde tuft. "I'm glad you're not shaved. I like it better this way."

"I kept it shaved for years."

"No, it's better this way." Now Kelsy touched Angela's thigh. She slid her hand up and down, teasing Angela by avoiding her pussy. The ice-cool lipstick lez with a blonde pussy. With a sigh, Angela turned to lie on her back.

"Why don't you make love to me?" Angela said.

Her asking for it like that excited Kelsy immensely. "Sure, baby."

She moved down the bed to kneel between Angela's legs. Again, Kelsy felt a strong urge to melt the ice. She leaned over Angela and slid her hands up and down Angela's legs. The pink light made Angela's creamy skin look even more delicious. Angela closed her eyes as Kelsy slowly stroked the insides of her legs. Angela opened her thighs wider, looking at Kelsy now to watch what she did. The blonde's face was impassive, which annoyed Kelsy, because Angela looked as though she were evaluating Kelsy's performance.

Silly bitch from Lake Forest, Kelsy thought. But with a sweet looking blonde pussy.

Kelsy was hot, feeling her own pussy heating up. She slid her hands up to Angela's breasts. The nipples were only half-extended. Kelsy jiggled the breasts with her fingers, and Angela appeared to breathe more heavily.

What did she like? What did she want? What would it take to make her scream?

Kelsy sensed the blonde's growing excitement, but it was too slow. She took the blonde's nipples between her fingers, rolled them, and pulled them outward. She pushed Angela's breasts together, played with them as Angela lay there inert with her hands at her sides. Angela would obviously remain passive while everything was done to her. Kelsy wasn't bothered by that, but it made her more determined than ever to melt the ice. She leaned back now to have a better look at Angela's crotch. The sparse blonde tuft stood up on the plump little mound. There was very little hair along the outer lips. The inner flaps were still hidden, even with her legs apart. The outer lips were a delicate light brown, almost pink, and not a sign of juice visible. Leaning forward, Kelsy touched the closed slit with her fingertips.

Angela made a sound of pleasure. Kelsy fondled Angela's breasts again, and then she bent her head to kiss a nipple. First one nipple and then the other. She kissed downward to Angela's belly. She skipped over the tuft to kiss Angela's inner thighs. She moved her lips with deliberate slowness, teasing Angela, grazing her skin to melt the ice. The blonde's body smelled of bath powder, a delicious smell that excited Kelsy.

But there was no scent of a hot pussy. Kelsy liked it when she could smell the desire in a girl, that hot smell that confirmed her skill. Kelsy now shifted her face forward to press her lips against the closed slit.

Angela gave a slight jerk, another sound of pleasure in her throat. The blonde moved her legs farther apart and drew her knees upward and to each side, her knees bowed out as she offered her cunt to Kelsy.

As Kelsy looked at it, the slit opened a bit, but not much. Some cunts opened easily, and some didn't. Kelsy backed up a little more to have a better look at the delicate coloring. She ran her thumbs along the almost hairless outer lips, rubbing gently up and down, wiggling them open until she could see the first sign of wetness inside. The pink in there seemed darker. Now she opened the outer lips completely to look at everything.

Angela still had her hands at her sides, no movement of her body, no sound from her mouth. She remained the ice blonde, inert and lifeless.

Time for the feast, Kelsy thought. She dropped her face, extended her tongue, and ran it lightly up and down the outer lips, then up and down between the outer lips and the inner lips.

Angela stirred a little and uttered a soft, almost inaudible moan.

Kelsy's tongue fluttered against the slit between the small lips. She slid her tongue into the groove, twisting her head, opening the small lips by using her tongue as a wedge.

Angela moaned again, this time with a slight lifting of her pelvis that encouraged Kelsy. She liked it better when they made noise and moved around. Such a delicate pussy this one had, a pussy that hardly smelled like a cunt. But Kelsy had known them as passive as this one. An Arctic pussy. Hell, she'd bet Eskimo women were as hot as blazes. Not like blondes from Lake Forest. Her tongue stroked up and down the inner groove, teasing Angela's clitoris, worrying the clit that was like a tiny pink pearl half-hidden by its cowl. Kelsy paid more attention to the labia now, her tongue working around the apex and then down to the opening, around the hole and then inside it with her tongue tip fluttering wildly in the tight pussy. Angela's hips moved slightly as Kelsy worked her tongue inside, in and out of the opening.

The blonde obviously liked it. She was whimpering now, which made Kelsy use more force. She fastened her mouth against Angela's cunt and sucked hard to pull some of the juice into her mouth. She felt a keen excitement as she swallowed the nectar. She could feel Angela heating up, but only slowly. She swabbed her tongue across Angela's clitoris again, and she thought that maybe the clit was swelling a bit. She tongued it now, pressing her lips around it, and then sucking it between her teeth. She dug her mouth into the soft flesh and continued sucking.

Angela's thighs moved, her knees rocking. But it was obvious that the ice wasn't melted yet, and Kelsy was more determined than ever. Now she used her hands to lift Angela's ass. Angela groaned, breathing hard as Kelsy slid her mouth downward to flap her tongue at Angela's anus. An instant later, the blonde suddenly cried out and shook from head to toe. Kelsy was amused as she understood she'd reached the magic place, the key to Angela's arousal.

Lake Forest girl who likes it nasty. "Roll over," Kelsy said. Angela groaned as she bounced out of Kelsy's hands to lie on her belly. Kelsy took hold of the blonde's hips and raised them, lifted her pretty ass and then pushed her thighs wide apart so she was now kneeling with her head down and her rear in the air, her sweet cunt pouting, and above that her anus appearing pink and dainty. The groove between Angela's buttocks looked virginal and perfect. With a low growl, Kelsy leaned forward to push her face into it, her tongue pressing against Angela's anus as Angela moaned and shook and cried out.

Now the blonde moved her body. She worked her ass, pressing herself back against Kelsy's face, moaning louder as Kelsy's tongue broke through the ring and began stroking in and out.

Melting the ice. Angela went wild as Kelsy tongued and tongued and tongued, working the tight orifice, Angela churning her ass around and around and then suddenly pulling away to roll over with her legs up and wide open.

"Get into me!" Angela cried. "Please get into me!"

"No, not yet. Open it first with your fingers. Come on, let me see you open it."

Angela groaned, blushed, and then did what Kelsy wanted. She slid a hand down to pry her cunt open.

Kelsy looked at it, the Lake Forest blonde lying there wide open.

"Use both hands," Kelsy said. Angela did what she wanted. She used the fingers of both hands to hold the lips apart. Now the pink interior of her cunt was completely revealed to Kelsy's eyes. The blonde's clitoris was swollen, visibly larger than previously.

Angela groaned. "Please do something!" Kelsy crawled up, slid over Angela's body at the same time as she pushed her fingers inside Angela's cunt. Two fingers inside Angela's vagina and her thumb on Angela's clitoris. Her fingers worked in and out, thrusting into the socket. Angela moaned, wild, hunching her pelvis upward as Kelsy kissed her mouth, possessed her mouth as her fingers possessed Angela's cunt. She kept her tongue deep in Angela's mouth as her fingers continued to fuck the now-dripping pussy.

Angela cried out as she came. Her heels drummed against Kelsy's thighs as her body jerked upward to meet Kelsy's fingers.

"Oh, God, don't stop!" Angela whimpered.

An hour later, Kelsy walked out of the high-rise into the cold March air and bitter wind on Lake Shore Drive. The doorman asked whether she wanted a taxi, and she nodded. The lake had some ice on it, but upstairs on the fifteenth floor where she'd come from, all the ice was melted. Kelsy chuckled and thought that was fitting. She still had the taste of pussy in her mouth, and she thought that was fitting, too. She tipped the doorman a dollar, climbed into the taxi, and went home.

CHERYL

The morning is the time that gives me the greatest sense of fulfillment. In the morning I feel more relaxed than at other times, so I accept everything without a struggle, accept Sabrina and everything we do together. I just let things happen. The pleasure washes over me, first in my head and then down into my sex. One minute I curl up like a lazy kitten, and the next minute I need to do things, anything, pleasure Sabrina in order to be certain she wants me, anything she wants, always anything Sabrina wants....

Last night the building's air-conditioning went out, and we had a difficult time sleeping. Sabrina tossed around all night and so did I, and at dawn I awakened with a pool of sweat between my breasts and under my arms. Now I'm lying at the foot of the bed like a perfect slave, my body twisted between

Sabrina's legs as I suck her cunt like an infant sucking at a breast.

She's always musky in the morning, the smell of her cunt like a ripe jungle. I put my nose in it. Then I pull my nose out and I push my thumb inside. She moves her thighs against my face. She has both knees up, and of course she's not sleeping anymore now that I've started this. But she does nothing to acknowledge me, no more than a slight movement of her thighs from side to side. I put my nose in it again. I know she likes that because she told me so. Sabrina is not in the least secretive about what she likes. She's not like some of the others. She always tells me what she likes and what she doesn't like, and maybe that's the reason I have the feeling things are coming to an end between us. Maybe it's time; nothing can last forever, can it? I don't want it to end, but maybe it's time. I have a sense that Sabrina will soon tell me it's over. She'll find some reason to throw me out. Or maybe she won't need any reason at all; she'll just do it.

Now my nose is inside her good and deep, and I'm sure she's feeling it. Of course I have to breathe through my mouth while I'm doing this, which means she's also feeling my breath on her anus. She's very sensitive there, but she never likes me to touch it unless she asks for it.

Her cunt is soupy, dark, lush, running rivulets of juice around my nose. The middle of August is such a rotten time for the air-conditioning to go out. I'm sweating again. I wonder what she's thinking now. Sometimes I have the fear she's not even paying attention to me when I suck her like this. She didn't ask for it—not directly, anyway. Maybe she'll slam me for not waiting until she asked for it. All she did was pull her knees up, and when I saw her do that, I scooted down on the bed to get my face between her thighs. She ought to kick me for it. I really like it best when she makes me do what she wants and not what I want. She knows that, so maybe she's not kicking me away now as a way of punishing me. If she looks down at me, I'll look back at her in order to get her annoyed. If I get her annoyed enough, she might show her anger by kicking me away and then making me beg to be allowed to eat her again.

Now she says, "Move it, pussycat." God, I love it when she calls me that! I get a long shiver down my spine, from the back of my skull right down to my tail-bone. I start moving, grinding my nose around in her cunt, rubbing her clitoris and stretching her vaginal opening, and blowing hot breath on her ass. I keep my nose deep inside her hole and do everything she taught me, everything she likes me to do. She starts heaving, bouncing her ass up and down so hard I have to hold on tight to keep my face in place. She comes fast and hard as she always does, pumping it at me, fucking my face with her cunt without making a sound, saying nothing, no crying out, no verbal sign of pleasure at all. The juice pours out of her like a faucet, drenching my face, and then, when she finishes, she kicks me away so hard I almost fall off the bed.

I lie there at the foot of the bed like a bewildered kitten. I'm afraid to look at her, afraid I'll see her looking bored, afraid I'll see her ignoring me again.

"Get a towel," she says. I hurry off to the bathroom. I bring back a towel and I climb on the bed again and start wiping away the mess on the insides of her thighs. When I glance at her face, I find her watching me with a lazy look that can mean anything. Now I'm praying she was pleased by the way I sucked her off, pleased enough not to leave me alone today. It's Saturday, and when she wants to punish me on Saturday, she goes off somewhere and she leaves me alone in the apartment. I hate that.

Sabrina says, "Is the coffee ready?"

I nod. "I've been up for an hour. Do you want your coffee now?"

"You don't need to ask that. You know I want my coffee." I feel myself blushing, the heat in my face, my heart pounding. I toss the towel on a chair and I hurry off the bed again.

But she stops me. "You're not wearing the heels."

"I forgot."

"Put them on." I hop to the closet to find the cute little Italian mules she bought for me yesterday. She likes looking at my legs, but I think my legs are ugly. They're not straight, and they're not long enough to be elegant. I wish I had Sabrina's legs. I put the heels on and I almost fall because the heels are high enough to make me unsteady on the carpet. I'm not wearing anything else—just the heels, my breasts drooping, my nipples stiff because I'm still excited. No, I'm excited all over again because of the way Sabrina is looking at me. I do a turn to show her my ass and my legs in the high heels. When I look at her again, she nods, and now I hurry away to the kitchen to get her coffee.

I don't know how old Sabrina is. Maybe she's forty-five, but she won't tell me. She has black hair, black enough so that sometimes I think it's dyed. I don't know about that either, because if it's dyed, she gets it done by a hairdresser. She's not thin; she has large soft breasts and round hips. When she's dressed for work, she looks authoritative, efficient, reliable. For the past five years she's been an assistant vice-president in the trust department of a large Chicago bank. She says the man she works for is due to retire soon, and when that happens she expects to get his job. That will make her the youngest vice-president in the bank and it's something she badly wants. Sabrina has an MBA from Harvard and she's smart, but when she's out of the office she plays tough. We met the first time in a lesbian bar on Halsted, and I was turned on to her immediately because of the heavy way she spiked me. After we'd known each other only five or ten minutes, I had a great rush when she whispered in my ear and said she wanted to fist-fuck me until I screamed. She took me home in a taxi, and that's exactly what she did. Three days later I moved in and now it's been almost two years.

I went to a shrink once when I was in college, a small woman with dark eyes and a New York accent, and she told me I'd always be an easy conquest for any woman who showed authority. After that the shrink fucked me with her fist. She had a small hand and she was able to get all of it inside me without too much trouble. That was the first time I'd ever had it, and it made me a little crazy. Sabrina does it to me often, but she has large hands and sometimes she hurts me. When I see her smearing olive oil on her hand, I know I'm going to get it, and I always start trembling. She does other things, too—things that hurt much more—but it's the fist inside me that always frightens me because I worry I might get damaged. I don't know if I'm being silly. I've talked to other slaves about it, but no one knows anyone who has been hurt by it. Not by fist-fucking in the cunt, anyway. Gynecologists stick their whole hands in there, don't they? Having it in the ass is something else. I've never had that, and I'm certain that if anyone did it, I'd pass out.

Sabrina likes red. She likes red silk blouses and red lipstick that matches the color of the blouse. She never wears much jewelry, even when we go to a party together. I'm the one who has to dress up. She chooses all my clothes and sometimes when we go out, she takes an endless time making up her mind what I should wear. She likes me to be as feminine as possible. She says she could never be serious with a girl who didn't have long hair. In the beginning she told me it was my hair that attracted her. But then later on she said it was my eyes. She said I have soft eyes. Sabrina's eyes are always carefully made up. She has dark eyes that turn beautiful when she gets angry. I'm always proud to walk with her, to be with her whenever she goes somewhere. I'm proud that people know I'm with Sabrina.

We have a simple lunch, a cottage cheese and tomato salad and rye toast. Then Sabrina tells me that an old friend of hers will be arriving soon, a woman named Billie. She hints that many years ago she and Billie were lovers, and of course that makes me curious and eager to meet Billie. I always want to know things about Sabrina; I want to know everything about her. But then she says wouldn't it be nice if when Billie arrives I play the part of a Roman slave and serve the drinks naked?

"Wouldn't that be nice?" Sabrina says. She looks amused, wicked, teasing me with slight smile.

"If that's what you want."

"Yes, that's what I want." She says she wants me in heels and with lipstick on my nipples. "Not too dark. We'll find the right color."

My cunt is already dripping because it's obvious I'm in for it. In the bedroom Sabrina chooses a pair of spike heels for me, and then she rummages in a box with lipstick tubes until she finds the shade she wants. She sits on the bench in front of the dressing table and makes me stand in front of her while she applies the lipstick. She holds one of my breasts in her hand, squeezing the nipple out as she paints it carefully. Then she does the other one. "There, that's better," she says. "Now down here also."

She wants my labia painted. She makes me raise one leg, and as my foot rests on the bench beside her, she starts applying the lipstick to make the inner lips more red than pink. Of course I get turned on immediately, and now I'm fearful I'll gush juice on her fingers. Sabrina makes it worse by deliberately teasing my clitoris, slowly rubbing the shaft with a fingertip until I close my eyes and moan as I feel the tip standing out.

"Poor little pussycat," she says. "But you can't have anything yet. Not until I say so."

"I need to pee."

"Go on, then, but don't smear the lipstick. I'll have a look at it when you come back."

What she really wants is to make sure I don't masturbate in the bathroom. I know Sabrina. She's not satisfied unless she has total control over me. When I'm in the bathroom, I don't lock the door because that's the rule. But I listen until I hear Sabrina in the kitchen, and then I carefully pull at the top of my cunt with my fingers to get my clitoris exposed, get the painted lips apart enough so I can rub the shaft without smearing anything. It doesn't take much. I haven't had anything all day, and in a few moments the orgasm is bursting out of me and my knees are shaking. After that I piss and then carefully wipe myself without smearing the lipstick. I toss the wad of toilet paper into the bowl, flush the toilet, and hurry back to Sabrina in the kitchen.

"Let's have a look," she says. When I raise one leg, she takes a good look at my cunt and she frowns. "You jerked off in there."

"No, I didn't."

"You're a liar, Cheryl. Don't worry, I'll fix you for it. Turn around and bend over."

"Please, Sabrina ..."

"I said, 'Turn around.'" I turn around. I know the routine and I'm already trembling, already humiliated because my being naked is not enough for her, she wants this also. I hear her open the refrigerator. Without being told, I bend forward and then reach behind me to pull my buttocks apart. In a moment I feel it, the point of the cold wet carrot sliding inside my ass.

"It's got some green on the end," Sabrina says. "It's pretty."

Billie is blonde. When she comes in and she sees me standing naked in the living room, she rolls her eyes at Sabrina. "You're at it again, huh? I see you've got a new dolly."

Before long I discover Sabrina has told Billie she has a surprise for her, and I'm the surprise. Billie is not only gay, she's also a toro; big shoulders, big breasts, a way of walking that makes you imagine she just got off a horse. I find out she's from Texas, but she's been in New York so long she's lost the drawl. She keeps looking at my nipples and at my cunt whenever she can see something. Sabrina tells me to turn around, and when Billie sees the carrot in my ass she snickers and tells Sabrina how much she envies her because I'm such a pretty piece. I serve them Black Russians, shaking my ass as I move back and forth on my high heels. I'm so hot now, I'm sure I'm dripping down the insides of my thighs. It's been sometime since I've been in a situation like this, and the heat hits me right in the belly and erupts up and down to make me burn all over.

AFFINITIES

For a while nothing happens, except I get looked at. Sabrina mentions the lipstick to Billie, and of course Billie wants a peek at it. So I have to get near them and raise one leg to show Billie my painted cunt. I can almost smell her turning on as she looks at me. She's a real bull. I bet if she had the chance, she'd pull the carrot out of my ass and fill me up with a long tongue while she pinches the hell out of my breasts. But she does her best to act sweet. She tells Sabrina how pretty I am, what a pretty slave, what pretty tits, what a pretty little cunt down there. She wants to know why Sabrina doesn't have me shave it clean. "She'd look adorable."

Sabrina laughs. "Would you like to fuck her?"

Billie seems flustered. She's known Sabrina long enough to realize that Sabrina doesn't give away her girls that easily. "You mean it?"

"She's been a bad girl. She needs a fist." I feel faint; the room starts to swim around me. "Sabrina, please …"

"Shut up, bitch."

"Oh, boy," Billie says. Her eyes are wide, expectant, happy because she's going to get something.

They take me to the bedroom. Now I clearly understand that Sabrina intends to throw me out soon. Otherwise she wouldn't do this. It's one thing to let one of her friends put her hands on me, feel me up a little. I'm a slave, and that's understandable. But fist-fucking is something else; fist-fucking by anyone but Sabrina is the ultimate abandonment because for two years I've had only Sabrina's hand inside me. Even if she hurts me sometimes, I've learned to trust her. Billie is a stranger, and I know hardly anything about her. Is she mean? I keep looking at her hands, gauging them, sizing them up, wondering whether she'll hurt me deliberately.

Sabrina tells me to get on the bed, and I when I do it, I roll over on my back and watch them carefully. I start trembling again the moment I see Billie smearing the olive oil over one of her hands. She looks at me and smiles. "Don't worry, honey. You're going to love it."

So she says. Sabrina seems amused. She goes to a chair near the window and sits down to watch. I lie back with one arm over my eyes, feeling helpless, resigning myself to it. Then I look at Billie again and I see that she's stripped off her blouse and bra. Her huge breasts swing from side to side as she approaches me. She wants to play a little first. She holds one of her mammoth tits with two hands and tells me to suck it. "It'll help you relax," she says.

I take the fat nipple in my mouth and discover it tastes of olive oil. I want to spit the nipple out, but I'm afraid she'll get annoyed and do something to hurt me later on. So instead I suck the nipple like a baby, tugging it with my lips, watching her face to see whether she likes it. After a while, she pulls the breast out of my mouth and feeds me the other one. I gorge myself on it, opening my mouth wide as she stuffs more and more tit down my throat.

"Oh, she's a sweetie," Billie says to Sabrina. Then, at last, Billie is ready for me. She makes me pull my knees back and starts fiddling with my cunt. I feel her fingers doing things, pulling at the lips, pinching my clit, then two fingers inside me. The olive oil makes it pleasant, greasy, slippery, hardly any friction at all. She adds another finger. Then another. Now comes the difficult part. Her hand is moving, turning, twisting me open. I don't want to look at it because I'm afraid I'll start begging her to stop. Sabrina hates it when I act disobedient. I feel Billie pushing at me, her hand pushing, twisting. Then finally she mutters something and my cunt suddenly stretches and then closes down again on her wrist.

"Beautiful," Billie says. She has her whole fist inside me. Now I crane my neck and I look down at it, getting a rush as I see only her wrist sticking out of me. It's like a big fat cock stretching me wide open. I can feel her fingers fluttering around inside me, her fingertips rubbing the mouth of my uterus. She looks at my and she smiles. "Hang on, baby."

She starts moving her wrist. With her free hand, she pulls at the top of my clitoris to get the head out. She has her whole hand moving, her wrist sliding back and forth through the big hole between my legs. I'm crying, but is it the pain or the pleasure? I hear myself sobbing. I hear Billie laughing, then Sabrina laughing. Billie keeps doing me, her hand and wrist moving like a huge log spearing my body. When I look at her arm, I see the muscles in it. She has her sleeve rolled up, and the muscles in her arm ripple as she does me. She pinches my clit, and I come again. I rock my legs, my head back, my mouth open, choking on my tears.

Then I see Sabrina walking toward me. She comes close to the bed and looks down at me. Billie still has her fist up my cunt, working it in and out. Suddenly Sabrina says something about me making too much noise, and she slams my face with her hand. She hits me again and again, slamming my face while Billie continues fucking me with her fist.

Sabrina asks Billie whether she wants a dolly, because if she wants a dolly, she can have me—she's kicking me out on Monday. "She's a piece of shit," Sabrina says.

Billie says no thanks, she won't live with a dolly because it's too much trouble. "No dogs and no dollies."

Rachel Perez

I start crying, and Sabrina hits me again. My cunt is numb. My whole face is one big lump of pain. I think I'm bleeding inside. I'm bleeding inside my brain.

DELORA

In the afternoon Susan decided she had too much sun on her desk and she proposed to close the blinds. Some of the other girls in the office protested. They said they liked the sun—the winter had been so dreary and now thank God spring was here. None of them liked Susan anyway. The problem of the blinds finally had to be settled by the supervisor, Ms. Malvados, who came out of her office and said, "Enough screeching—we'll close half the blinds, and that's that. Is this entire accounts department to be paralyzed by bickering?"

The accounts department was on the second floor of the bank, and Ms. Malvados—Delora, as she liked the girls to call her—was in charge of it. There were six girls, each girl at her own desk, a water cooler and a copy machine and a long row of metal file cabinets whose drawers contained copies of everything that moved in or out of the office. The single most critical rule enforced by Delora was that copies be made of every scrap of paper that passed through her department. "We play it safe," she told the girls. "We always play it safe."

Delora was a brunette, well past forty, tall and stately, always dressed in conservative clothes, her sleek dark hair always pinned up and crowned with a tight chignon. She liked to wear small pearl earrings and bright red lipstick. Her grooming was always perfect, her makeup perfect, her nails perfect, every small detail exactly as she wanted it; all of this a great problem for Susan, because Susan was madly in love with Delora and Delora's apparent perfection made Susan desperate.

Susan, however, lived with it; not a word, not a gesture ever communicated to Delora. She watched Delora whenever she had the chance and she thought about Delora constantly.

Susan was twenty-four, unattached now after a disastrous two-year relationship with a neurotic social worker named Wilma who finished by telling Susan that she was too flighty, too interested in freaked-out dykes in chains and leather, too incapable of understanding what really counted in this world, especially how much a serious lesbian like Wilma could do for her if only Susan would focus on what was important. "You bore the hell out of me!" Wilma screamed, angered by the reality that it was Susan who had the lease for the apartment and therefore it would be Wilma who had to pack and leave.

Good riddance, Susan thought. She never cried when an affair ended. Her attitude was that if it had to end, it ended, and that was that. She hardly thought of Wilma anymore, except during an occasional lonely evening in her bed when a sexual memory involving Wilma would flash across her consciousness; a remembrance of Wilma naked, with those huge breasts swinging back and forth as she did a crazy little dance coming out of the shower, or Wilma huffing and puffing with her face between Susan's legs, huffing and puffing and complaining because Wilma always found it so difficult to get Susan to climax. She started calling Susan "the girl with the iron clit," and this Susan would not tolerate. Whenever Wilma said that, a bitter fight would follow.

Good riddance and the hell with Wilma. All Susan cared about these days was Delora Malvados. Susan suspected Delora was gay, but she had no proof of it; no clear indication, no distinct evidence. All Susan had was a feeling, but most often she told herself the feeling was nothing but wishful thinking because Delora was so definitely her type. Oh, yes. The most passionate entanglements experienced by Susan were always those with dominant women like Delora, the women dominating her completely, body and soul overwhelmed, and any individuality Susan had drowning in a sea of erotic chaos.

Delora knew about Susan because at the first interview Susan had with Delora, Susan had more or less revealed everything by explaining the reason she was still unmarried was that she preferred living with a woman. Delora hadn't batted an eye, showed no concern at all, no interest or scorn ever evident then or afterward; and of course this aloofness made Delora even more appealing to Susan, a gnawing challenge to Susan who had experienced enough success offering herself to dominant women to think that she might be successful again.

No matter that Delora gave her no encouragement, Susan would not give it up. She occupied her mind with fantasies, images of Delora's body, Delora's attitudes. During the working day, Delora's presence no more than twenty feet away in her private office, distracted Susan completely, and at night the obsession became even worse because there was no office routine to interfere, no paperwork on Susan's desk, nothing to prevent her mind from running wild with obsessive imaginings. Night after sweaty night Susan lay on her bed masturbating as she thought of Delora dressed, half-dressed, undressed, making love to another woman or making love to Susan or sometimes even making love to herself, the two women, one imagined and the other real, fingering themselves with identical movements of their hands until finally Susan exploded in a great volcanic orgasm.

One evening Susan was at her favorite bar, a place called Angie's, the room packed to the rafters with women, smoke, leather, vinyl, and a smell of feminine sweat. Susan sat alone at the bar, not at all happy to be alone, but satisfied that at least here there were others just as lonely as she was; women alone, women cruising, women out merely to be in a group of women like themselves, the bond of the underlying camaraderie almost palpable. Each time Susan came to Angie's, she hoped she would find someone interesting who would take her to bed. But this evening there were too many punk-looking women for her taste, too much cruelty in their eyes, and the few butch beauties in the place seemed already involved, already half-possessing someone on the dance floor or in the shadows of one of the booths where it was possible to kiss and fondle and even cry out in a climax without anyone seeming to care one way or the other.

Then suddenly, unexpectedly, Susan caught a glimpse of Delora Malvados.

Yes, it was she, all right, Delora over there on the other side of the dance floor, not dancing, merely standing there alone and watching the dancers—Delora, of all people, dressed like a confirmed butch in tight jeans and a red silk shirt and hardly any makeup, neither dress nor stockings nor high heels, nothing like what she wore at the office every day, even her lipstick looking subdued at that distance across the crowded room.

Susan was too shocked to do anything but stare, the idea of approaching Delora totally unthinkable. Half-turned away from the bar, Susan sat quivering as she watched Delora until eventually they made eye contact. Now at least Delora knew that Susan was there and maybe something would happen. Delora recognized her, of course, and the idea that something might indeed happen made Susan groan inside. Oh, Delora's dark eyes!

It took a while, but finally Delora walked around the dance floor and approached the bar where Susan sat trembling, waiting.

"An unexpected encounter," Delora said with a smirk. "Are you with anyone?"

Susan shook her head. She imagined that she could smell Delora's perfume. What was she wearing? Her pulse pounded as she gazed at Delora's blouse and discovered that she could see the points of Delora's nipples. "I'm here alone," Susan said.

"Surprised to see me here?"

"Yes."

"Well, you ought to be. I've never been here before. I don't like these places, but I heard about this one and I thought I'd try it. I think it's awful."

Susan thought of asking why, if that were true, was

Delora still here? But instead she said nothing, nodded acceptance when Delora offered to buy her a drink, closed her eyes a moment and resolved to get herself together enough to stop trembling. Since there was no place for Delora to sit, she rose and offered her stool to Delora, but Delora refused and made Susan sit on the stool again. "You're too pretty to stand," Delora said with a smile, an overt flirtation that caused Susan to start trembling again. The tension continued to build, but it lasted no more than ten minutes, for at the end of that time Delora took Susan's hand and led her out of the bar as though nothing in the world existed except the two of them.

Susan was afraid the bubble would pop, the dream splinter into shards of colored glass.

Delora had a car parked outside Angie's, a sleek gray Corvette that made Susan clench her teeth to avoid gasping like a teenage drugstore bimbo. She hadn't known this about Delora, nothing about a Corvette. She'd seen Delora once or twice in a dull Ford. Did she own two cars? Delora answered the question without Susan's asking it. "This one is for fun," Delora explained. "The problem is I don't get to use it often enough."

The inside of the car was all plush leather and deep comfort. Susan sat in the bucket passenger seat, wondering where they were going and afraid to ask, but Delora never bothered to start the motor. Instead, Delora leaned across the console that separated passenger and driver and she kissed Susan's mouth.

"I've been wanting to do that for a long time," Delora said. Susan said nothing, still feeling the touch of Delora's lips and wishing the console between them would disappear so she could throw herself in Delora's arms.

Then Delora said, "Don't you have anything to say?"

"I'm too afraid."

"Afraid of me?"

"Yes."

Delora chuckled. "Is it the bank? Forget about the bank. Right now we're just two dykes sitting in a car. Did you know about me?"

"No."

"But you know now, don't you? Listen, before this goes any further, it's not going to develop into anything important. I never mix my personal life and business life. Whatever happens tonight, it's just tonight and never again. Are you understanding me?"

"Yes."

"I hope so. When I saw you in the bar, I thought maybe I should ignore you and walk out. That would be one way to avoid trouble." She leaned closer to Susan and touched Susan's cheek. "But the problem is you're too fuckable."

Susan shuddered. "Do something to me."

"Like what?"

"I don't know, anything." Delora leaned across the console and kissed her again, this time sliding a hand down from Susan's shoulder to cover Susan's right breast and fondle it through the knitted tank top. Susan groaned against Delora's mouth as Delora pinched her nipple; and, as Susan's mouth opened, Delora's tongue quickly entered to explore everything within reach. The wet kiss demolished Susan completely, left her shaking and more than ever afraid to say something wrong and inadvertently ruin the moment.

"I'm also a little too old for you," Delora said.

"No, you're not."

"I can be very demanding."

"I don't care, that's what I want."

Delora sighed, her body turned so that she faced Susan.

"It's dark enough here and no one can see us. Why don't you lift the top and show me something?"

An instruction rather than a question. Delora already knew that Susan wore no bra under the tank top. Susan hesitated only a moment, and then she did what Delora wanted. She slowly lifted the bottom of the tank top until her breasts were revealed in the dim light like two silvery globes capped with tender points already stiff and tingling.

Delora leaned closer to Susan and stroked one breast with her fingertips, slowly, casually, around and around the breast and then out to the tumescent nipple. Holding the nipple between her thumb and forefinger and gently pulling it outward, Delora said, "We can go to my place if you want. Would you like that?"

Delora's apartment was like Delora; functional, uncluttered, and a great deal of red everywhere—the paintings on the walls, the framed posters, the red velvet sofa. Susan stood in Delora's living room, disbelieving she was actually there. She watched Delora fix drinks at the small bar. The stereo was already switched on, a Spanish dance of some kind performed by muted guitars.

Still at the bar, her back turned to Susan, Delora said, "I'm telling you again I never get my personal life involved with people who work for me. I think it's bad policy and I don't do it. It's a rule with me."

Susan gazed at the curves of Delora's ass revealed by the tight jeans, and she felt a keen and sudden sexual excitement. She had never before seen Delora in jeans or tight clothes of any kind.

"I don't do it," Delora continued. "But since we met the way we did at that bar tonight, I'll forget my rule just this once." She turned now and walked toward Susan carrying the two glasses filled with scotch and ice. "Just this once, okay? And no involvements." Her eyes locked with Susan's. "Can we agree on that?"

Susan nodded. How does a serf argue with the lord of the manor? All she cared about now was the sexual tension that had her tuned up like the strings of a violin about to snap. Her eyes were on Delora's breasts, on the shadows of Delora's nipples. "Yes, that's fine," Susan said.

Delora kissed her again, one hand holding her drink and the other hand sliding around Susan's shoulders as she aggressively pushed her tongue inside Susan's mouth and washed her teeth with it. Finally she took Susan's drink away, put both drinks down on a nearby table, and took Susan in her arms again. "Drink my mouth instead."

Susan quivered and yielded, a total yielding, a complete acquiescence. Now the complete femme, she leaned against Delora, waited for Delora, quivered as she waited for Delora to lead them onward. Susan's pussy gushed as she sniffed at Delora's perfume. Delora fondled her now, stroking her breasts through her tank top, the breasts that she'd already seen naked in the car, tickling her nipples through the knit, pinching them, tugging them, letting Susan know that she wanted Susan's body and expected to have it any way she wanted it, her hands sliding down Susan's back to possess Susan's ass with strong clenching fingers.

"I bet you were surprised to see me in that bar," Delora said with a soft laugh.

"Yes, I was."

"Our little secret."

"I won't say anything, if that's what you mean."

Delora laughed. "I don't care one way or the other what you say—they all know it anyway."

"They do?"

"Darling, believe me they do. I'm forty-six and single, and the president of the bank sees me in restaurants with dreamy little girls half my age. What do you think he says to himself? He says, "Delora Malvados is a dyke'—that's what he says. But he doesn't care because she runs the best department in the company. Doesn't he say that?"

"I guess so."

"Just remember that. Be the best there is at what you do, and keep your private life private. Will you remember that?"

"Yes."

"Now let me undress you, because for the rest of the evening you belong to Delora."

Susan trembled, immobilized, waiting, trembling again as Delora's hands at last began working to get her undressed. The first to go was the tank top, tugged over Susan's head and past her raised arms, Susan's breasts jiggling and causing Delora to murmur something about how pretty they were, and then Delora bending to kiss Susan's nipples for the first time, those full red lips grabbing at a nipple and chewing it not at all gently, chewing and sucking one breast and then moving on to the other breast, Delora's mouth active enough to make Susan's nipples swell out like a pair of ripe berries.

"Perfect," Delora said with a happy smile, her fingers bouncing Susan's breasts from side to side as if to test their resiliency. "Now let's get everything else off."

She stripped Susan quickly, efficiently, tugging the

clothes off Susan's body until Susan stood there wearing only her tiny gold earrings and her black watchband. Delora wanted to look at her, and Susan had to stand motionless while Delora walked around her as though she were some Turkish sultan deciding whether to purchase a girl for his harem. The fantasy caused Susan to quiver, and when Delora came around in front again to gaze down at Susan's auburn tuft, Susan blushed as though she were indeed on the slave block. She wanted Delora to touch her; she was dying to be touched by Delora. But Delora did nothing, merely looked at her, remained dressed as she was with her bright eyes feasting on Susan's nakedness.

Then finally Delora reached out to stroke Susan's breasts again. "What do you like?" Delora asked.

Susan faltered. "I don't know."

Delora toyed with one of Susan's nipples. "Don't be so shy."

Then she kissed Susan again, flooding Susan's mouth with saliva, her hands stroking Susan's buttocks. Susan shuddered as she felt Delora's fingers in her cleft, fingertips stroking her anus, tickling it, pushing at it, but not really penetrating. Delora kept one hand back there while her other hand slid between Susan's thighs to find her slit and the opening and push two fingers inside Susan's wet vagina. "You're creaming," Delora said. "You're a hot little pussycat."

Susan opened her legs. The insides of her thighs were drenched, glistening with her juices. She wanted desperately to come, but she was afraid to ask for it. But there was no need to ask. The next moment, Delora's fingers started thrusting in her vagina, the two fingers sliding in and out with an audible sucking sound while at the same time she rubbed the ball of her thumb over the shaft of Susan's swollen clitoris. Susan groaned as she came, her knees trembling, her pelvis humping against Delora's hand, until finally Delora pulled her fingers away and laughed softly. "Oh, I like that. That was lovely, darling. I love the way you come so hard." Her eyes meeting Susan's, Delora licked her wet fingers to get the taste of Susan's cunt, her pink tongue sliding over the fingers to clean them thoroughly. "Wait here," Delora said. "I've got some slippers I'd like you to wear."

Slippers? Susan watched Delora leave the living room. Now she was alone, her pussy drenched, her face still flushed from that violent orgasm she'd had. She walked over to a mirror and looked at herself, at her breasts and then at her belly as she rose up on her toes to be able to glimpse her thatch.

Delora returned naked, not a stitch on, whatever makeup she'd worn completely removed. She had small breasts, small dark nipples, and a carefully trimmed dark bush. In her hand she held a pair of high-heeled slippers, and now she held the slippers out to Susan. "Here, put these on. You've got the most gorgeous legs, and these are perfect for you."

Susan took the slippers, put them down, and slipped her feet into them. The heels were high enough to be sexy, and she enjoyed the feeling of suddenly being taller and her body more poised. Delora seemed pleased with the effect, too. She walked around behind Susan to have a look at her from the back, and then she came up behind Susan and ran a hand over Susan's ass. "Delicious, darling. You've got this old dyke hungry for you. But first you do me, okay? Turn yourself on a little more before Delora gets to you."

She left Susan, walked to the sofa, then sat on it and opened her legs. Suddenly her sex was exposed, a ripe thick-lipped flower in stark contrast to the neatly trimmed triangle of hair above it. The invitation to Susan was both obvious and irresistible, and she quickly moved to kneel in front of Delora and gaze entranced at the hairy mouth of Delora's sex.

Delora smiled and widened her knees, the movement visibly stretching her wet labia apart. "Hurry, pet."

With a soft moan, Susan dived in, rubbed her face along the inside of one thigh and moved forward to smell Delora, to sniff the perfume of her bush. Delora sighed and pulled her knees up far enough to put the soles of her feet on the sofa cushion.

In the quick of it now, Susan started licking the drooling cunt, fluttering her tongue over the thick lips, licking softly along the groove, getting into it, licking around Delora's strong clitoris whose tip protruded like a pink bean out of the darker hood. More than anything, Susan wanted to make Delora come to prove her skill. See how clever I am? She licked the oozing opening, ran her tongue over Delora's glistening flesh, licked her vagina, tasted her, pressed her mouth into it as Delora creamed heavily on Susan's lips. She licked down to Delora's anus, licked around the ring, tickled it, nibbled at the dark tendrils as Delora whimpered with delight. Delora's knees opened wider, her knees pulling back to her breasts, her eyes fixed on the pretty mouth now sucking the flesh just above her vaginal opening. Susan whipped Delora's stiff and swollen clitoris with her tongue, as now Delora groaned and slid both hands down to hold Susan's head. Rocking her knees, her voice hoarse as she cried out, Delora pulled Susan's face more firmly against her sex and came hard on Susan's mouth.

The shaking of Delora's body lasted for some

time, but finally it stopped, and she dropped her legs to hold Susan prisoner.

"That was wonderful," Delora said.

Susan wiped her mouth and beamed. "I'm glad."

"Come up here and kiss me." And when Delora opened her legs to release her, Susan climbed up to straddle Delora's lap and kiss her.

"You're a pretty girl," Delora said, her hands now sliding around to take hold of Susan's buttocks. She worked her fingers into the crack, found Susan's vaginal opening and swiftly penetrated her from behind with two fingers. "Pretty girl with a pretty pussy," Delora said.

Susan leaned over Delora's shoulder and smiled to herself as the fucking started, as Delora's fingers started thrusting in and out of her flooded sex. It would take time of course, but Susan was certain that in the end she would make Delora forget her rule about not getting involved with people in the office. Oh, yes, Delora would forget the rule, all right. Susan closed her eyes and licked her lips and groaned with happiness as Delora's fingers churned and churned and churned.

EVELYN

Evelyn calls me at ten in the evening. At first I don't recognize her voice, and then when I do, an abrupt shock passes through me as I realize who it is, that it's really Evelyn.

"Are you alone?" she says.

"Yes, of course."

"Why 'of course?' You might be with someone."

"I'm not with anyone." Is that what she expects? She's been resisting me for months, avoiding any contact with me at parties, allowing me to make a fool of myself because it's obvious to everyone that I want her. I dream about her. Of course she knows everything. She can't pretend she doesn't know. Now she says she wants to come over, her voice sultry. "I'll find a taxi."

I'm dubious, wary of being hurt by her. Everyone knows how fickle Evelyn can be. But I agree. Do I have a choice? I hang up the phone with my hands shaking.

And I wait. I sit there in the living room totally uncertain about what will happen now. Will she actually come to me? I see my face in the mirror looking so pale, almost like a ghost. I tell myself that I need to make a decision about the mess in the living room. Should I get the place in order? Does it matter? No, I don't care. I'm stubborn. I don't give a damn what she thinks. Not after all these months of making a fool of myself.

Then finally the doorbell rings, the sound shattering the silence, shattering my thoughts. I can feel my heart beating. God, I do want her! I go to the door trembling and open it, and there she is.

"Hi," she says. She stands there in a long raincoat, a slight smile. She's wearing red high-heeled pumps that catch my eyes as I glance down. She isn't that tall—five or six inches shorter than I am—but with more height now in the high heels. I love it. I feel an intense excitement as I stare at the red nylons that complement the red pumps.

Without another word, she comes in, walking past me into the apartment, the heels clicking on the parquet floor. My hands trembling again, I close the door.

"Let me take your coat." She shakes her head.

"No, not yet."

Why? Does she intend to leave soon? I follow her to the living room, my eyes on the red pumps, the red nylons, her lovely legs. She knows that red is the perfect color for her, the red of her shoes the same shade as the red of her lips.

In the living room, she leans against one of the bookcases. I'm sorry now there's no fireplace or fur rug. I don't have the trappings. I never do have the trappings. Maybe that's the reason I'm never successful with women like Evelyn.

As she continues leaning against the bookcase, she slides her hands out of the pockets of her raincoat and unties the belt. Her eyes on me, she slowly pulls the raincoat apart and in a moment I freeze and my heart pounds again.

The raincoat is open enough to show the red garters and the red lace garter belt and the red stockings pulled tight, high on her round thighs. That's all she's wearing, nothing else. My God, how delicious she is! The shock of it keeps me frozen, immobilized.

Her eyes question me. "What do you think of it?" I say nothing, remain silent as I continue staring at her.

All I want to do is look at her, keep my eyes on the vision of loveliness. And I do that, staring at everything, at the garter belt and stockings and red heels and sheer red nylon through which her white skin gleams. And the bush of dark hair that looks brushed out, fluffed. Her breasts are still covered because the upper part of the raincoat is still buttoned, but I can see her navel above the lace garter belt, the slope of her belly.

Now she unbuttons the top of the raincoat, her fingers working at the buttons, and in a moment she pulls the top part of the raincoat apart to reveal her breasts and the now-continuous white of her body running from the tops of her thighs upward to her throat.

I've never seen any of it, never her breasts that are now revealed. I've always guessed about her breasts, stealing glances at them at parties, wondering about the shape and look and the size of her nipples. Now I feel a wild excitement as I gaze at the succulent tips, the brownish nubs. She's as beautiful as I expected her to be. I study the way the weight of each breast pulls it downward a bit, the perfect lines. I could go to her and touch her, but I don't want to. I'm afraid. Instead I just stand where I am, hypnotized by the picture she makes.

She slips out of the raincoat and gracefully drops it to the floor. "You haven't said a word," she says. "I'm going to think you don't like me."

"You know that's not true."

Naked except for the garter belt and stockings and shoes, she leans languidly against the bookcase again and says, "You could take your shirt off."

I'm nervous. "I'll open some champagne."

"Yes, but first take your shirt off." She smirks at me as my fingers fumble at the buttons of my shirt. In a few moments, I'm stripped except for my jeans, my breasts exposed, swinging. Does she approve? My nipples are stiff like turrets, tingling with excitement as I keep my eyes on her. Now she turns to walk across the room, and I have a view of her legs, her lovely ass seen from behind, the cheeks framed so provocatively by the red garter belt and red nylons.

The high heels make a clicking sound on the floor, an enticement, an inducement to madness.

She turns and smiles at me, aware of my eyes on her, amused. "I thought you're getting the champagne."

Furious with my own weakness, I hurry away. In the kitchen I open a small bottle of champagne and pour the pale liquid to fill two glasses. The wine bubbles. In a hurry now, I carefully carry the two glasses to the living room only to find the room empty and Evelyn gone.

She's nowhere in sight. Have I been dreaming? After an instant of fear, I call out, "Where are you?"

Her voice comes from another room. "The bedroom." Relieved, wondering, I carry the champagne to the bedroom down the hall. And there she is on the bed, flat out, on her belly, her body arranged neatly in the center of the bed, a pillow under her belly to lift her hips, to lift that luscious ass, her forearms and head resting on another pillow.

The pose is a shock. This is her first time on my bed, and the way she has arranged herself is a deliberate attempt to drive me wild. Her knees are wide apart, but her feet have been brought together, the high heels gone now, her feet touching each other through the red nylon.

Her cunt is exposed from the rear, everything visible, the hair-lined outer lips, the puffy flesh, the red in the long groove between the lips, the long slit, and above that her ass, the moons, the winking eye of her anus. Like a brown eye.

She turns her head to look at me. "Champagne? If you have the champagne, I want it."

"Don't move."

"But I want some champagne."

"I'll bring it to you." And I do that. I carry the champagne and extend a full glass to her. She turns only the upper half of her body, her breasts hanging, and she takes the glass from my hand and giggles softly. "Do you mind me coming in here?"

"All I care about is looking at you." She wiggles her hips. "Is that all? I hope there's more than just looking." She keeps her eyes on me as she sips her champagne, her red lips at the rim of the glass, her lips wet with wine and pouting. Then she hands the glass back to me, and I put it on the night table.

"Your nipples are so big," she says. It's the areolas that are big. The points themselves are tiny. "Big and ugly," I say.

"No, I like them."

I sip my champagne, and then I move down to the foot of the bed to look at her from the rear again. She sighs and rests on the pillow. The view of her open cunt puts a fire in my belly. I can see the glistening in the groove, the wet flaps. For a moment the silence is heavy, only a slight movement of her legs to alter the pose, a slight movement that make her folded legs appear to beckon to me. What I would like to do is dive in there and feast on her for three or four days, lose myself in it, wallow in that lovely open cunt whose lips pout at me with such provocation.

I climb onto the bed, push her legs apart and kneel between them, and then I slowly pour some of the champagne I'm holding into the crack of her ass.

She gasps. She wiggles her hips, whimpers into the pillow as the champagne streams down the valley to the open maw of her red cunt. "Oh, God, I love that!" she says.

I leave the bed and, with deliberate slowness, I walk to the night table and put my champagne glass down. Then I return to the foot of the bed, gaze at her wet ass a moment, and then climb onto the bed again between her legs.

This time I bend my head and get my face against her ass. I start kissing her buttocks, first one and then the other, licking the smooth flesh, then gradually sliding my face into the crack to flutter my tongue at her raised cunt. She squirms and moans as she feels it. I find her wet vaginal opening, and I taste her juices mixed with the champagne.

Which is stronger; the taste of her flowing cunt or the taste of the champagne?

My tongue is inside, twisting and turning inside her. She moans continually now, a soft pleading sound as she slowly wriggles her ass against my face.

I hold her cheeks with my hands, nibble at one lip, pulling at it with my teeth as she churns her ass with more vigor. Another gasp comes out of her throat as I lick upward to her anus and tickle my way around it, tease it, bedevil it, then stiffen my tongue and push the tip of it inside the dark ring. She groans as she feels my tongue slide inside. She loves it. I get myself all the way inside her, my mouth pressed into the groove between her buttocks, my tongue foraging in there with constant movement.

Finally I pull away and roll over onto my back beside her. "Get on top of me," I tell her. "Get over me, and I'll eat you that way."

She hurries to climb over me, facing me, her knees on either side of my chest. She gazes down at me, the hairy mouth of her cunt so close that I imagine I can feel its heat on my face. Now she slides forward to give it to me, pushing forward to mash her clitoris against my mouth as she starts grinding the lower part of her cunt against my chin.

"Go on, lick the bowl clean," she says with a soft laugh. My reply is to dig my fingernails into the cheeks of her ass until she cries out.

She begins a rhythm, humping at my mouth, but it doesn't work for her, and soon she stops it and she pulls away. "I'm turning around."

Now her ass is presented to me, her cunt revealed again from the rear, the wetness everywhere, the inner lips swollen and distended.

Instead of shifting backward to get her cunt on my mouth, she bends forward to get my jeans unbuttoned and unzipped. She pushes my jeans and panties down my hips, down my thighs, and off my legs and feet, as I fix my eyes on the crack, on the two openings, on the pouting hairy lips.

When I'm naked, she scoots backward far enough

to find my face again. "There, that's better," she says.

I don't argue. I pull at her ass to get her down to my mouth more firmly, and after that's done, she leans forward to get her face between my thighs.

Why am I afraid? I have her wet gap on my face as she starts licking me, my hands on her ass as her crotch grinds against my mouth. I feel her tongue working even as my own tongue works. I feel the wetness, the inundation, the drenching of my lips and chin.

Why am I afraid? This is Evelyn. This is Evelyn in a garter belt, Evelyn moaning against my cunt, Evelyn's wetness dripping on my face as I hump myself at her mouth.

We come one after the other, the bed shaking as we heave up and down, and afterward we lie head to toe and hugging each other. I lie with my arms around her ass, hoping she won't move until tomorrow.

FRANKIE

When Frankie walked into the party, she was in one of those moods she called "tough and true," disliking everything in existence including herself. She walked into the room crowded with women and headed straight to the bar. She avoided eye contact, thinking about her love life and aware of the eyes on her, eyes that knew who she was, some of the eyes fawning and other eyes envious. She was in between "serious relationships," drifting nowhere, and in this room there was no one she knew well. She told herself what she really needed tonight was something quick and lovely, something to get her mind relaxed, a one-night stand without commitment, nothing ponderous beyond a good time in bed. Maybe she could find a woman here, someone hot and lovely.

Unfortunately, the party seemed dull and insipid. She found some red wine, filled a glass, and then turned and stood there to accept an occasional hello from occasional acquaintances. The room had everything in it; swaggering dykes, emaciated dykes, lipstick dykes, and nearly all of them looking completely wrung out and unsuitable for what she needed.

Then, as she turned to walk closer to one of the windows, she saw the blonde.

She was a tall girl with long blonde hair, a fluff in a blue party dress, busty and with a perfect face. She was alone and she was staring at Frankie with eyes that said, "I'm here if you want me. I'm all yours."

Frankie strolled across the room. She never lacked confidence when she played like this. Tonight she was decked out in a black shirt, tight black jeans and black cowboy boots, and she knew she looked good enough to make some of them quiver. Was this the one she wanted?

"Hi," Frankie said. The girl had creamy skin and large breasts, an abundance of deep cleavage revealed by the low neckline of her short party dress. She wore spike heels that gave her an impressive height, and above the sexy shoes the perfect legs were sheathed in sheer black nylon.

"Hi," the girl said, a faint blush rising to her heart-shaped face.

Frankie sipped her red wine, her eyes dropping to the full breasts and then lifting to the blonde's eyes, Frankie's nose now aware of the sweet scent of Shalimar. "Do you know anyone here?"

The blonde smiled and replied in a sweet voice, "It looks like I've been deserted."

"My name's Frankie."

"Yes, I know. You're Frankie Dellum, and you're an actress. I'm Sheila Kay."

"Hello, Sheila."

The sweet voice again: "Hello yourself."

Frankie wondered whether she belonged to anyone. She imagined the blonde naked, those lovely breasts swinging from side to side as she ambled across a room. Never mind who she belonged to if she'd make herself available.

They flirted, the eye contact remaining tight, portentous.

Frankie said, "Whoever it is who abandoned you is silly. You're too beautiful."

Sheila blushed, the color making her face look even prettier. "I like your haircut."

Frankie nodded, twisting her head to get the lock of hair out of her eyes. "It's getting too long." And then she added, "But don't you ever cut yours."

Sheila blushed again. "I guess you thought I was giving you the come-on before when I was staring at you."

"Well, weren't you?"

With a shy smile, Sheila nodded. "Yes, I was."

"And here I am."

"I'm feeling very nervous."

"Not too nervous, I hope."

Her lips were as perfect as the rest of her, the lipstick exactly the right shade for her coloring. Her submissive femme attitude filled Frankie with an intense excitement as she imagined the blonde's peaches and cream sex open and waiting.

Sheila said, "I saw you in a play once. I really liked it."

Frankie was amused to find a fan. She had the feeling she could have the girl if she wanted her, no matter whom she belonged to or who had brought her to the party.

"What do you do?" Frankie said, her eyes deliberately fixed on Sheila's breasts. "Do you work?"

The blonde looked coy. "I'm a secretary with a hobby."

"And what's that?"

Meeting Frankie's eyes, Sheila said, "My hobby is enjoying life."

Frankie chuckled. "Sounds interesting."

And Sheila said, "I've never made it with an actress before."

Which produced in Frankie a sudden extreme hunger for the blonde. Oh, yes, she wanted her. Her voice low, Frankie said, "There must be an empty bedroom upstairs where we can get to know each other better. Why don't we find it?"

Frankie expected a refusal, but her policy was to never miss a good opportunity for want of an attempt. Try not and have not, she thought.

But Sheila did not refuse. The blonde hesitated, looked around, and then nodded in agreement with her blue eyes sparkling. "All right, why not?"

They left the crowded room, Frankie not caring whether or not they were noticed. They wandered upstairs and passed two women on their way down, which made Frankie suspect that she and Sheila were not alone in what they wanted. They finally found an empty bedroom at the end of the hall, a room small but tidy, two small lamps casting a yellow light over a bed with a patchwork spread. The shades were already down, but as far as Frankie could tell, no one at the party had used the room yet. At least it smelled fresh.

Sheila walked past her, looked at the bed and then casually reached behind herself to unzip her dress. Frankie suddenly felt it was all a wild fantasy to be here in a strange room with this gorgeous girl. But no, it was very real. What a lovely thing she was! Frankie closed and locked the door, thankful now that the noise of the party was gone. When she walked up behind Sheila, she could smell the Shalimar again. The blonde's dress was already unzipped and open down her back, her pink skin and the black band of her bra revealed. Sheila gave a short gasp as Frankie slipped her hands inside the dress and around her body, nuzzling Sheila's neck as she pushed the dress away from her shoulders.

Sheila murmured, "I hope no one barges in on us."

"I locked the door."

Sheila's breasts were supported by a delicious low-cut bra that barely covered her nipples. Frankie now dipped her hands into the cups of the bra to free the blonde's breasts. The two globes felt lovely in her hands, heavy and firm with nipples already spiking. Sheila gasped, then whimpered and leaned back against Frankie as Frankie held her breasts up with her palms.

"Feel good?"

"And how!" Sheila said with a groan, her sudden desire obvious. "You're getting me hot."

Frankie chuckled against her ear. "That's what I'm aiming for."

She kneaded Sheila's breasts, then stroked them lightly with her palms, her fingers gliding over the firm flesh and then dancing out to the large well-formed nipples that were like pink candy topping the two luscious globes. The nipples rose quickly in Frankie's palms, stiff nuggets of pleasure, Sheila moaning as Frankie's clever hands brought her a feverish excitement. "God, I love the way you touch me!" She pressed back against Frankie with more urgency, swaying her hips from side to side. Frankie slid a hand below Sheila's bra to her belly, her fingers stroking the soft skin where the dress was still snug at her waist. Only half the package was unwrapped, the blonde's dress still covering most of her body.

"Let me get out of these clothes," Sheila said, her voice plaintive.

"No, let me do it." Frankie was amused by Sheila's need to get naked. She was hot, all right, and the idea excited Frankie. She imagined the blonde's cunt flowing, the pink flaps flaring, the flower dripping its nectar. The image threatened to force her to be hasty, but what she wanted was something else. Delaying the main event would only make it better.

Sheila shivered as Frankie withdrew her hands from inside her dress, and then the blonde groaned as Frankie bent down and unexpectedly lifted her body to carry her to the bed.

The blonde was thrilled, crooning against Frankie's neck as Frankie brought her to the edge of the bed and then gently laid her down on the colored spread.

Sheila giggled. "Hey, you're strong!"

Frankie gazed at her. Lord, what a lovely little fluff the girl was! She bent over Sheila to peel the top of the dress down below her waist. Sheila wriggled as Frankie bared her from shoulders to waist, Frankie again thinking of her as a confection, aroused by the blonde's luscious milk-white skin spiced with cute freckles at her collarbones. Sheila's face was flushed pink with excitement. Frankie had an urge to lick every inch of her skin, every square centimeter from her neck down to her painted toenails.

Gazing up at Frankie, Sheila's wide blue eyes were filled with admiration and expectancy. Now, with her eyes heavy, she suddenly extended her arms to Frankie and said, "Kiss me."

Frankie gazed at the blonde's parted lips and the moist pink tongue just visible between them. She bent to kiss her, the first kiss, their tongues tangling, the kiss wet and erotic. Frankie felt her own passion boiling. She smeared Sheila's mouth with her own as she stroked Sheila's full breasts and tugged gently at her stiff nipples.

Then she broke off the kiss and pulled back a moment, only to drop her face again to take one of the nipples in her mouth and suck it. Sheila moaned as Frankie's mouth moved from one breast to the other, her lips sucking at the points, tugging at them, her tongue running over each breast like a cat licking a kitten. Whimpering with pleasure, Sheila threw her arms back on the bed and squirmed under Frankie's wet mouth.

Sheila's body delighted Frankie. The blonde was simultaneously slender and curvaceous, a slender frame with full prominent breasts and a luscious ass. She moved her hands down to Sheila's waist, and Sheila now raised her hips as though to signal how badly she wanted to be taken. Frankie worked the dress down past Sheila's hips, tugging at the rustling material, now revealing black lace panties and a skimpy black garter belt, the panties almost completely transparent, sheer enough to show the blonde curls that covered the mound of Sheila's sex. Frankie pulled the dress all the way down Sheila's legs, uncovering the black garters and the tops of the sheer nylons. As she pulled the dress past Sheila's legs and feet, she chuckled. "Do you know how gorgeous you are?"

Sheila whimpered with happiness. "Turn you on?"

"You look like a centerfold girl."

Sheila seemed amused. "Oh, you look at those, do you?"

"Every chance I get, honey." Frankie tossed the dress onto a nearby chair, and then she leaned back to get a full view of Sheila on the bed. What a treat she was lying there in nothing but high heels, dark stockings, black panties with garters. Her legs were folded to the side. She still had the black bra under her breasts, but the full mounds were completely free.

Frankie now leaned over her to work the bra around and free the clasp. Sheila lifted her back to make it easier, and in a moment Frankie had the bra unhooked. She pulled it away from Sheila's body.

Now Sheila was naked from the waist up, blushing, her wide blue eyes fixed on Frankie. Frankie next removed Sheila's shoes, the fuck-me stiletto heels that were so sexy. She slipped them off Sheila's feet and tossed them into a corner. How would the blonde ever get dressed again? Sheila giggled, her face flushed. Frankie undid the black garters, thrilled by Sheila's sleek thighs. She glanced at the crotch of Sheila's panties and quivered when she saw the wet spot. The blonde seemed in a fog of desire, moaning softly, her legs moving continuously. Frankie felt an intense animal urge to have her, to possess her totally. With a soft groan, she bent to sniff at the crotch of Sheila's panties, the blonde gasping, whimpering, opening her knees and pulling them back to make herself available.

"Oh, God, you're something!" Sheila said with a moan.

Frankie bit gently at the plump flesh under the nylon. "You're dripping in there."

Then she pulled back and started working at the stockings, undoing the garter clasps one by one, getting the stockings free, pulling them down Sheila's legs one after the other, rolling the wisps of nylon past the blonde's knees and down to her slender ankles and off her feet. She tossed the stockings into the air one after the other, where they seemed to float like dark wreaths before falling to the floor.

Sheila puckered her red lips. "You're teasing me." She lay there stretching her arms as Frankie unhooked the garter belt, removed it, tossed it away over her shoulder. The blonde's eyes were heavy with desire as she waited for Frankie's next move. She lay on the bed supine, submissive, totally feminine. And naked now except for the transparent black panties that showed everything. The lace panties looked so flimsy that Frankie thought she could tear them with her fingers and penetrate the blonde at the same time.

Now she slid a hand over Sheila's belly and bent to kiss her navel. She slid her hand under the elastic waistband of the panties, teasing the blonde, inching her fingers down closer and closer to the treasure, Sheila quivering with desire, trembling, her skin hot. Frankie's hand moved deeper inside the panties until she felt the first tendrils of soft pubic hair.

"Want something?"

Sheila groaned. "You're teasing again."

Frankie's finger found the top of the blonde's slit and hooked into it, just grazing the shaft of Sheila's clitoris, hooked in there and pressing down.

Sheila moaned, turned her head to the side, then looked at Frankie again and licked her lips. "Please ..." She reached out with her hands, begging Frankie to kiss her again. "Don't be mean!"

Frankie laughed. "But that's what I like." She drew back, at the same time sliding her hand deeper inside Sheila's panties until she had her fingers between the fat labia. With her hand curled into the blonde's crotch, she began a slow rotation of her palm over the swollen cunt. She gradually worked the panties down, making a game of it, enjoying the power she had over the blonde. She did everything deliberately, slowly, her own lust heightened by the scent of the blonde's hot sex. As she gradually pulled the panties away, more and more of the blonde triangle became exposed; the wisps of blonde curls, the plump and firm mound, the blonde's prominent pelvic bones. Sheila opened her legs as though to cool the heat of her cunt. Frankie restrained herself and continued pulling the panties down the blonde's long thighs, down her calves and ankles to the red painted toenails.

She tossed the panties away, and as she did so Sheila slowly opened her legs and writhed on the bed. "I'm so hot!"

Frankie ignored the pleading. She rose now to strip her clothes off. Her eyes on the naked blonde, she peeled everything off her body; her boots and socks, her jeans, shirt, and underpants. She glanced at her body in the mirror; the long lines, the muscular thighs, the firm small buttocks. Her nipples were pointed and stiff and, as Sheila watched her, she flicked them with her fingertips.

"Please …" Sheila opened her legs wider to reveal more of her wet cunt.

Still toying with her own nipples, Frankie said, "Open it with your fingers. Get that little clit out."

Sheila blushed and did what Frankie wanted. "Okay?"

"Spread it more. Take hold of the lips and pull them out."

"Oh, God."

"Come on, do it."

Using the fingers of both hands, Sheila tugged the pink flaps out and held them there. "Do something to me."

"Not yet. Get your fingers inside. Do you do that when you rub off?"

"Yes."

AFFINITIES

"Okay, do it. Show me two fingers in the socket." The blonde groaned, closed her eyes, and pushed two fingers inside her vaginal opening. She started thrusting the fingers in and out rapidly in an obvious attempt to make herself climax.

Frankie immediately went to the bed and pulled Sheila's hand away. Then she climbed on, half-covered the blonde's body with her own, breast against breast, her hips fitting between Sheila's spread thighs as the blonde groaned and raised her knees.

They kissed, Frankie's wet mouth pressing against Sheila's wet mouth, Frankie devouring her, biting on the blonde's full soft lips. Sheila humped her pelvis to meet Frankie's body, groaning, her hands feverishly stroking Frankie's back and buttocks. After positioning herself accurately between the blonde's open thighs, Frankie pressed her cunt against Sheila's cunt, wet flesh against wet flesh, grinding, thrusting, feeling her clitoris mash against the blonde's pubic bone, Sheila crying out with pleasure, her knees up, a fast humping, Frankie grinding into her, Sheila grinding back in response, squealing, wild with desire and incoherent as she cried out again and again.

Frankie adored it this way, the savage thrusting, the blonde's eyes slitted with pleasure as she begged for more. Frankie continued thrusting, and then finally she slipped a hand between their bodies, her fingers seeking the blonde's wet cunt, two fingers pushing into the swollen slot, thrusting with her fingers now, her knuckles spreading Sheila's labia as she worked the two fingers in and out with the movements of her body. She moved her hips up and down, held still a moment, then started moving again, stretching the opening farther, teasing the blonde, dominating her, reveling in the complete power she had to bring the blonde girl pleasure.

Sheila cursed, groaned, rocked her knees as Frankie's fingers pummeled her vagina again and again. Frankie kept her pinned down, immobilized, possessing the blonde with her hand as their bodies writhed together.

Sheila cried out as she came again, her blue eyes rolling upward as she felt Frankie's knuckles mash against her clitoris.

Frankie exploded in an orgasm against her own hand, her mouth now clamped against Sheila's mouth, tasting the blonde's lipstick, vanquishing the lipstick femme with her body and hand.

One last grind, cunt against cunt, the two bodies now covered with a film of sweat as they held each other.

After that they collapsed side by side on the colored patchwork bedspread.

When Frankie caught her breath, she said, "How was that?"

Sheila sighed, giggled. "I really thought you would eat me. But I like what you did better."

"Really?"

"Yeah, I love it."

Frankie suddenly abandoned the idea of a one-night stand. With a soft voice, she said, "I'd like to see you again."

Sheila hesitated, then pulled away and sat up. "I can't. Really, I can't."

"Why not?"

"Because I'm involved with someone else, that's why. All I wanted tonight was something like this, a one-time thing. You know what I mean?

"A one-time thing."

"Don't think I'm a bitch, but that's the way it is. Listen, I think I'd better get dressed and get back to the party."

ILENE

(from the novel *Black Velvet*, to be published by Spectrum Press)

My name is Ilene. I'm in a crevice at the foot of the mountain of white rock, huddling in the crevice, naked except for the iron slave collar that circles my neck. The sun is shining, but the crevice is in shadow, and I'm cold. I've been here two days and two nights, every moment filled with misery, every moment unbearable.

I've had enough; I've truly had enough. The rock in front of me gets wet in the evening, and if I lick the stone, I can gather enough water to survive another day, and maybe another. No, I don't want that; I want to die. But then, as this thought forms in my mind, I reject it as well. Are there people who accept death easily? I'm not one of them. I'm not yet thirty, too young to accept the nothingness of death. The black void of death is a total impossibility, unacceptable. But yet ...

Of course they'll find me. They'll find me and they won't force anything. They never actually force anything because there's no need for it. They know that.

I slept awhile, and then I heard a noise. Now I hear it again. Oh, yes, it's them. I hear the chopping sound of the helicopter. I can't see it, but I can hear it. I've heard it every day, but this is the first time I'm certain they'll find me. Why? I don't know. It's possible they've looked everywhere, and now this is the last place to look. They know all the places; they told me that and they never lie. Not about that, anyway.

The helicopter again. I cringe as it passes directly over me. I'm afraid to look at it, afraid I'll see someone looking back at me. Instead, I huddle deeper into the crevice and start shivering again.

Something moves against my foot. It's a tiny gray lizard with red eyes. The lizard turns its head to look at me. Then it scurries away and vanishes.

The helicopter is landing. It settles down like a great metal creature fifty yards away. The dust flies as it comes to rest on a flat place in the scrub. The rotor blades stop turning, and the dust settles again.

And now they wait for me. A seabird passes overhead, turning, gliding over us, and then turning out to sea again.

They wait for me and do nothing. I can make out two figures in the helicopter, but the distance is too great to see more than that. I crouch in the shadow of the crevice, but after a time I know it's useless, finished, and I rise and walk toward them. I walk naked toward the helicopter.

The two figures are two women, both wearing sunglasses, both looking at me, their faces flat, expressionless.

They say nothing as I arrive at the machine. I put

my foot on the boarding step and one of them extends a hand to help me aboard. For a brief instant her eyes glance at my breasts and sex. Then I'm inside. The rotor blades are whirling again, the dust rising. I look in the sky for a seabird, but I can see nothing. The sky is blue and so terribly empty.

Michiko sips a glass of champagne as she looks at me. "Why did you do it?"

She wears a white dress and white sandals. The room has only one chair in it, and Michiko is sitting on it near the open window. I'm in the center of the room, naked except for my iron slave collar, squatting on my heels with my back straight and my knees apart.

Michiko says, "Why did you do it?"

"I'm sorry." She's not much older than I am, but the difference between us is as great as that between night and day.

Or between master and slave. Michiko does not wear an iron slave collar. She wears a white dress and white sandals. As I gaze at her knees, I can think of nothing except the terrible need I have to push my face between her thighs.

Her cunt is thick lipped, the hair on her mons like fine black silk.

Now Michiko rises and she walks out onto the terrace that overlooks the sea. She stands there a moment with her face lifted to the sea breeze, and then she returns to the room and she looks at me again.

"They've ordered me to whip you, but I've arranged to have one of the servants do it."

I fall prone at her feet. "Please, only you!"

"No," she says.

And so I'm denied Michiko's punishment. Instead, one of the servants will whip me. To be whipped by a servant here is the worst of all possible indignities. For the servants here are not masters; the servants are mere servants. When I first arrived on the island, I thought all the servants would be Greek locals, but none of them are Greek; the servants are Malays, brought all the way from Malaysia—silent slender women with no expression in their eyes. Sometimes I think their tongues have been removed, for they never speak. No, that can't be; I've heard them talk among themselves. Are they cruel? I don't know if their cruelty is any greater than that of the masters. I've been whipped by both servants and masters and I think the masters are always more diligent. The problem is not the cruelty; the problem is the indignity, the absence of a master, the absence of Michiko's love. If Michiko would whip me, her love for me would be a solace. With a servant there is no solace at all; with a servant there is only the pain and the indignity of punishment by someone who is not a master.

Two of them come for me and they attach a chain to my iron collar and they lead me away from Michiko. At the last moment I turn to look at her, but one of the servants pulls at the chain and my neck is abruptly jerked forward.

Oh, my love!

This is the way they do it: I'm standing in the center of the whipping room, my arms raised above my head, my wrists bound and attached to a chain suspended from the ceiling. The chain has been pulled to bring my heels up and only my toes touch the stone floor. My neck is already tired and my head bends forward. The iron slave collar still has the chain-leash attached to it, but the chain drags on the floor behind me. I don't want them to lift that chain. I remember the one time I was whipped with the chain-leash and the pain was awful.

No, they won't use the chain. I hear them behind me as they talk in their language, an easy sing-song interchange. They may not be talking about me after all; they may be discussing their next meal, or their next trip to the mainland when they have time off. Then one of them touches my buttocks, and I know that something will happen soon. The only time the servants are allowed to fondle the slaves is when the slaves receive punishment from them. I should imagine they want to do more than merely fondle the slaves, but it's never allowed. I would reveal it. Or maybe I wouldn't reveal it under the right circumstances. I don't know because it's never happened; I've never been taken by a servant, and I can't imagine it. Would the masters ever allow it?

This room is dank, gray, the stone walls glistening with moisture. I've seen other whipping rooms that looked less forbidding. Is there any significance in my being in this room and not in one of the others? I don't know; I don't know very much. I know hardly anything, and at the moment I'm afraid because the degree of pain is always unpredictable. Even if they don't draw blood, the pain can be horrible.

But first the fondling. They always fondle from behind, as if to avoid looking at my face, as if to avoid my eyes. One of them now slides her hands around my body and, as she presses against me from behind, she puts her hands on my breasts. I feel the hands gripping my breasts, a hand for each breast, then the fingers finding my nipples and twisting them. As I bend my head farther, I can see them, see the hands on my flesh. The hands are slender, feminine, and the first awakening of desire begins in my belly.

But then her hands are withdrawn. Whoever she is; the Malay servant; the unknown. She moves away, and I feel the other woman press against me now. This one wants something different from my body. Her hand pushes between my thighs from behind, her fingers pushing forward to find my sex. I feel the fingers parting the lips, pushing between them, pushing inside the opening. She says something to the other woman. She slides her fingers in and out of my vagina a few times, and then finally she pulls her hand away completely.

Silence now. I hear them moving behind me, doing things, and my skin begins to crawl, the tingling feeling spreading across my shoulders and down my back to my buttocks.

I listen. All my attention now is focused on the sounds in the room.

One of them speaks in their language. The other one answers, a guttural sound.

I hear it suddenly, the sound of the whip cutting through the air, and the next instant an intense burning streaks across the skin of my buttocks.

What orders have they been given? Will they mark me? Michiko promised I would never be marked, not like the some of the other slaves I've seen here. But maybe they were also promised; maybe the marking is simply another stage in the progression. To where? Where are they taking me?

The whip strikes again. And again. After the fourth blow, the burning is constant, hot, spreading up the lower part of my back like a slow fire. And between my thighs. At the next strike of the whip, I feel the heat in my sex, the first tingling.

And again the whip strikes. I moan. My head

hangs forward, my body turning slowly, a quarter-turn to the left, a quarter-turn to the right, only my toes touching the floor, and the ache in my shoulders intensifying with each movement.

I lose track of the whip, the strikes, the number of blows. I hear moaning, my own voice. I feel a drenching wetness between my thighs; that, too, is my own.

Michiko lies naked on her belly on the air mattress as I kneel straddling her legs. Is she sleeping? The window is open, the warm air carrying the sound of the surf beating on the rocks below.

I dip my hands in the warm oil and slide my fingers over Michiko's shoulders. My hands mold the muscles, coaxing them, urging them to relax.

As I work down her spine, I shift backward. I stroke her flesh gently with my fingers, rubbing, squeezing, stroking the oil on her perfect skin.

My sex is wet. I want very much to rub it against Michiko's leg, but she'd be aware of it in an instant and berate me for it. Instead, I allow my hunger to continue, daring no more than a subtle pressure of my knees against her thighs.

She moves. She stretches and arches her back in response to my touching her. She undulates her body, a lazy rocking movement, and then she lies still again.

I slide my hands over her buttocks, over the firm flesh, the sweet globes. Is she breathing harder now? I feel the sweat rolling down between my breasts. Then her body stiffens as I grip her buttocks in my hands and begin stroking them with the warm oil. My palms roam over the twin globes of her ass. Nowhere has her skin been touched by the sun, but the skin of her buttocks is a lighter shade than the rest of her. Only in the groove does the darkening begin again.

I shift backward. I raise my left knee and change my position so that now I'm straddling only her right leg. She responds by spreading her legs slightly, and then even farther as my fingers rub deep into the valley between her buttocks. I take her movement as an invitation, a sign of permission, and now I lean forward and I graze the tips of my breasts over her ass. I slide my palms between her thighs and fill them with her warm flesh. My face pressed against her buttocks, I begin to gently bite the globes.

My sex is on fire, my cunt ravenous and dripping as I move my lips over Michiko's skin. The heaviness is unbearable, the flames of desire leaping through my veins to the tip of my clitoris. I bite harder at Michiko's perfumed flesh. The musky scent of her cunt is now in my nostrils as I plunge my tongue deep into the crevice between her buttocks, searching, then finding the ring of her anus. I prod the opening, then hold still, waiting for a sign, waiting for Michiko's permission. She wriggles gently; her hips move; her ass rises to meet my mouth and a wave of happiness washes over me.

Now my belly jerks with an unleashed frenzy. My body shakes as I push my tongue deep into Michiko's ass, my face pressed against the sticky groove, my chin rubbing her thick-lipped sex. Suddenly she lifts herself against my mouth, and my tongue slips down past her anal passage to the wet slit of her cunt.

Her taste inflames my senses. Oh, the marvel of it! What a wondrous feeling it is for a slave to dip her tongue into the well of her mistress and find the liquid evidence of acceptance and love!

Michiko writhes as I push my head deeper between her thighs. She lifts her hips to roll her buttocks against my face. I plunge my tongue inside her anus again, and immediately she captures it and cries out, a soft cry, then another, the sounds of pleasure muffled in her throat.

Later, when I try to rub myself against her calf, she kicks me away. "No," she says.

My clitoris is a hard marble; my destruction is total.

These are the Rules of Engagement: The slave speaks only when ordered to speak. The obedience of the slave is always complete. The punishment of the slave is never questioned. The pleasure of the slave has no meaning. I first learned them in New York when Michiko wrote them down on paper and taped the paper to my bedroom mirror.

The chastisement for my attempted escape lasts three days. Each day I'm whipped in the morning and then again in the afternoon; always by two servants, sometimes the same women and sometimes others. The routine of the whipping is always the same: first the fondling of my body, fondling of various kinds, and then the whipping from behind, the blows on my buttocks and thighs. So far they haven't marked me; they've been careful not to draw blood. But I cry nevertheless. The pain is awful, and at the end of each whipping, I'm a sobbing wreck, shattered, trembling, too weak to stand.

Concerning damage: If the skin is brought to a deep red color by the whip, the color will fade in an hour.

If welts are produced by the whip, the welts will be gone in a day or two.

Soreness produced by a beating doesn't last; the tissues heal themselves within two or three days.

Blue marks are the worst; they last longer, and they look ugly. I don't like them.

After my three days of punishment, I'm allowed to rest for two more days, and then Michiko tells me I'm to be used by the masters again. "You'll be called in a few hours," she says. "Make yourself ready, and come back to me."

The room where I sleep is in a wing added to the main building some years ago. The stone walls are whitewashed, and the wooden floor is covered by a worn rug. I sit at the small dressing table and prepare myself for the evening. I work a long time on my makeup, my eyes and lashes, my cheeks and lips. When I have the coloring of my face just right, I apply rouge to my nipples and then just a hint of it to the outer lips of my sex. After that I pin up my dark hair in a chignon, and I clip pendant earrings to my earlobes. I turn my head from right to left and back again in front of the mirror. Yes, it's fine; it's the look that Michiko favors. After that I rummage through a dresser drawer to find a red French cache-sexe. It takes but a moment to put that on, to adjust the thin strap in back between my buttocks and the triangle in front so that it completely covers my pubis. I find a pair of red shoes with spike heels, and I put those on and inspect myself in the mirror.

What I see is a naked woman wearing a black choker necklace. Except the necklace is made of iron, and it's a slave collar.

"Yes," Michiko says. She has me stand in front of her as she looks at me. She wears a white evening dress, and her beauty is so exquisite that it makes my hands tremble. She tells me she's flying to a party in Athens this evening. She won't be on the island while I'm being used. The idea frightens me—makes me desperate—but I do my best to conceal it.

One of the servants is waiting to escort me. "Don't

misbehave," Michiko says. She waves a hand, and I'm dismissed.

I feel alive only when Michiko is angry with me. If Michiko is not angry with me, then she must be thinking of other things, and I'm not the center of her existence. When Michiko is angry with me, all she can think about is me. Nothing else is on her mind. I adore that; I adore Michiko's anger.

But this evening, Michiko is in Athens.

This master has not told me her name. The room is sparsely furnished, but a thick lamb's-wool rug covers the floor, and in the center of this I squat on my heels in the usual position, my back straight, my knees apart, naked except for the red cache-sexe and the red heels. She manacled my hands as soon as I entered the room, and now I'm finding it difficult to maintain the posture without discomfort.

Against the far wall is a bed, the mattress covered by an embroidered white counterpane. I know the riding crop is on the bed, but I don't want to look at it. I don't want to look at anything, least of all that.

So far she hasn't said much. She speaks English with a British accent, but I don't think she's British. She's been sitting in that chair for the past ten minutes, and all she does is look at me. She's about forty, strong looking, wearing a dark blue suit, a red string tie, a white shirt with a bit of lace at the sleeves. She has short dark hair and green eyes and a cruel mouth. I suppose that if I saw her on the street or at a party, I would say she was beautiful. Here that doesn't matter; the only thing that matters here is that we both know she'll soon be very nasty to me. Michiko says I can always trust them to go only so far, but I'm never certain of it. Maybe this one will be an exception.

Finally she speaks to me. As she sits with her legs crossed, she tilts her head to the side and says, "I like your breasts."

Is it my rouged nipples? I feel the heat in my face as she gazes at me. I'm afraid to look down at my breasts for fear I'll see my nipples erect. I want Michiko. I feel abandoned, lost, unwanted. Will my love return?

Now the master rises and begins to undress. She does it slowly, methodically, removing each piece with care, her jacket draped over the back of the chair, her tie untied, pulled out, draped over the jacket. She continues to gaze at me as she removes her clothes, no expression on her face, no way to read her, a great threat because when they don't talk, you never know what to expect.

But then she says, "I'll flog you first. And then we'll try some other things. Have you had any experience with alligator clips?"

"Yes."

"That's why you've painted your nipples, isn't it? You want them attended to."

"Yes."

"That's fine." Meanwhile all her clothes have been removed, and now she's naked. She has square shoulders and small, firm-looking breasts, the brown nipples unusually long. Her pubic tuft has been clipped to a narrow triangle. She walks to the bed and picks up the riding crop. Now I'm forced to look at it, forced to see my punishment rod.

"Over here," she says. "Kneel on the bed." It's not easy to rise from my knees with my wrists manacled behind my back, but I try to manage it without being too clumsy. When I'm on my feet, I walk to the bed while avoiding her eyes. Climbing onto the bed while not using my hands is not easy, either, but I manage that, too.

Now my head and shoulders are down on the counterpane, my ass up, my knees spread. Of course she can see everything. I've seen Michiko's photographs of me kneeling like this, and I know what I look like.

She says nothing. Then I feel something graze the inside of one of my thighs. It's the tip of the riding crop. It moves up and down slowly, and then it moves upward to make contact with my sex. She gets the rod between my labia and spreads them. Is she looking at me? When I first arrived here, I thought they would shave me completely, but they didn't. Only the lips are shaved, and I'm thankful for that because I think having some hair in front is attractive. I've seen several slaves here who are shaved completely. All of them are blonde except one English girl, who's a brunette.

The master is still prying my cunt open with the riding crop. Now she moves it again, and I feel the tip entering the outer rim of my vagina. She holds it there, moving just the tip of it to produce a tickling sensation. It's almost like the tip of a finger, but not quite. Am I wet? I suppose that if I'm wet she can see it clearly. But she says nothing. It's maddening. I feel my belly quiver. I try not to move.

Now she withdraws the tip of the riding crop from my vagina and slides the length of the rod between my buttocks.

"You've been flogged recently," she says.

"Yes."

Then she pushes the tip of the riding crop at my anus. "And what about here? Do you like it here?"

"Yes, if the master wishes it."

She chuckles. "I'll draw some stripes first."

My belly is quivering again. I feel the riding crop sliding in the groove between my buttocks, and then a moment later it's gone. I remain motionless, waiting.

"Now," she says softly. And the next moment I hear the sound an instant before I feel the stinging pain across my buttocks.

"You're a lovely bitch," she says. She hits me again. And again. She whips me with a measured pace, each blow causing a great burning pain across my buttocks. She continues whipping me until I groan.

She says, "Yes, that's better." She whips me again. Then three more blows with the riding crop, and she stops it.

I hear her toss the riding crop away, and then I feel her fingers unlocking the manacles that bind my wrists together. When she has my wrists free, she pulls the manacles away. "Turn around," she says. "Sit on the edge of the bed."

I turn my body and take the position she wants, glancing at her, fixing my eyes on her sex, on the dark, narrow triangle. Will she be rough with me? I gauge my vulnerability. She comes forward with an easy stride, approaches me close enough so that her legs touch my knees and the dark tuft sways only inches from my face. "Go on," she says.

I touch her mound with my mouth, stroke the triangle of hair with my lips, exciting myself. The smell of her sex fills my nose as I lean forward to lick her. She arches her back, pushing her pelvis forward, pushing her cunt against my upturned mouth.

Michiko likes to tease me about the way I suck a cunt. She says I have a gluttonous mouth and I look whorish when it's covered. Oh, my darling, where are you?

The master remains motionless as I move my head from side to side. I forage in the groove with my nose, find the stiff clitoris, and begin rubbing it as my tongue flaps against flesh below.

Suddenly she begins to move. She takes control of me. She holds my head between her hands as she moves her loins back and forth. Her wet cunt slides over my mouth. Her thrusting becomes more determined, more brutal.

Will she come? My mouth is filled with her. She holds my face in her hands as she slams forward again. I hear the noise of it, the slurping noise of her cunt on my wide open mouth. The pace increases, her pelvis ramming, ramming again, and then abruptly she stops and groans and begins coming, coming into my open mouth while she grips one side of my head and my chin with her strong hands.

She strokes my throat with her fingers as I swallow her thick syrup. "Thirsty little whore, aren't you?" I suck her dry, and when it's finished, she pulls her cunt from my lips. "Stand up now," she says. When I rise, she lifts my breasts in her hands and she looks down at them. Then she takes hold of my nipples between her thumbs and forefingers and she pinches them. "How much can you take?"

"I don't know." I'm afraid now. She's a total stranger, and I have no idea about her capabilities. I have to trust them; I have no choice but to trust them.

She leaves me and goes to the dresser, then returns to me with the clips in her hands. "All right, let's try these."

The clips are chrome, the jaws serrated. I'm frightened of them. I've had alligator clips before, and they can be awful. They can tear the flesh if you're not careful, and the wounds don't heal well.

The master sees my fear and strokes my face gently. "Relax. We'll try to do everything right, won't we?"

When she attaches the clips to the points of my breasts, I know immediately that the springs are strong and the pain will soon be difficult. But I say nothing. She seems amused when she finds me trembling. "Relax," she says again. Then she wants one of my legs raised to get my cunt exposed, and when I do that, she bends to clip my labia. I feel the teeth of the alligator clips immediately, a sharp, stinging pain that quickly becomes a constant agony.

She straightens up and looks at me up and down, and I see the interest in her eyes. Her eyes are my reward. I withstand the pain in order to have her eyes like that.

"Now kneel on the bed," she says. After that it's ordinary. She fondles my buttocks, talks to me about the stripes produced by the riding crop as she moves her hands over my hips. Then it's my anus that becomes the focus of her attention. She says she wants my ass while I'm clipped. "Hold yourself open," she says.

I do that. I rest my head on the counterpane, and I reach back to pull my buttocks apart with my hands. I think of nothing but this. I feel the oil when she applies it. And then I feel her fingers pushing inside me, pushing through the ring relentlessly. She embeds her fingers completely in my ass and purrs with pleasure as she starts fucking me.

"Don't move," she says. But I'm not moving. I remain motionless, totally numb, the image of her fingers sliding in and out of my rectum burning through my brain.

Then I feel her hand sliding under my body to find the clips attached to my nipples. She twists one of the clips, and the searing pain causes me to cry out. Her hand slides back to find one of the clips attached to my labia, and she twists that clip also. The pain is total, overwhelming, like a thousand brilliant lights flashing all at once.

I hear moaning, but it's my own voice. The master continues to take her pleasure. The slave's pleasure has no meaning.

In the morning, Michiko holds me in her arms. She says, "Tell me everything."

And so I tell her everything, all of it, from the first moment to the last moment. When I finish the telling, she says nothing. She pushes me away and opens her knees to expose her cunt.

I take my reward. I suck the juices, bury my face in it, keep doing it until she pumps against my mouth and comes. I adore it.

I'm not good. I'm not virtuous. I'm not sympathetic. I'm not generous. I'm nothing but a creature of intense feeling. I feel everything, and it burns me like a fire. I have a marvelous capacity for misery and happiness. I go into the deep shadows, places that most people avoid. For example, Michiko would never do what I do. She says she's a top and not a bottom, and she could never do it. She could never do to me what I do to her. I suck her cunt whenever she wants it. I suck her ass whenever she wants it. She treats me like garbage, and I adore it. She whips me, and I want more. Whatever we do together, I can't get enough of it. I need it every day, but unfortunately Michiko is not available to me every day. So I make do. Doesn't everyone? Sometimes I think I've reached the edge of the world: one step more and I fall off.

I had a vapid and lonely childhood, and my father died when I was eight. Does it mean anything?

One evening Michiko tells me that we'll have dinner in the master's dining room. The slaves are usually not allowed in there, and I'm surprised. Michiko wants me to dress carefully. My slave collar will not be removed. She finds my labial ring on the dresser, and she makes me attach it to one of my sex-lips. She helps me with my makeup. She chooses my underwear. The pink panties are nylon lace and show my pubic hair. The matching demi-cup bra is cut low enough to expose my nipples. She wants me in sheer pink thigh-high stockings with rubber grips concealed by the lace tops. She has a time finding the right shoes for the ensemble, and she finally decides on a pair of white high-heeled sandals. I don't think the white shoes go so well with the pink stockings, but I say nothing. I'm too excited at the idea of having dinner with Michiko, and I don't want to get her annoyed. Over the underwear, I wear a white summer dress with spaghetti shoulder straps. Now the shoes look more appealing. Michiko makes me do a turn, and she seems satisfied. "I'll call for you after I dress," she says. But I start trembling and she notices it. "What is it?"

"Don't leave me alone now."

A shadow of annoyance passes across her face. "Sometimes you're a bother."

"Please, Michiko …"

"Shut up, won't you?" She turns away from me and walks toward the open window. Then she moves from the window to the mirror and touches her hair as she looks at herself. "All right, come here. Let's see if you can do it through my panties."

She lifts her skirt and puts one foot up on the chair. Fearful that she'll change her mind, I hurry to get between her legs. But as soon as my mouth clamps on her cunt through the gusset of her panties, I know I'll be allowed to finish it.

AFFINITIES

She moves as I do it, rocking her hips back and forth. It's a problem getting enough friction on her clitoris to make it good for her, but I do my best, use my teeth and nose, rub her legs with my hands as my mouth sucks the wet pulp of her cunt through the nylon. But she stops me after a while. Still holding her skirt up with one hand, she uses the other hand to pull aside the crotch of her panties. "Finish it," she says.

I'm at her again, this time with my mouth working at the flesh itself, the hairy grotto, her wet cunt covering my nose and tongue. When I delay sucking her clitoris directly, she slaps my head with her hand and shouts at me. "I'll hurt you if you don't hurry!"

Finally I make her come, a torrent of juice now bubbling out of her as fast as I can suck it. When her climax is finished, she kicks me away and she laughs. "Now look at you. You're a mess, darling. If you're not perfect in an hour, you'll be sorry for it."

She wipes her cunt and the insides of her thighs with a towel and then tosses the towel at my bed. When she leaves me, I hurry to the mirror to look at myself. Of course my makeup is ruined, nothing left of it, my mouth a smear of lipstick and Michiko's juices, her drippings glistening on my chin above my slave collar. Do I really love her? I gather some of the moisture with a fingertip and then slowly clean the finger with my tongue.

And I weep.

A thousand treasures that I want are lacking. My life is filled with misery—the misery of nothingness. I want to be beautiful this evening. I want to be lovely, vivacious, sparkling for Michiko. I'm fundamentally an egoist. When I look in the mirror, I see a slut filled with vanity and self-conceit. Every pain, every humiliation I experience is well deserved. Michiko knows that. The others know that, too.

But really, it's only a small step between the great and the small, the tender and the contemptuous, the sublime and the ridiculous, the aggressive and the humble, the master and the slave, the paradise and the hell.

It's true, isn't it?

Michiko leads me into the dining room, and when we arrive at our table, I'm chagrined to find two women there waiting for us. The women rise; they treat me like an equal; they each take my hand. Don't they know I'm a slave? I'm wearing the slave collar. It's not possible that they don't know it.

One of the women is younger, thin-faced, Nordic-looking. The other is an American of fifty or so, and before long it occurs to me that I know her face. She's in politics; I'm certain of it. No, I'm not certain of it. How can I be certain of anything here? In any case, everyone who comes here is more-or-less incognito. Their true names are never revealed, and if you do recognize someone, the rule is that you say nothing. So I say nothing. Whoever she is, the American calls himself Georgina, and the one who looks Nordic has been introduced to me as Petra. I sit opposite Michiko and between the two women, and the four of us have a clever little dinner, as though we're dining in a cozy restaurant in Manhattan. The people at the other tables ignore us; they see three masters and a slave, and it's ordinary. The Malaysian waitresses come and go; the open windows bring a breeze from the dark sea. Petra talks about the topography of the island as if this island is like all the other islands. Georgina asks about scuba diving. She says she'd like to get some of that in while she's here. Scuba diving. She looks at me occasionally, an examination, her eyes on the slave collar. Petra, on the other hand, looks at me only casually. So now I understand that Georgina is the one who will have me. It's Georgina's capabilities that concern me now.

After the dinner is finished, we leave the dining room and walk in the gardens. The women talk. Michiko walks with me and holds my hand. After a while, we move indoors again, and Petra leads us to a room on the first floor. It's a living room, furnished more elaborately than most of the other rooms I've seen. I don't think I've been in this room before, but I'm not certain.

Petra pours some brandy into four glasses, and we drink a toast to the island. I feel absurd. Not long ago I tried to escape, and now I'm drinking a toast to the place. Then Michiko leaves my side for a moment, and when she returns, she attaches a leash to my collar. The make-believe has ended, and I start trembling.

They talk about me. Petra and Georgina and Michiko sit down, but Michiko signals me to remain standing. I feel the heat in my face; no matter how often I do this, it still rattles me.

Then Michiko tells me to show everyone how perfect I am. "Show them your marks, darling."

My hands are shaking as I lift my skirt to show them the welts on my thighs. Meanwhile Georgina is getting an eyeful of the lace tops of my stockings. Michiko wants more; she wants me to show the marks on my buttocks. But I can't do that unless I first remove my panties. When Michiko's eyes meet mine, I understand she wants that. I slip the panties down quickly, step out of them, hold them crumpled in my hand and raise my skirt again with my back turned to show my striped buttocks.

"Oh, my!" Georgina says. Is it shock or arousal? In another two days, the welts on my buttocks will be gone, but now the stripes are still there—something to look at. Is it a pretty picture? My buttocks haven't received any sun since the day I tried to escape, so I suppose the tan has faded and the skin is pale. Does Georgina enjoy the color of the stripes against my pale skin? Or is it my ass that interests her?

My equilibrium is like a sand castle; one more breath, and the whole structure might collapse. I'm on the verge.

Then Michiko tells me to show them the ring. I do a turn, face them now, and part my legs enough to make the gold ring visible. Georgina's eyes are bright with desire as she looks at it. She also looks at my belly and thighs. Does she find the lace tops of my stockings appealing?

Then Georgina says, "How obedient is she?"

Michiko's response is to hand Georgina my leash and tell her to have me do whatever she wants. "Try her," Michiko says.

Georgina snickers. She pulls at the leash and tells me to get on my knees in front of her. "Bow low," she says.

I do it. I bow low in front of her feet like some ancient Oriental slave. Then she spreads her knees under her dress to suggest that she wants a more blatant indication of my servility. I move forward to get my face under her dress, and immediately I find that she's without underwear, her stockings gartered high on her thighs, her cunt naked, hairy, the scent intoxicating.

I suck at the wet pulp of her sex. She groans. She's pleased. She murmurs her pleasure to the others. Meanwhile I have the warm taste of her cunt in my mouth, her flesh like a soft fruit between my lips.

She tells me to stop. Now she wants me to rise and remove my dress. Michiko and Petra looked relaxed as they sit back and watch us. I avoid Michiko's eyes. Whatever I do, I do for Michiko. The humiliation I feel is a gift to Michiko. So I tell myself.

I strip my dress from my body. Georgina says she wants to see my ass again, and obediently I turn my back to her. She tells me to bend forward, and I do that too. Without being asked, I use my hands to pull my buttocks apart and reveal the focus of her interest. Is she pleased?

I hear Georgina chuckling. "She looks used. But I like those marks on her ass."

Petra says, "Why don't we get our clothes off?"

"Sure, why not?" As the women rise to undress, Michiko rises also. But she's leaving. She comes to me, and she kisses my cheek and leaves us. I begin trembling immediately, shocked by her exit, disconsolate, confused, fearful.

I watch the women undress. Petra has a thin body. Her skin is fair, pink, her breasts small and drooping. Georgina has large ripe breasts with enormous nipples.

I'm nothing but an amusement for them, an abject toy groveling at their feet. As I squat on my heels, they approach me together to have me suck them one after the other.

My cunt is dripping but it means nothing. The pleasure of the slave has no meaning.

"And then what happened?" Michiko says. "Did they have your ass at all?"

"Georgina did."

"Tell me how." I tell her. After I finished sucking them, Petra left and Georgina took me to a room. She had me everywhere with her fingers, mouth and cunt and ass, until I was sore. Then she whipped my thighs with a belt. I sucked her again. She choked me with her juices. She pinched my nipples until I cried, and then she threw me out of the room and shut the door.

"That woman is a toad," Michiko says. She opens her thighs. She wants me to suck her again. I press my mouth against the open clam and do my best to think of nothing else. I think of Michiko. I think of Michiko's cunt. I think of Michiko's taste. I think only of Michiko.

There are things in my life so vague, so opaque, so undefined, that I find it impossible to grasp them. I analyze and analyze, and it goes nowhere. There are feelings that rise and rush over me and overwhelm me. I'm helpless, crushed, defeated before them. My soul goes blindly seeking, seeking. And nothing answers.

One morning when I awaken in Michiko's arms, she tells me for the first time that I may be leaving the island. "I think we have the ideal person for you."

I feel a bolt of fear in my chest. "Who is it?"

"I won't say anything now."

"Please, Michiko ..."

"You agreed to it, didn't you?"

"Yes, but—"

"You agreed."

"Yes, I agreed." And so it goes. She won't say anything more than that I was chosen from the photographs. It was Michiko herself who took the photographs in New York.

I plead to get more information, but it's useless. She won't say anything. I pass hours of unhappiness thinking about it. Then, three days later, I'm told to prepare myself. I move like a zombie as I gather my few possessions and stuff them into a small valise. Michiko comes to me and takes me in her arms. "I'm going to Athens with you," she says. "She's waiting for us at the Hilton."

"Who is it?" Michiko smiles and mentions a name. I laugh. "The actress? You can't be serious."

"But I am, darling. Aren't you happy?"

I'm stunned, too stunned to think clearly. "I never knew she—"

"She visited here a year ago."

"Not as a slave."

Michiko laughs. "Don't be silly. Anyway, I'm sure you'll have a lovely time with her. We've arranged for six months, but it could be more if you behave yourself. You will behave yourself, won't you, darling?" She pinches my cheek affectionately.

I feel dizzy. When Michiko leaves me, I sit down and stare at the sea. I watch a gliding seabird in the distance, and I start crying. The tears stream down my cheeks and drip onto my breasts. Of course they won't take me to Athens wearing a slave collar. I'll wear a choker of some kind, but not a slave collar. Michiko will see to everything. I might get some new clothes if they decide it's necessary. But she's already chosen me, hasn't she? Or maybe there's a final decision to be made after meeting me in person. I can't imagine myself meeting her. I'm fearful I'll act stupid and she won't want me. But of course she doesn't care how stupid I am; she cares about other things. I try to imagine the other things, and I start trembling, shuddering from head to toe. Is the air too cold? Then I think of leaving Michiko, and the tears begin to flow again.

Oh, my darling Michiko!

I'll call her Ramona. She's more than a movie star, she's an institution; a brilliant dramatic actress, a fading beauty well past forty but undeniably still lovely, elegant, magnetic, and most captivating when she's on the big screen. They say something comes off the screen when she's on it, a special magic that no one else—no other female star—can produce.

I'm trembling again. When Michiko and I walk into Ramona's suite at the Athens Hilton, Ramona is there waiting for us. She rises, and I'm immediately surprised at how tall she is. Tall, slender, perfectly dressed. She takes Michiko's hand. She takes my hand. Her eyes linger on mine, but her face says nothing, no hint of anything.

Ramona offers us cold white wine, and I make an effort not to spill it as I hold the glass. Ramona looks at me and then at Michiko. "I'm certainly not disappointed."

And Michiko says, "I didn't think you'd be."

"She's lovely, much lovelier than I thought she'd be. Photographs don't do it, do they?"

Michiko laughs. "I did those photos myself."

Ramona waves a hand at her. "Oh, they're fine. All your stuff is good. But it's only a photograph and the real thing has more ..."

"Impact?"

"Exactly."

"Well, I'm glad you're pleased." Ramona looks at me again.

"Very pleased."

I'm blushing; I can't see it, but I can feel it in my face.

I can feel the heat in my face, feel the sweat dripping under my arms and down my ribs under my dress. As I sip the wine, the surface of the liquid vibrates with my trembling.

Oh, my darling Michiko!

The arrangement is uncomplicated. I'm to be with Ramona at least six months and maybe more than that.

I'm to be her slave in all things. I'll be known to the outside world as her "personal assistant."

Ramona will be completely responsible for my existence. Michiko has brought the papers with her, and Ramona signs them. I myself have nothing to sign. I watch the signing, and I feel a great agony in my heart as I face the loss of Michiko.

But not her love. When Michiko kisses me farewell, she whispers in my ear, "I love you."

Isn't that enough?

After Michiko leaves, Ramona shows me a small room adjoining the suite that she's arranged for me. I suppose it's a servant's room. The suite itself has three rooms; an anteroom, a living room, and a bedroom. In the suite, we sit in the living room. I take the chair I'd been sitting in previously, and Ramona sits on the sofa with one leg folded beneath her and a glass of wine in one hand. "I'd like to tell you a few things," she says, a quiet firmness in her voice. "It's better to get them out now and avoid difficulties later on. First of all, don't expect me to do much for your sake because I usually won't. You're not here for that; you're here to please me. You're here for me and for me only. The best attitude you can have is to expect nothing. I'm bothering to tell you this because I had a girl with me not long ago who turned out to be a great deal of trouble. She was a lovely little slave, but she expected things I couldn't give her, and that becomes a pain in the ass. Am I getting through to you?"

I nod. I'm frozen, stunned. "Yes."

"Good. The second thing is the whipping shit. I'll whip you, but *I'm* the one who decides. Don't ever ask for it. When I feel like doing it, I'll do it. Michiko says you need it often, but it's *my* call. If I don't feel like it, you won't get it. Don't try to seduce it out of me because you still won't get it. If I'm not in the mood, you don't get it. The one thing I don't like is a bottom who thinks she's going to manipulate me. You try that, and you're out the door immediately. Okay?"

"Yes."

"The next thing is clothes. I won't tell you what to wear. You get an allowance, and you dress yourself. Just look your best, and everything will be fine. We're about the same size, and it's all right to ask me if you can wear something of mine if you need it and I haven't been wearing it. But don't overdo it, and don't wear anything of mine without asking me first. Are we clear?"

"Yes."

"Finally, there's the problem of appearances. Which means you take extra care about keeping things private. You wake up in your own bed every morning. I'll let you know when I want you, and then you make damn sure you get there. If it's the middle of the day, it's your job to make sure we're alone, and no one is around who can make trouble for me. The last thing I need is the *National Enquirer* telling the world I'm a dyke. No matter what, they'll say it if they get a line on you. Just remember that and be careful, okay?"

"Yes, I'll try."

"Maybe we'll get along."

"I hope so."

"You're afraid of me, aren't you?"

"Yes, I think so."

She smiles. "Come over here and cuddle with

me." I go to her. I stretch out on the sofa beside her, and I lie with my back against her chest as she takes me in her arms. I feel small and vulnerable, like a child in the arms of her mother. It's a new feeling; first it unsettles me, and then I adore it. How strange it is to be lying in the arms of this famous woman! A few days ago, I couldn't have imagined it. I can smell her perfume. I can feel her arms holding my body. Unable to remain silent, I blurt out: "I love you."

Ramona chuckles. "You don't even know me yet. Which of my films did you like?"

I mention one. "You were marvelous." She seems pleased, and she wants to hear more. I talk about other films, all her great successes. The words bubble out of me uncontrolled, admiration, adulation, an adoring fan at the feet of her goddess. The more I talk, the more in love I am.

Then finally I stop talking. A shudder passes through me as I feel her face nuzzling against my neck. I cuddle against her, overjoyed, wondrous. Her arms are divine! Another shudder as she passes her hands lightly over my breasts.

Ramona says, "Do you have something to wear this evening?"

"Yes, but I'd like to shower first. Can I do that?" She laughs as she pushes me away. "Go on, do it. We'll have dinner on the Plaka. We'll sneak out of here and pretend we're ordinary tourists."

I hurry to my new room, quickly strip off my clothes, and step into the shower. In a daze of happiness, I turn on the spray and lean back against the wall as the water cascades over my body. How glorious it is to have a new love! Will she be kind to me? When she's not smiling, there's a definite hint of cruelty in her eyes and around her mouth. Or am I just imagining it? I feel my breasts tingle as I remember the way she stroked them gently.

Suddenly the shower door slides open and I see Ramona standing naked. Her eyes meet mine; she looks amused; she steps into the shower beside me. "Tell me about Michiko," she says.

Under the shower, I tell her about Michiko, how I met Michiko in New York, how Michiko took me in, took me under her, took over my life completely. And as I talk, Ramona holds me in her arms again, her breasts pressed against my back, her arms folded around my body.

Then the talking stops and Ramona soaps my shoulders. I tremble as I feel her hands and fingers on my back and waist. The hands are everywhere, at last on my hips and then on my buttocks.

Ramona says, "What did she use on you?"

"Usually a whip."

"I have something I bought in Mexico. Cured leather, flat, smooth enough so that it takes forever to cut the skin. Do you want me to mark you?"

"Only if you want to."

"No, I don't want to do that. We'll just be careful." Then she reaches around to cup my breasts in her soapy hands. She holds them, squeezes them gently, and drops one hand down to my belly and then to my cunt. "Keep this without hair," she says. "Everything off, okay?"

"Yes." Her hands return to my breasts, and she kneads them with increasing pressure. Her fingers tug at my nipples. The points are already erect, burning with impatience. She pinches them, and that brings the first moan out of my throat.

She laughs, whispers in my ear. "Easy, love. You're not coming, are you?"

"Almost." She laughs again. Her left arm in front

of my body, she runs her right hand over my ass. She holds one of my breasts as the hand behind me fondles and squeezes my buttocks. Then her fingers are in the crack, rubbing soap up and down in the valley, and then finally zeroing in on my anus. She pushes one finger inside and holds it there.

"Lean forward," she says. "Put your hands on the wall and spread your legs."

After I do that, she starts fucking me. First it's one finger in my ass, then two fingers. She bites my earlobe as she slides her fingers in and out of me. She asks me about Michiko again. She asks me whether Michiko did this. She tells me how tight I am. She says she has a dildo she'll use when she feels like it. I'm groaning. She wants to know whether I'm coming. Yes, I'm coming. The top of my head is gone, and I'm screaming with joy as she works her fingers in my ass.

After it's finished, she pushes me down. She opens her legs and, as I tilt my face upward, she fits her cunt to my mouth. I start sucking it. She moves on me, her hips moving, her cunt moving on my face. She bucks her hips when she comes, grinding her clitoris on my teeth, and then, at the end, she pisses, and the urine and shower spray wash over my upturned face like holy water from heaven.

I'm consecrated. I have a new life. Everything up to this point is a bundle of trivialities.

ISOBEL

In the real estate office where she works, Isobel has been reading the same listing over and over for the past five minutes as Charley walks up to her desk. Charley is as sleek as they get; a woman who has everything going for her, always hurrying around town in a flashy little sports car with some exotic creature beside her, always dressed in nothing but the latest fashion and knowing every hot place in the city. Where does she get the time to sell any real estate? Girls go crazy over Charley, fawning over her, the femmes quivering in the aura of Charley's butch confidence. All of this making Isobel envious because her own life seems so empty by comparison. If Charley is sleek, Isobel sees herself as dull, gray, pushing forty, and generally hopeless.

Charley says, "I'd say from the looks of it you could use a drink." She has the kind of smile that makes you think nothing can hurt her. "I've got a date for lunch, but why don't you come along for the ride and get your mind off the office?"

Isobel shakes her head. "No, I'll only get in the way."

"Don't be ridiculous. Besides, I want you to meet this girl. She's a real knockout."

Which Isobel doesn't believe. If Charley's date was a real knockout, Charley would never be so magnanimous. From the beginning they've had a mutual understanding: two dykes in a straight office, let's just keep it between ourselves and don't expect me to make it with you. This unspoken agreement has always been accepted by Isobel. On occasion she sees Charley in a bar and they wave to each other, but it's never more than that. And now this offer that ought to be declined. But Isobel tells herself she needs it; she needs to be with people; she needs something. She'll be better off having lunch with Charley than eating alone again.

"You sure she won't mind?"

"Of course not. Come on, let's get out of here."

Twenty minutes later, Isobel is sitting across a restaurant table from Charley and her date. The girl is indeed gorgeous, a blue-eyed blonde in her midtwenties, long hair, a heart-shaped face, and red rosebud lips. Isobel thinks the girl looks a great deal like a former lover who broke Isobel's heart. This girl's name is Lauren, and she works nights as a dancer in a topless bar, the required assets for the job now barely concealed by her low-cut dress. Isobel finds it difficult to take her eyes off Lauren's breasts. Looking at those breasts makes Isobel more envious of Charley than ever.

Now Isobel gazes down at her drink in order not to seem too obvious, too blatantly hungry for something. After all, Lauren belongs to Charley, and it's bad form to intrude into someone else's relationship. Charley is rambling on about something, but Isobel isn't listening. In the back of her mind she imagines that Lauren is laughing at her, and she wishes she were more of a conversationalist. Tonight, when she thinks about this, she'll regret every moment she was awkward. Charley always knows what to say.

Now the waiter approaches the table and says to Charley, "There's a phone call for you at the bar."

Charley rises and she smiles at Isobel and Lauren. "I'll be right back."

Suddenly Isobel is alone with the beauty on the other side of the table. Isobel has no idea at all what they've been talking about, and she struggles to fill the awkward silence.

Isobel says, "Charley tells me you were once in a centerfold."

Lauren nods. "I was Miss August. I was a cowgirl with a ten-gallon hat and two six-guns. Maybe you saw me."

Isobel shakes her head. "No, I don't think so. I think if I'd seen you, I wouldn't forget you."

Isobel is surprised to hear herself say such a thing. Will Lauren think she's flirting?

Lauren smiles. "Well, it was a long time ago. I was just out of high school and still living with my parents." Then Lauren jumps into a nonstop monologue that begins in the cornfields of Iowa and follows her life through succeeding chapters to the present. Isobel is spellbound. If Lauren would go on and on like that all day long, Isobel would sit there without once taking her eyes off Lauren's face. But Charley returns and interrupts them.

"Hell, I'm sorry," Charley says. "I've got some pressing business at the office, and I'm afraid I'll have to leave. Why don't you two stay on and have lunch together? It's on me."

Lauren smiles. "I'd love to."

"Then it's settled," Charley says. She turns before Isobel can say anything and she gives Isobel a sly wink, an invitation that tells Isobel, "Go on, do what you want." Then Charley leaves. The waiter returns, and Isobel and Lauren order lunch.

They talk. They eat. They have some more wine. Before Isobel is aware of it, an hour has passed, and they're on their feet and leaving. Both are a little tipsy from the wine, and Lauren is hanging onto Isobel's arm to keep her balance. Isobel is amazed at herself for drinking so much and not feeling it.

Lauren says, "I've never had such a good time. It's so hard to find people you can talk to. You're really a good listener."

"You're an interesting girl."

Lauren giggles. "And you're the strong, silent type, and I love that."

Isobel doesn't usually think of herself as very strong and silent, but she lets it pass. She's willing to be anything Lauren wants. Every time she glances at Lauren, she needs to make an effort not to look down the front of Lauren's dress.

People are staring now, and Isobel feels a bit foolish, about to stagger out of the restaurant in the middle of the day with a beautiful girl on her arm. She thinks the waiter smiled a little too much when she paid the bill. So what, let them look, Isobel thinks. She decides she doesn't give a damn. This is the first time she's felt really alive in months and months.

"Come on, I'll take you home," Isobel says.

"Don't you need to go back to the office?"

"I'll call in sick." And they walk out.

AFFINITIES

Lauren has a small apartment in a building for young singles. The apartment is on the second floor; and rather than wait for the elevator, they climb the stairs with Lauren hanging onto Isobel's arm to keep from falling. "I've had too much wine," Lauren says with a giggle. Isobel is completely sober now, worried about how far to go and how much of what happens will get back to Charley. Did she read Charley wrong in the restaurant? She's not certain; she's never certain about anything. That's her big problem, isn't it? Not enough certainty.

When they reach the door to Lauren's apartment, Lauren fumbles in her purse for the key. "Don't mind the mess—I'm not much of a housekeeper."

Inside the apartment, Lauren picks up a stocking lying on the floor in the small living room. Isobel sits down on the sofa and she looks around at the clutter, the various articles of clothing scattered everywhere, every available surface piled high with an assortment of junk. Isobel is amused as she takes it all in. So what if the girl is a slob. With that body, she can be anything she wants.

"I love it," Isobel says.

Lauren blushes. "I know it's a mess but I just hate doing housework. There's so much more to life." She kicks off her shoes, and then she sits on the sofa near Isobel and lies back with one leg dangling provocatively over the edge of the sofa as she throws her arms back over her head. "God, I'm dizzy. I sure did drink too much wine."

Isobel gazes down at the luscious figure stretched out before her. Lauren's skirt has pulled back to expose her firm thighs, and those lovely breasts seem about to pop out of her bra any second. Isobel stares at the deep neckline of the dress, and she imagines Lauren's hard little nipples right there where the stitching converges on each side. Thinking about Lauren's swollen breasts makes Isobel's pussy twitch, and with a sigh she leans back and she casually places one hand on the crotch of her own tight slacks. Lauren seems oblivious. Isobel gazes at the ceiling as she carefully presses her palm against her crotch, and then finally she pulls her hand away, sits up, and tells herself to relax. Take your time, Isobel thinks. Don't ruin it.

Now Lauren shifts on the couch and she raises one knee, her skirt sliding the rest of the way down her smooth legs to expose the milk-white crotch of her panties. Her creamy inner thighs are so incredibly appealing that Isobel can barely control herself. She has an urge to dive between those legs and rip the flimsy material away with her teeth. She tells herself Lauren can't possibly be ignorant of what she's doing to her. Is it some kind of game Lauren is playing, some kind of teasing idiotic game?

At last Isobel reaches out and gently rests a hand on one of Lauren's knees. Lauren takes a deep breath, but she says nothing. Isobel's fingers inch a bit higher, and she lightly strokes the girl's tender flesh. The satiny feel of Lauren's skin sends an electric chill up Isobel's arm and down into the pleasure center between her legs.

Lauren's response is more verbal. "Mmm, that feels good." Then she spreads her legs and adds, "Do it some more."

God, she really wants it, Isobel thinks. She feels her belly tingling as the erotic heat builds inside her. She licks her lips, and she slides her hand farther along the girl's exquisite flesh until her fingers are almost at the treasure between those lovely thighs. Tiny golden curls are visible peeking out from beneath the tight edges of Lauren's panties; and now, for the first time, Isobel sees that the thin cotton is wet with the sweet juice of Lauren's cunt, right there where the swollen lips are no doubt pouting open. Isobel is almost drooling as she imagines the cunt exposed and the slick lips sucking at her thrusting tongue.

Lauren moans, "Oh, baby, you make me feel so good!"

Isobel feels the room begin to spin. She imagines that she feels a wad of juice gush out of her own pussy and soak the crotch of her pants. With a groan, she slides off the sofa, sliding down on her knees beside Lauren with her right hand stroking the insides of Lauren's thighs, her fingers digging into the yielding flesh and rubbing the smooth skin with her open palm. "Do I?" she whispers. "Do I make you feel good?" And, as she says this, her left hand travels over Lauren's body to slip inside the open neckline of Lauren's dress. Carefully, gently, her fingers trembling, Isobel pulls the neckline of the dress away, and she eases Lauren's breasts out of her bra one after the other, the lovely globes jiggling on Lauren's chest like two mounds of jelly, the hard little nipples standing straight and begging for attention. Lauren shudders as Isobel brushes her nipples with the tips of her fingers. Lauren spreads her legs farther, and now Isobel's right hand is toying with the edge of Lauren's panties, stroking, teasing with her right hand while she uses her left hand, her thumb and forefinger, to roll one of Lauren's erect nipples.

Lauren purrs like a kitten, the pink tip of her tongue licking her wet lips. She starts gyrating her hips seductively, her eyes half-closed, her ass moving on the sofa, all of it driving Isobel to the edge of madness.

Suddenly, with a husky groan, Isobel bends to take

one of Lauren's nipples between her lips. Lauren sighs and immediately she takes hold of Isobel's gray head to pull Isobel's face more firmly against her chest. "Mmm, I love that."

Isobel's tongue rolls over the hard little nipple, around and around in ever larger circles until she's licking the entire breast. She moans as she tries to suck all of the breast inside her wide-open mouth. But the breast is much too big, and she finally returns to the nipple to suckle it again. She squeezes the nipple between her lips, flicks her tongue over the tip and around the areola. Lauren squirms on the couch as Isobel teases the nipple with the sharp edges of her teeth. "Oh, baby, I want you!"

With her free hand, Isobel yanks back Lauren's skirt to completely uncover Lauren from the navel down. Isobel sits up and pulls the girl closer to the edge of the sofa, positioning Lauren's legs on either side of her own body. Lauren makes no move to resist, but instead watches with enthusiasm as Isobel now stands up and fumbles with her belt to get her pants down.

"Keep your legs open," Isobel says, her voice throaty as she pushes her slacks and underpants down at the same time.

Lauren snickers, her eyes narrowed as she gazes at the abundant bush of hair at the joining of Isobel's thighs. "I'm still wearing my panties."

"Just wait." Isobel gets her slacks and underpants off, and then she strips her knee-highs off her legs and she stands there naked from the waist down, her eyes fixed on Lauren's panty-covered crotch, her fingers sliding down over her own belly and into the heavy bush between her legs. "God, you turn me on," Isobel says in a rasping voice, her forefinger and middle finger now squeezing her clitoris between them, jerking the flap up and down without caring what Lauren thinks. Lauren's eyes open wide with excitement as she watches it.

Isobel pulls her cunt open, her fingers forcing her clitoris to protrude. "Here, what do you think of this?"

Wide-eyed, Lauren stares at the big clit. "God, it's huge." Take your time, Isobel thinks. Make it last. She drops down again and she runs her hands over Lauren's legs and then over the mound of Lauren's pubic arch. Isobel's fingers take hold of the white panties and she slowly pulls them down, down over the golden triangle. Lauren moans and closes her eyes as she lifts her hips to make the unveiling easier.

Slow down! Isobel thinks. She bends forward to get her face against the golden bush, nuzzling it, getting the smell of it, sniffing at the powerful hot woman-smell. She blows her hot breath on it and feels Lauren shudder in response.

Now Isobel pulls back and gets Lauren's panties down, and Lauren raises her knees to help Isobel slide the panties over her lovely legs. The panties dangle on one slender ankle until Lauren kicks them free. Then, her eyes heavy with passion and her rose-bud lips pouting, Lauren spreads her knees apart to show Isobel everything she has.

"And here's Lauren," the blonde says with a soft giggle.

Isobel gazes down into the most beautiful cunt she's ever seen. It's perfect, everything perfectly formed. It's a blonde cunt, blonde hair, pink lips, a bright pink interior now revealed as the inner wattles are flaring outward, the short clitoris completely covered by its hood, the opening showing an oozing of white, and below that the tight pinkish-brown anus already receiving the juice streaming from the vagina above it.

Lauren groans, half-lying on her back, her chin pressed down against her collarbone, her knees up and wide apart to make everything she has available to Isobel. "Eat me," she says seductively. "I'm dying to feel your mouth on my pussy."

With a soft growl, Isobel bends forward to press her lips directly on the open slit.

Lauren gasps, closes her eyes, shakes her knees back and forth. Her legs drop to wrap around Isobel's waist and pull her in. Now Isobel is covering all of Lauren's cunt with her mouth, the slippery outer lips hot beneath the broad surface of her tongue, Lauren's pubic hair tickling her lips and teeth as she blows her breath into the oozing sex.

Lauren groans, cries, digs her fingers into Isobel's short hair as she squirms her hips on the cushion. Quickly, Isobel slips her hands under the girl's ass, her fingers clutching the buttery globes as her mouth simultaneously presses down with her tongue sinking into the sticky-sweet pudding of the open cunt. Lauren rolls around in Isobel's hands as Isobel laps and licks and stirs the slick inner walls of her vagina, pushing forward with the pointed tip of her tongue until her mouth is completely engulfed by Lauren's hot flesh. Without reserve now, Isobel uses her nose to rub Lauren's swollen clitoris back and forth until Lauren cries out and heaves and shoots her legs up in the air as her cunt explodes again and again.

Isobel continues to suck as Lauren comes down, Isobel's lips pulling at the flowing cream, savoring it, gorging herself.

Finally Lauren drops her legs over Isobel's shoulders again and sighs. "Oh, God, that was something." The blonde giggles. "You really did me, didn't you?"

Isobel pulls away, wipes her mouth with the back

of her hand, and rises to find her purse. "You're a lovely girl."

Lauren gazes at Isobel's full ass as Isobel crosses the room. "Thank you."

"It's too bad you're Charley's girl."

"But I'm not. Did she tell you that?"

Isobel finds her purse, extracts a Kleenex, and wipes her chin. Then she turns to face Lauren again. "She didn't say it exactly, I just assumed it."

Her legs crossed, Lauren shakes her blonde head. "I'm not anybody's girl. In case you're interested, I've never done this with Charley."

Isobel sits down in one of the easy chairs, and she crosses her legs to hide her sex and make her thighs look more firm. Now she wishes she had her pants on. "Say that again."

"I said I've never done this with Charley. She tried, all right, but it never happened."

The next day at the office, Charley winks at Isobel. "How did it go with the blonde, Isobel? Nice time?"

Isobel blushes. "Interesting, yes."

Charley laughs. "Interesting? Yeah, she's that, all right. Sweet, isn't she?"

And, as Isobel watches Charley walk away, she wonders how many of Charley's other girls are interesting and sweet and untouched by Charley. Maybe it's the sports car, Isobel thinks. Maybe there's something about a flashy red sports car that gets in the way. She smiles at her own silliness and starts reading the latest listings again.

JAMIE

One day I'm wandering around the Neiman-Marcus department store on North Michigan Avenue, wandering for no reason at all, just looking, wandering and wondering if I ought to become a shoplifter, a low-life thief, because it looks like that's the only way I'll ever have anything nice in my life. I'm at a sweater counter touching, feeling the cashmere, my God, it's tempting to steal, and then, when I back away from the sweaters, I get slammed by someone from the side; a woman with packages crashing into me, her arms filled with packages, the woman crying out, all the packages falling out of her hands, an absolute chaos, and me almost knocked over on the floor, holding onto the counter to keep upright.

"Oh, my God, I'm sorry," she says. She's a plump blonde in a sweater and slacks and a butch haircut, past forty, bright red lipstick, dangling earrings, and money written all over her. Just my type. Blonde hair and blue eyes like a Norwegian, the breasts like honeydew melons under the sweater, big and hanging low enough to make you think of them swinging around when she's naked and without a bra.

She helps me straighten up. "I hope you're not hurt." She has strong hands, the fingers gripping my elbow.

"No, I'm fine." After that we scramble around to get the packages in her arms again, her laughing because she's really overloaded. For the first time I notice the shoes, her dainty little feet in strapped sandals with pointed Italian heels. A blonde with a big bust and pretty little feet. As we get the packages in her arms again, I manage to get the back of my hand against one of the honeydews.

And I say, "Can I help you go somewhere? You've got all these packages."

She throws a smile. "Listen, I owe you a cup of coffee, don't I? Let's go to the store coffee shop."

Of course I'm happy about that; a free cup of coffee is always welcome when you walk around with ten dollars in your pocket. Like a good little girl, I take some of the packages to help her, and we're off to the coffee shop on the fourth floor.

Is she for real? Maybe I'm only imagining things about her. Her breasts do get to me, and the way she looks at me. Yes, she's real, all right. It's so obvious she's a dyke, and a heavy butch, too, when she has the chance at it. She's married, with an engagement ring, a wedding ring, a home in the suburbs that I learn about when she starts talking about herself, all of that, but a heavy butch, too, even if she pretends otherwise at home in Highland Park. She says she came to Neiman's in the city today only because she had a doctor's appointment a few blocks away. Every moment her eyes show an interest in me, an interest in my furry little thing that she wants to hold in her hand and pet. God, the big breasts turn me on terribly, a pair of big honeydews like these. We make trivial talk about nothing, all the time her working on me.

And then I tell her I'm gay; casually, as if she knows it already.

Yes, of course she does. She smirks at me. "Yes, I thought so. That's why I invited you for coffee." The eyes with a steady gaze as she looks at me, connecting, putting the wires together, letting me feel the electricity between us. No need to ask about her, not now. She talks about her life in the suburbs, says she likes the city better, but she has two boys, teenagers now, and the schools are much better in Highland Park, you know. Her husband is an executive for some corporation out there and he knows nothing about the way she often cruises on Halsted and on Broadway. Now I'm wondering maybe I've seen her before, once or twice, but of course I'm always so preoccupied with my latest passion that I don't notice much. She talks on and on about Highland Park, blah, blah, and me not caring one way or the other because all I'm thinking about is how far will this go, will it go where I want it to go?

Then she looks at me and says, "Suppose I come into the city tomorrow. Will you be free?"

Meaning will I be available for fun and games. She smiles at me. And I say, "Why don't you meet me at Angie's on Halsted?"

"Yes, I know the place."

"How about three o'clock?"

"That's fine." She gives me the eyes again, silent for a long moment, and then she smiles, spreading those pert red lips, and says, "I bet you're delicious."

That makes me blush. That makes me want her

very much. But I say nothing. I'm too afraid that if I say something, it will come out stupid.

We leave the coffee shop, ride the elevator down, and say good-bye in front of the store entrance. I walk away without looking back, not wanting to look back because then I'll be too vulnerable. Do I want to be vulnerable? I don't know. I don't know anything.

At night I lie in bed rubbing my clit and thinking about her breasts, thinking about getting my face between those two pillows, thinking about her nipples, wrapping the honeydews around my ears, her breasts so warm and soft, anticipation making me rub off again and again, my clit stiff and long and hot and tingling as I jerk around on the bed giving it a rat-tat-tat with two fingers pumping in and out of Jamie's little wet socket....

The next afternoon, I go to Angie's early. The place has a smell of last night's beer covered over with rosewater, hardly anyone there, and no one I know. God, how I hate being alone! I hate getting the once-over in a bar, the eyes going up and down as they tear your clothes off your back. I sit down at one end of the bar, resolved to make one beer last. I sip the beer, stare at nothing, avoid any eye contact with the two bulls at the other end, two bruisers who look like they could take a girl apart and then make her beg before they put her back together again. Not this afternoon, Sam.

Finally Helen walks in, my Highland Park date, the blonde shorty haircut, the body in a tight red blouse and striped white slacks that show her lovely hips. She's wearing the bright red lipstick again, and that's a nice touch; a fringe benefit because it prevents her from looking too much like a bull, which I never want.

"Hello, Jamie."

"Hello, Helen." The blouse is tighter than the sweater she wore yesterday, the big breasts on display; and as soon as she sits down on the stool beside me, the electricity starts flowing again. Her face is fresh, smiling, appealing. She orders a bottle of Heineken, then leans toward me and says in a half-whisper, "I thought a lot about you last night."

"Mmm." Her eyes are hot, her eyes on my face, my breasts in this little black tank top I'm wearing. She pays no attention to anything around us. She's not cruising today. All she wants is me, which makes me feel very warm inside. She strokes my hand on the bar as we talk, and that makes me hot. I always get hot when they want me. She's more butch today, no qualms about showing it here in Angie's, talking about how pretty I am. "You're like a young Mia Farrow," she says. She talks about my "figure." I could be her daughter. I get a rush each time she drops her eyes to the front of my tank top, where I know my nipples are showing. I like turning her on, imagining her sucking my nipples.

I look directly at her breasts and say, "You're the one with the figure."

She laughs. She likes the attention. "You like the big ones, do you?"

My mouth waters as I look at the front of her blouse to see whether I can discover the size of her nipples. She leans against me to let me feel one breast against my arm, rubbing it against me, the tension building and getting me so hot that I think I'm shaking. I rub my arm back and forth against her breast while I sit staring straight ahead and pretend that nothing is happening.

Her face flushed, she whispers, "You're turning me on." And all this time my pussy is dripping like a faucet. Will she be mean?

Finally, her voice husky, she says that we ought to go someplace and get more comfortable. "I need to get back before six," she says.

I tell her that my place is a dump, which it is. And I tell her that I'm living in a girl's flophouse, which I am. She ponders that a moment, and then she says, "All right, there's a motel on Diversey."

Is that where she usually goes with her girls? As I walk out with her, the two bulls at the other end of the bar both turn their heads and look us up and down. Do I feel taken? I don't know what I feel.

Helen has her car parked on the street outside, a maroon Cadillac, almost new. "It's too big," she says. "Next year I'm getting a small Mercedes."

Who cares? Inside the car the seats are brown leather, plush, soft. I love them. When we're on the front seat together, she wants a kiss, and immediately her warm lips are against mine. As she kisses me, I get a hand on one of those honeydews, and I squeeze it. I like it. Sometimes they don't let you touch them too much. But Helen doesn't mind it. She likes it. "You're a doll," she says. "Going to Neiman's yesterday was one of my better ideas."

And so we drive down Halsted to the motel, the radio blaring a sexy beat, me dripping with anticipation. There is really nothing in this world lovelier than an afternoon fuck. Usually you have only a few hours, and that keeps the tension good and high. What I'm doing now is quivering with expectation, hoping she knows how to handle me, hoping she knows everything.

Yes, she does, all right. When she gets out of the car and I see her swaggering to the motel office, I know without a doubt I'm in for a time with her. She comes back in five minutes with a key, her small white teeth showing in a satisfied smile.

"One room left," she says. "We're lucky." We leave the car and we find the room on the first floor.

When we're inside the room, she pulls the blinds closed and draws the drapes, and then she comes up behind me while I'm standing at the dressing-table mirror. We're about the same height. She leans to the side and smiles at me in the mirror. Then she puts her arms around me and slides her hands up to cover my breasts. She bends her head, and the next moment I feel her lips, wet and hot, at the place where my shoulder and neck meet. She kisses me and whispers, "Let's get rid of some clothes."

She squeezes my breasts, brushes aside my hair with her face, and then runs her tongue over my ear. I get an instant rush up my body, and my pussy begins to tingle as she rubs her front from side to side against my denim-covered ass.

I always heat up so easily, and I'm always asking myself why it is because it makes me so vulnerable. Is everyone else this easy? Maybe it's no good to be so easy, no good at all. But of course I want it. I can't possibly tell myself I don't want it. Then, as I'm thinking about this, I feel her hands unbuckling my belt to get my jeans down. "Come on, do it," she says. And she steps back, steps away from me to begin stripping her clothes off. I turn around to watch her, taking my time with my own clothes because I want to see her. She gets the slacks off, and then she walks over to one of the easy chairs, and she carefully folds the slacks over the back. Her panties are white cotton, and as I'm looking at her from the back I can see her full ass, not big enough to be sloppy, but broad enough to be strong-looking. That gets to me, too. But what I really want a look at is up front; and now, when she turns to face me, she slips off the blouse and I get my first look at the honeydews in the bra, the two breasts pushed together to make a deep cleavage, the cups bulging with her beauties.

Smiling at me, she runs her hands lightly over her bra-covered breasts. "Hurry, doll. Get your things off so I can look at you. Or would you rather I do it myself? Want me to undress you?"

"No, I can do it." I start pushing my jeans down, and as I do that she reaches back to unsnap her bra, and she pulls it away from her breasts. There they are, the two honeydews, big and round and capped with perfect wide areolas, the nipples thickly extended and delicious to look at. She tosses the bra onto the chair, takes her breasts in her hands and massages them, and then she smiles and she comes toward me. "You want my help, don't you?"

So I let her undress me, first the jeans, and then the tank top, and now I'm standing with only panties while she cups her plump hands over my breasts and squeezes them gently. "Beautiful," she says. And then in a more husky voice: "I bet you're terrific in bed."

She kisses me, an open-mouthed kiss, her tongue licking my tongue and then her tongue licking the roof of my mouth. What I do is melt completely, turn into a soft jelly as I keep telling myself this is what I want, this is what I want, this is what I want, my knees shaking as I feel the big honeydews rubbing against my breasts, rubbing from side to side as she deliberately moves her body around. Then she pulls her mouth away from my mouth, and she bends her head to kiss and suck my nipples until they tingle, her face now flushed and her breathing heavy. "You're adorable," she says. She gets my panties down over my hips, and then she forces me backward against the dresser and starts kissing me again, pressing herself against me so I can feel the two pillows and the heat of her body. Now I've reached a point of confusion because I'm not sure in my mind what I want from her, to be cuddled against the two honeydews or to be slapped around, if she likes that. No matter what, I do need something to put the fire out, the raging fire now in my belly as she continues thrusting her tongue in my mouth, her hand sliding down and down, farther over my belly and into the quick of me, her fingers squeezing my love-lips, tugging at them, pinching them, and as she does that I part my legs farther and start humping her hand, moaning and humping because I want to get off so badly that it's making me crazy.

But she pulls her hand away and steps back. "Not so fast," she says with a soft laugh, her voice suddenly coarse, as if she's done this a thousand times, fingered off quivering little femmes and now she's tired of the ordinary and she wants something quite different. Like what? What does she want? "I like a buildup," she says. "I like it when it gets really hot." She lifts the hand she used on me to her mouth, sniffs at it, licks her fingers as she looks at me with amused eyes. She comes forward again and puts an arm around me and slides her hand under my armpit to one of my breasts. She pulls me back away from the dressing table. "The hotter you get, the better you screw," she says with a chuckle.

"You're still wearing your pants." She gives my breast a squeeze. "Go on then, get them down for me."

And that's what I do. I move around in front of her and crouch down and slide my hands up to the waistband of her white cotton underpants. Real butch Jockeys. Does she wear these at home, too? I get the underpants down her hips and there it is like a dream, completely bald, the upper part of the slit showing, no hair at all anywhere, and now my knees are shaking, I'm so hot, I'm afraid I'll fall over on the carpet.

I pull the underpants down her legs and off her feet, and when I look up again, she moves her legs apart and tilts her pelvis forward to offer it to me if I want it. "Be my guest," she says.

She has a plump little belly, and maybe her thighs are too big, but between them is that heavenly split fig, the outer lips so smooth and clean, the slit showing the pink inner lips protruding out just enough to make my mouth water. What I want is a look at the jewel, and now I run my hands up the curves of her calves and thighs, and when my fingers reach her pussy, I pull it open to look at her clitoris that points downward like a tiny pink tongue between the pink flaps.

She makes a noise, a throaty sound of pleasure as she hunches her pelvis forward to encourage me. "Go on," she says.

I move in, and I kiss it. I work my tongue between the flaps, and then up and down and around her clitoris, and then I open my mouth wide to suck everything, all of the soft flesh and the smooth, hairless outer lips, sucking everything, urging the fountain to flow, feeling the first stirrings, the first gushing on my probing tongue. I imagine I even feel her clitoris enlarge, but I'm not certain. My head is bent back, my neck arched as she pushes forward and forces me to sit on the rug; and then the next moment she moves her legs even farther apart, and she more-or-less squats on my face as I continue sucking the now-running brook.

AFFINITIES

I know she's looking down at me doing it, and I'm wondering what she thinks. Does she think I'm good at it? Does she like the way I move my mouth around to give her pink flower a firm massage as I nibble and suck it? She takes hold of my head, guiding the movements of my mouth, hunching back and forth as she gives it to me and moans, "Oh, yes! Jamie, baby, that's the best!" And my response is a more vigorous sucking, cannibalistic, gluttonous, without reservation, my lips now sliding over her swollen clit to feel the tip and beat it with my tongue, whipping it from side to side as she cries out and hunches and comes on my face with a tasty lovely waterfall.

She pulls back, her breasts wobbling. "Oh, Jamie, baby, that was so good for me. Come on, get up. Get up and let me do you. Let me screw that sweet pussy."

Hearing her talk like that turns me on. Trembling, my knees weak, I rise from the carpet, and she maneuvers me around so I'm facing the mirror over the dressing table with her behind me and her breasts pressing against my back. She pushes me forward a little, and then she gets a hand between my legs from behind. "Mmm, you're dripping," she purrs. "You're a wet little bitch." And then she makes me bend forward and put my hands on the dressing table as she pushes three fingers inside my pussy and starts giving it to me.

She's good at this. She knows everything. She knows exactly how to do it. As I stare at the mirror, I watch my mouth hang open. Her fingers punch in and out of me, the strokes long and deep and hard, and before long I'm lunging my ass back to meet every stroke, moaning and wailing as she gives it to me, and then crying out with a crazy delight as she pushes her thumb inside my anus to hold me like a bowling ball in her hand, thrusting at me, pulling back, thrusting forward again, my internal muscles gripping her fingers front and back, my cervix feeling as though it's exploding, the great white waves washing over me, drowning me, tossing me up on the beach like a helpless clump of soggy seaweed.

Afterward she takes me to bed, and I get to press my face between the pillows, roll my nose around the honeydews, then suck at those fat nipples while she does me with her fingers again. After two hours, we're both exhausted, sweaty, completely demolished.

"I need to get back by six," she says.

I watch her pack the honeydews into the big white bra. "Yes, you said that."

"It's been fun, hasn't it?"

"Listen, can you lend me some money?"

She turns and looks at me. "Sure, honey. Is twenty all right?"

"Well, I was thinking of fifty."

Silence. She finds her blouse and slips into it. "I'll write you a check," she says.

"You can always find me at Angie's on Saturday afternoon." She says nothing, and I don't care one way or the other. She continues buttoning her blouse, and all I'm thinking about is how that big white bra doesn't do much for her in the way of support. God, I love it when they have honeydews!

LINDA

(from *Linda Baby,* published by Spectrum Press)

Let's go out, Margo said, let's go out somewhere and eat. I've got to unwind.

All right. Where would you like to go? Margo said. I don't know, maybe the Village, let's go to Roz's. You know I don't like those places. Come on, Margo, nobody knows you down there. Short blond hair dyke WASP attorney Margo. Like a husband, Linda thought, she's my fucking husband look at the gray flannel suit the black string tie the way she does the makeup with just the right amount of blusher so you don't see it they must be crazy about her on Broad Street the hotshot female corporate lawyer out of Westport and Bennington and Yale Law School they ought to know about the little Puerto Rican Jewish wife she's got they'd flip down there what do you think.

Baby, Margo said, I don't like the lez hangouts, I just don't. Be nice to me, won't you? I had a really rough day, three fucking meetings and nothing gets accomplished, we just crack the yellow pencils on the yellow pads and it's all for nothing, my head was just empty today just empty that's all. So why don't we go to Ricky's on 65th Street, we'll sit in a corner and have a lovely salad and some cold wine. Are you ready for that?

The Village, Margo. Definitely not. Oh shit. Are we going to fight, baby? I'm not fighting, you're fighting. You're the one who's being difficult. I don't like Ricky's, it's too much uptight East Side shit, I don't like it.

Oh, God. Linda started to cry. She did a lot of crying these days, she didn't know why, she just started crying for no reason this was no reason they wouldn't go to the Village anyway she could never stand up to Margo with her black string tie.

Linda said, Okay. Now come over here and give me a kiss, Margo said. That's better. Don't you feel better now? What's this, no pants? My little bare-assed pussycat. You've been horny all day waiting for me haven't you baby, no stop don't move let me do it, open up a little that's it, God look at this the poor thing is dripping like a faucet, come on baby come on my hand just a quickie before we go to Ricky's just an hour or two at the piano bar and then we scoot home and I'll fuck your brains out, come baby come on my fingers come on come for me.

Linda groaned hunched closed her eyes gave in and made it with her head up her eyes on the ceiling Margo's fingers slapping in and out of her cunt oh Jesus oh Jesus fuck it's good oh Jesus it's good.

For some reason in the taxi beside Margo she thought of Max wondered what he was doing now did he still have his beard did he have a new girl taking the phone calls between blowjobs in the office? Listen

AFFINITIES

it's no good your life is no good it's a pile of shit, but she did like having Margo next to her the way Margo took care of her it was nice wasn't it she couldn't deny how nice it was maybe the nicest part was that she was clean now clean clean East Side clean with Margo making a hundred thou a year it's not like with Hector is it? It's not Chinatown no more stinking subway she rode the taxis now wiggling her ass in the department stores Margo telling her to look good dress up for Margo make Margo cream her Jockeys just thinking about her on the way home from Broad Street perfume and high heels I don't care about the face Margo said all I care about is the body the tits the butt the legs the cunt never mind the face baby it's not that bad anyway maybe not like it was before but it's fine I love you I love the face. And she'd go on and on like that and Linda would melt and cry and then stop crying and then melt again and believe her about the face no it didn't matter did it anyway never mind don't think about it think about Ricky's oh shit in the land of the uptight WASP Connecticut asses.

When they walked in, the Wednesday-night asshole was playing some stupid ditty on the piano, God, she hated ditties, with the white teeth shining at you as he goes through the dumb lyrics. Thank God they could get a corner table far enough away from the piano so she didn't have to look at him. The waiter was new, a red face licking his lips as he gave them the once-over like maybe he had it figured out the blond butch and the Spic-looking femme this is Manhattan lady you can do any fucking thing you want here you like pussy go on be my guest it's a free country she hated guys like that the way they stared at her looked her over looked at her face the messed-up Spic with the curls and the blond butch hey did you get a load a that pair how do you think they do it gobble gobble or maybe the blond one fucks her with a Coke bottle Jesus Mary why didn't she go to the Village instead of coming here I hate it hate this place really all these Yale boys with pink cheeks the way they looked at Margo she drew the eyes all right sleek well dressed the ascot just right the long earrings they ought to see her shaved pussy drop a load in their pants the jerks what are you looking at fuckface? His hair just as blond as Margo's that's the way they grow them between Rye and Hartford, honey.

You look far away, Margo said. No, I'm not. Are you angry at me for bringing you here? It's all right. Anyway, you look pretty tonight. Just the way I like you. You, too, Linda said. Really? I like the jacket. Is anyone standing behind me? No, Linda said. I'd like to suck you off right here. Do you think they'd mind that?

Linda giggled. Then she thought of Margo's friends the girls who came down from Westport married now to stockbrokers investment bankers assorted Wall Street pig-fuckers coming into the apartment to meet Margo's Spic roommate who they think is the daughter of a rich Puerto Rican hotel man because she doesn't work I don't want them to know, Margo said, please, Linda that's the way it is, anyway, it doesn't happen that often she certainly doesn't encourage them to visit her in Manhattan she belongs on the moon really and then some of the other friends a few heavies a woman who used to be her therapist one or two girls from the Village even one dyke attorney who came to dinner one night and started drooling over Linda's tits whenever Margo was out of the room her tits and legs she got hot thinking about that one sucking her off right there in the living room.

Now Margo smiled at her across the restaurant table: Home, baby?

Let me finish my coffee. In the elevator going up to the apartment they were alone after the fifth floor and Margo put a hand on Linda's ass rubbed it around got her hot through the dress before they were even inside the front door then Margo's hands all over her as they kissed Margo's hands on her asscheeks the fingers pushing squeezing probing between the cheeks pressing her asshole through her panties tickling her asscrack to get her hot Margo knew everything every move to get what she wanted like the superdyke she was the mouth working her tongue in Linda's mouth sucking her tongue getting her hot the fingers pushing down there Margo's thin body pressed against hers then a hand in front rubbing her crotch pulling up the dress the fingers finding her cunt through her panties her clit Margo snickering because she was so wet down there, Mmm my baby's hot, Margo said, using all of her hand now the flat of her hand the palm rubbing hard to give her a quick one get her primed for the bed making Linda spread her legs so she could get her wrist rubbing up against her cunt through the panties hard and fast, Come on make it baby come for me, then leading her to the bed undressing her undressing herself showing her shaved pussy the tits nonexistent only a pair of soft nipples making Linda stretch out on the bed with her knees up kneeling in front to work her fingers in Linda's cunt again smiling at her the fingers inside her pussy a thumb on Linda's clit biting her lip her face flushed God I adore fucking you, she said, one two three orgasms then finally dropping down to suck at her wet snatch the tongue the mouth the lips sucking at her like crazy making her go off again she heaved her ass off the bed cried out when it hit her clamped her thighs around Margo's head to hold her there forever it's all I have isn't it this face fucked over the scars the nose broken in two places they had to put a wire in her jaw oh God no I'm coming again oh shit her body shaking as she held on and rode with it.

One day Margo said: I'll buy you a present, what would you like?

I don't know. Isn't there anything you want? A camera. Really? Do you know how to use one? I used to sell them, remember? Oh yes, I forgot. A Nikon, get me a Nikon. Just the camera? No, everything. So in a week she had everything, the camera the lenses the accessories 1500 dollars' worth of black magic she had no idea why just a lark no it was more than that something to do maybe something she could get serious about instead of just sitting around and waiting for Margo like a sweet little pussycat I'm her cunt that's what I am the little woman waiting at home for the busy attorney she didn't want that she had to do something play with the camera the gadgets shoot pictures anything she found a lab on Lexington Avenue to develop the negatives for her proof sheets prints everything she learned from Lenny and the store coming back to make her happy for a change Margo saying Yes it's good I like to see you smiling. She took pictures of flowers dogs cats children old people Margo dressed Margo undressed Margo vamping Margo playing the coy dyke Margo giggling in he bathtub squatting on the bed to show her shaved pussy, You can't take those to that place to develop, No I'll do it myself I'm fixing up a darkroom you'll see just a few trays in the kitchen, Oh God you'll make a mess, no, I won't I promise, like a little pussycat begging for the darkroom you're crazy Linda what the hell are you doing this for going crazy with the fucking camera like this no she liked it she really liked it she liked the control the looking the images the little technical problems maybe it was time she used her brain for something that's all she had left wasn't it the face wasn't worth shit anymore just the brain and her pussy even her tits were going dropping down getting empty you're past thirty kid when she looked in the mirror she saw what the motherfuckers did to her she took pictures of her face set the timer shot her face front and profile my face my Spic Jewish face the bones in the nose never healed right they said it had something to do with dehydrated cartilage the scars where they cut her weren't too bad if she used a heavy base they said plastic surgery might help a little but she wouldn't let Margo pay for it fuck that well what do you care you lousy cunt you're not a model anyway just a pussy-wife for a Wall Street dyke lawyer at least she keeps you in clothes pays the rent buys you presents like a good husband sucks you off when you feel like it doesn't ask for too much she didn't like it she liked to whack off while Linda watched her legs up shaved pussy wide open hand rubbing her clit like crazy bouncing all over the bed when she went off just once she made her talk about the banging the three of them on her in the alley, Just so I know, Margo said, telling her about it crying in her arms oh fuck don't think about that never mind go out and buy something a new pair of shoes Margo likes her in spike heels when they play around prancing across the room to show her legs and ass get Margo hot for her hot enough to suck her off from behind when she was real hot she liked to do it that way give her some Bennington WASP face against her Puerto Rican

Jewish ass hey knock it off you'll get hot thinking about it go out and shoot some pictures dummy.

One night she woke up screaming Margo shaking her, Baby baby what is it? holding Linda in her arms Linda shaking from the nightmare not the first time a black alley and her running from them the hands reaching out slamming her against the brick wall her head knocking her back cutting her clothes the knife in one corner of her mouth lick it baby lick the blade I'll give you money here take the money one of them choking her another one digging fingers in her cunt and ass at the same time hitting her getting her down her knees scraping on the filthy concrete then one cock after the other in her mouth holding her ears to fuck her face You bite it I'll cut you baby Hey man I'm fucking her ass hey shit look at this look at this ass man fucking her ass fucking her mouth fucking her cunt one after the other shooting off on her face laughing hitting her again cutting her up hey shit look at the blood man then pissing on her all three pissing on her until she passed out like a dead rat in the black alley left her there like a dead rat her eyes open her face sliced up the blood running into her eyes from the cut on her forehead her face bashed in by the brick wall the blood running out of her broken nose her mouth hanging her jaw broken her ass bleeding like she was dead bleeding like she was dead no she wanted to be dead that's what she wanted she wanted to be dead I'm dead I'm dead I'm dead....

    Crying in Margo's arms. I'm here baby, everything is all right now. Calling her baby like they called her baby, Oh, God.

She never liked to cry, never never in her life did she

like to cry. Some people liked to cry but not me not Linda Rodriguez she didn't like it she was a street girl from the Bronx fuck the crying she didn't want the tears on her face what was left of her face the motherfuckers no I'm not crying.

La-di-da look at pictures now okay? She pulled the box down from the closet why not now she was the hotshot little photographer now with her Nikon around her neck look at the pictures she had here this high school graduation Evander Childs High School seventeen almost eighteen years old the way the schmuck photographer tilted her head to the side to make the picture dramatic my God what a baby face she had the hairdo yuk who wants to be seventeen again no but look at the eyes she already had a look of sadness in her eyes like if you look deep in her eyes you can see the future come on Linda that's bullshit anyway what happened to the others the other girls the guys how many dopeheads maybe she passes some of them on the street they wouldn't recognize her anyway not now and this one how old maybe seven years old sitting on the floor in a striped dress a doll in her lap smiling at the camera happy little girl nice teeth long black hair happy happy you never get it back you never get back what you had at seven years old not her anyway who is it this little girl she's a stranger now no she's not a stranger it's you dummy and this one nineteen years old who took this one? wearing hardly anything kneeling on the floor high heels a bikini bottom pasties on her nipples oh yes that was Sal the New Year's party when she came out like a stripper caused a riot and this one oh shit look at this one she looks like hell when she was living with Hector sitting in the kitchen when one of his friends came in with a camera look at her eyes she looks so fucking strung out wait baby you don't know the half of it and here what's this one of Lenny's against that patch of brick wall in the studio wearing nothing but white slacks her ass against the wall her tits hanging her head up smiling she never liked her nipples they were too dark but at least the tits weren't bad Lenny had a way with black-and-white good contrast he knew how to use the paper to make the picture something and here again this time dressed a studio shot with her wearing a red blouse tied up at the diaphragm the shot taken from the side so that half her right tit was hanging out the hair long maybe just washed she doesn't look too unhappy a little pensive but not too unhappy nice backlighting anyway and now here one of the beaver shots God why does she keep them? the bastard knows how to do it doesn't he? with her legs up like that a dark polka-dot blouse a black garter belt the black stockings the black high-heeled sandals and there between her thighs (they look too fat she's not that fat) her plump little hairy beaver she remembered this one she didn't want to look at the camera he kept telling her to look at the camera and she didn't want to fuck him and this one now he has her lying on a fake tiger rug on the old sofa one leg hanging her ass up nothing on top a white garter belt and white stockings the angle just right to catch part of her cunt from behind the way it sticks out from the back it always amazed her her little pooch sticking out like that so tender no wonder Margo liked to get at it from behind rub her nose in it stop it you're getting turned on looking at your own ass dummy that's what they call unbridled narcissism and this one in the park a yellow T-shirt and skimpy white shorts and bare feet sitting on a wooden bench with her elbows on the table her face in her hands she looks pretty doesn't she the long hair the eyes looking at the camera and here a black-

and-white again just from the waist up her tits lit from the side the nipples sticking out like that her face half in shadow and this one in a black leotard standing in front of the mirror one hand on her ass the back thong drawn up tight between the cheeks like that the bastard knew how to make her sexy didn't he and here in a bubble bath just her boobs sticking out her dark nipples her hair wet a look of surprise on her face and this one a shot of that antique mirror showing her naked with her back turned the long hair in back the deep cleft of her ass looking at the camera over her right shoulder she looked younger here she was already twenty-eight but she looked twenty-two not exactly the pose of a nun was it showing her ass like that the hell with them the nuns and priests the bullshit they hand out to the kids the crazy rabbis the wild ass motherfucking rabbis who think they talk to God while they shit the priests jerking off in the confession box the nuns fucking their cunts with a little statue of Jesus come on honey get the feet in there fuck your pussy with the feet of Jesus God has to spit on them if he doesn't spit on them he's no god or if it's a she a she-god spitting on them they think they know something about God they know nothing they're so fucked up in their heads what do they know they know nothing.

In a boutique on Lexington Avenue she flipped through a rack of Caribbean skirts reds yellows white and red stripes, then a tall woman wearing a white jumpsuit came out of the back office talked to the girls at the cash register walked around the shop around the rack to where Linda was standing. Need any help? the woman said. Linda shook her head, I suppose I'm browsing. You have a marvelous figure. Thanks. If you need any help let me know. All right I will. The woman moved away only a few customers in the shop Linda gliding from the skirt rack to a line of silk dresses, then after a while the woman in the white jumpsuit was back again pulling out a wild print in blue and black. This would be lovely on you. Linda looking at the price tag, It's too expensive. Try it on, will you? I'd like to see you in it.

Their eyes met, Linda silent, saying nothing for a moment. Maybe some other time, Linda said. Do you dance? No. Maybe you ought to, are you sure? No, I don't do anything. You were in an accident, weren't you? I mean your face. Something like that. I thought so, I love the way you walk, the face never matters, you've got the body, why don't you let me help you into one of these dresses? Linda looked away, then looked at the woman again: I've got a feeling you want more than that. The woman smiled: Okay I do, I'd like to ball you, you can tell that can't you? would you like some coffee? I've got a fresh pot ready in the office. Just like that, Linda thought, why not? maybe she needed it yes it didn't happen that often did it?

The woman took her hand led her to the back of the shop a small office with art nouveau posters on the walls telling her to sit down on the black leather sofa then bringing the coffee pouring the coffee into two small cups on the low coffee table, It's Italian coffee, very strong. She sat down beside Linda, the two of them sipping the coffee. It's good, Linda said. And you're good, too, good to come in here with an old dyke like me. You're not that old. Darling, I'm old enough to be your mother. You don't look it. Let me ball you and you can have anything in the store. Linda laughed, Anything? Anything at all. That Uchino dress you were looking at. That's 800 dollars. It's yours. I won't do anything myself. I don't want you to, what's your name? Linda. I'm Arlene. The name of the shop. Yes it's mine. She watched Arlene walk over to the door to close and lock it then move to the desk open a drawer to bring out a small tube of the white stuff. I'm having some of this, Arlene said, why don't you join me? No I'd rather not. She watched her do a sniff then another sniff looking at her throwing her head back smiling at her, Let me see it. Linda looked at the door: Will anyone come in here? They won't try and they couldn't anyway, not as long as the door is locked. Fuck it, Linda thought, she unlaced her tennis shoes slipped them off worked at the buckle of the belt around her waist pushed her jeans and panties down to her ankles then off her feet turned on the sofa so that she faced Arlene opened her thighs raised one knee to show her pooch, It's cold in here, Linda said, can't you turn down the air conditioning? Arlene laughed, walked to the thermostat to turn the knob, then walked back to Linda with her eyes on the target, her eyes bright. Go on, Linda thought, suck me off I don't care she looks like she'd be good at it anyway that white jumpsuit she must be pushing sixty the old bitch the way she looks at it now spreading her legs a little more as Arlene sits down on the sofa near her feet kisses one knee then the other knee then the insides of her thighs sniffing at it mumbling something her tongue out the old bitch's tongue finding her gash finding her clit nuzzling in there lapping it oh shit yes looking down to watch it the pink tongue in there flapping around like crazy then the fingers tickling probing fucking inside sliding in and out of her cunt as the tongue works on her clit to get her off more do more yes I'm coming oh shit the way she always shakes like that it's awful.

Wow look at the crowd, Margo said, her excitement

so obvious Linda wanted to laugh the East Side blonde who liked to look down her nose at the Village now with her in a lez bar in the West Village packed to the rafters with hot pussy like a supermarket every color every brand baby you name it we got it here the long bar with all the glasses on it the butches and femmes leaning over it the lighting kind of dramatic she could shoot this with Tri-X speed it up in the tray the music making her deaf Margo holding her hand pulling her along to a booth at least in a place like this when they look at you the look means something no chickenshit wondering she didn't mind it she hated pushy dykes and they were all over the place here but really she didn't mind it because her face passed here just a few years ago her face wouldn't pass here they'd take her for a slumming bimbo but now with the face she had she was just another one here a gay girl with her blonde dyke lover, I want beer, she told Margo let Margo have her gimlet what she wanted was a cold beer my God the noise in this place maybe she was too old for this scene but when she looked around at the crowd she saw most of them were like her past thirty some kids twenty some older dykes with gray hair the women dancing in the big open space between the booths and the bar the tables on the other two sides Hector would like this the way they danced with their hands on each other's asses Margo looking at her smiling, It's almost too much isn't it? and Linda rolling her eyes, Come on Margo you've been here before. No, not this place. What's the difference they're all the same, Linda said, she thought of Alan where was he now maybe here in the Village maybe down the street with the guys in a gay bar lining something up or maybe he was living with someone now she watched the women dancing the hands the bodies

pressed one against the other the hands on the asses
the femmes wiggling their butts wearing spike heels
she could imagine them getting sucked off later
maybe after they were freaked out on dope shit you
could smell the pot all the asses wiggling like that
Margo the WASP attorney doing her best to look so
cool they ought to see the cool attorney's shaved
pussy and the way she pisses when she comes pisses
all over the fucking mattress that's the way they do it
in Westport when they finally get off a big one they
piss now the eyes on them some of the dancers looking at them looking at Margo looking at Linda whatta ya looking at cunt haven't you ever seen a broken
nose before what have I got, she thought, I've got
Margo the apartment the camera the other photography shit no money in the bank no bank anyway I'm
her little wife look at the way they sweat what she
had was a busted up face a body that still looked
good sometimes good enough to get a tight-ass dyke
like Margo sucking her pussy when she wanted it all
she had to do was be there in the apartment wearing
a leotard and high heels when Margo came home and
she'd get her plumbing worked over before dinner
her pussy sucked out dry now she wondered how
many of the dykes here were better at it than Margo
you can't blame a girl for wondering can you, I'm
going to the john, she said, Margo turning up her
flushed face. Don't get lost, will you? Fuck you,
Linda thought, you don't own me, then pushing
through the crowd to the back where they had the
two johns pushing the door open walking in the place
dirty grime on the walls paper towels on the floor in
the sink shit what a hole they could at least clean up
the place it's like everywhere the whole fucking city
is like this like a dirty john then a dyke in leather
coming out of one of the stalls looking at her the

black eyes looking at her face at her legs the high heels smiling at her then two girls pushing in laughing at something kissing in front of the mirror not looking at her as she closed the stall door to piss but they were still there when she came out the two girls still kissing they're so fucking crazy for it sometimes these were street girls not rich bimbos not like Margo no old money here no money at all no nothing two New York girls making out in a dirty bathroom in the Village, then when she went back Margo said she wanted to leave, I can't take it I've got a nasty headache from the noise, the East Side look on her face oh shit, No let's stay awhile, Linda said, Maybe you'll get used to it anyway I like it here, and then out on the dance floor a girl who looked Puerto Rican dancing with her hand between the legs of a Chinese girl and then the dyke in leather from the john approaching the table with her eyes on Linda, How about a dance baby? Margo giving Linda an icy look, Well, fuck you, Linda thought, nobody owns me no they don't nobody owns me as she rose up left the table to dance on the floor.

You're a sweetie, Patti said. This was the second month they'd been together, two months with blonde Patti, all her shit now in Patti's place, a new beginning she was new now she was different not the same Linda oh no times have changed baby time marches on getting all her shit together Patti sitting there looking like sugar candy in those red-and-white panties the T-shirt with the big T between her tits the banner on the wall behind her head HUNTER COLLEGE oh Jesus well here she was looking at her blonde dolly what would Max say he'd say Linda how come you're a butch dyke is that what you want what do you think if that's what I am that's what I want isn't that the way it goes all the rest is bullshit what she had now was a blonde tootsie hooker with a fantastic ass and tits with those puffy pink nipples that always drove her wild blonde Patti darling Patti her life and love now my one and only my true love femme the perfect face the eyelashes the painted fingernails the pink heels of her pretty feet when she stood in those bareback mules that Linda loved the way she wiggled her ass when she walked enough to give Linda's tongue a hard-on.

You're a sweetie, Patti said. Listen, Linda said, I don't like it when you stay away a whole weekend, I think it's rotten. But you know I was working, honey, they had three of us corralled on that fucking estate, I mean shit it pays the rent doesn't it? What did you do with them? You don't want to hear it. All right, I don't want to hear it. I thought you loved me. I do love you, that's the trouble, if I didn't love you I wouldn't give a shit.

She tried to imagine what they did with her fucked her brains out that's what they did the three girls providing the weekend entertainment for the North Shore WASP pig-fuckers screwed them every which way they could even the wives of the pig-fuckers the lady pig-fuckers maybe the girls eating each other for the delectation of the assembled crowd in black tie oh shit don't think about it don't ask her you know what she is you knew it all the time didn't you she had such a lousy ride on the subway from her job the sweat the stink the old turd pushing against her ass until she had to move away but at least she had a job now enough to pay her part of the rent buy clothes buy things for Patti make Patti happy that's what she wanted to do make Patti happy you're crazy Linda crazy crazy for a blonde hooker what is it some kind of psychoanalytic bullshit wish-fulfillment projection Jesus maybe what she needed was a shrink again dear doctor these days I find myself a butch lesbian and even if I like it I'm not sure I can handle the spiritual consequences if you know what I mean what was she now a spic-looking dyke with hair almost a crew cut dressing in black pants and black boots with a blonde pussy hooker cuddling up to her when she came home from the job Lenny had arranged for her as a still shooter with an ad agency but of course the cuddling etcetera never lasted too long because Patti was usually on call after seven o'clock the hotels and such sometimes a convention sometimes a flight to catch on a call out of town why the fuck did she think they called them call girls in plainspeak have holes will travel right? mouth cunt ass they dialed a number and imported two or three holes for the evening. Patti liked posing for the camera and Linda didn't mind that, gave her a buzz now and then to see her little blonde pussycat acting sexy for the lens her tits her ass her legs in white stockings sometimes showing everything not for public consumption anyway she wasn't into that except for shooting Patti all she did outside the job these days was shoot bums on the streets in the subways in the alleys bums and beat up broads the knocked-out scum the city left behind on its way to nowhere.

She felt a vague tension now, a tightening in her belly. Listen, she said to Patti, how about if you just take calls during the week and forget about the weekend stuff? Patti stopped filing her nails, looked at Linda, shook her head: It won't work. Why not? If I'm not on call once in a while for a weekend, she'll take me off the list. Oh shit. What's the matter, are you feeling rotten again? What do you think? Come on, I'll go down on you and you'll feel better. Stop it, will you?

She caught a glimpse of herself in the mirror on

the wall near the kitchen table, the short hair the face with lines around the mouth she looked like hell these days the broken nose looking worse than ever Patti liked to kiss it when they cuddled kissing her busted nose the scars this face that looked fucked out and fucked up by something people never guessed what all they thought about was accidents not an alley job in broad daylight on 14th Street Patti had listened to the whole thing once and then she started crying both of them crying holding each other Patti cursing them saying she hated all her johns hated their guts all she ever wanted was another girl in her arms then turning around so they could suck each other at the same time Linda losing herself in the blonde cunt and ass the damp flesh and skin surrounding her face blotting out the world losing herself in Patti's wet cunt it was better wasn't it? she'd rather do that than suck a cock or get fucked by one rather lick a pussy fuck it with her fingers watch Patti's eyes roll up when she came she said she never never made it on a call or with any man ever she promised swore to it said it never happened just with you baby you're the only one I come with I mean it the only one.

You could stop it if you wanted to, Linda said. What about the money? Patti said. I make enough. Patti laughed, Come on, Linda, be reasonable. Let's go to the bedroom. Patti giggled, I thought you're mad at me. I'm thinking about it.

When she had Patti naked on the bed she lifted one of her legs up spread them out to make the pink slit gape like a hungry mouth oh she was hungry all right the blonde pussycat was always hungry for it the bald pussy-lips the pink in there the clit already sticking out the juice running she licked her lips as she went down Patti's hands on her head pulling at the short hair her nose sniffing at it her mouth opening to take the whole fat twat inside like sucking at an open peach Patti moaning telling her how good it was calling her sweetie the clit stiff under her lips she was an expert now the best Patti said hot pussy sucking hard now using her hand her fingers in the wet Patti humping her ass off the bed as she took three fingers inside telling her to do it then another finger sliding down to find the asshole four fingers working in the blonde cunt and ass while she sucked her clit used her tongue in the hole worked her mouth washed the open gap her fingers pumping her face her nose her mouth in the puddle of love Patti's hands holding her head her knees rocking back and forth as she cried out humped her ass shook all over on the bed like an epileptic in a fit my God what a come then she wanted her own wiped her mouth crawled up to kiss Patti's eyes and mouth and neck and mouth again then sitting up to get her pooch over Patti's face the blonde groaning grabbing her ass to bring her down sucking at her twat the hands squeezing her ass the blonde head down there between her thighs.

So what have I got? she thought, riding more gently now on Patti's face fucking her nose and mouth a job at least thanks to Lenny they liked the pictures she did they told her so oh fuck who cared about them they could go fuck themselves all she wanted from the job was the money to pay the rent buy supplies equipment clothes when she needed them of course if she had more then maybe Patti wouldn't need to sell her pussy mouth ass sometimes when she came home from a call Linda had to wonder which hole was the last one they used which hole took the load Patti would never talk about it she said it was disgusting to talk about it like that it was just something she did for money the fucking bastards this piece belongs to me and they fuck it on call how could she stand it how could she let Patti go out in the evening like that knowing everything oh fuck and here she was riding the blonde face what do you want Linda I don't know what I want I'd like to do something with my camera I'd like to do something with my life just something it's me this is Linda Rodriguez humping up and down on a girl's face what would Hector think would he say she was exploiting Patti fuck Hector she loved it she didn't care Patti loved it anyway always said she did said she liked being the femme showing her body off wearing teddies and high heels around the apartment teasing Linda with her tits so Linda would suck them getting Linda to fuck her from behind with her fingers that gorgeous ass hiked up by the high heels all the holes plugged and reamed making her come over the coffee table or the kitchen sink or a chair or once while she was half hanging out the window to look at an accident in the street.

Oh God I'm coming, Linda said, I'm coming on your face Patti I love you.

They went down to Acapulco for Christmas, Patti happy to get away from New York and Linda happy that Patti was happy smiling at each other on the plane holding hands when no one could see Linda didn't care but Patti cared said she didn't like to be stared at all the people would stare at them the two lezzies maybe the asshole on the aisle over there already guessed it.

As soon as they arrived at the hotel in Acapulco they went to the room stripped their clothes off put on bikinis and went downstairs to the pool took a dip ordered a couple of daiquiris while they lay on a pair of poolside lounges how crazy it was to be so close to the ocean and the beach and be sitting beside a pool but nobody used the beach all the beaches were public beaches crowded with characters selling blankets earrings hats anything you like always bothering you saying *chinga* if you shook your head *chinga* yourself motherfucker she liked the pool better anyway God it was great to relax like this with Patti right there beside her in the sun the heat of it on her skin Patti looking so sexy in the bikini the long legs the blonde hair the tits they ought to see those nipples on her but it's not for them it's for me. She sipped the drink looked at the pool at the people swimming around in the water the guys flirting with the girls Patti's fear was that she would come to a place like this and meet one of her johns they could be anywhere Linda hated the idea of it pushed it out of her mind pretended they were just a pair on a vacation but all the time she couldn't help thinking about the johns Patti fucking nearly every night in New York my God it's got to stop it can't go on maybe when they got back she'd try again to stop it she couldn't take it any more it was too much wasn't it too much she looked at Patti her blonde hair in the sun her breasts half-uncovered by the bikini top her love for Patti like a lump in her chest God it's crazy if the people around them knew what was going on here two lezzies in the middle of suburbia transplanted south of the border ay ay ay.

I like it, Patti said, her eyes hidden by the sunglasses, uncrossing her legs then crossing them again, I love the sun here. Me too, Linda said. It makes me horny. That figures. Patti laughed, What does that mean? It means it figures, I know all about you, I should shouldn't I? I don't know.

Linda licked her lips to let her know she was thinking about her pussy, Patti smiling at her the eyes unseen, all the rich bimbos around them showing their tits and asses to their husbands and boyfriends Hector would go crazy here call it a convention of pig-fuckers they wear the fucking jewelry down at the pool here look at that one the fat ass hanging out the gold bracelets oh Jesus what are we into here now there's more of them where do they come from maybe California they look California they have the California look don't they it's not New York it's California.

Up in the room she stood in front of the mirror looking at herself while Patti took a shower looked at her body her face in the mirror the short hair the lines the scars the nose she looked like hell didn't she but the haircut was good just right for the face she thought she looked tough as nails just the way she wanted it holding her tits in her hands getting hot baby? she wouldn't mind it the sun always made her feel horny put the edge on her the tension in her belly what she needed was a workout heavy sweating with Patti right there on the bed oh God look at the face if she turned her head that way you could see the scar on the side right through the makeup she grabbed a towel rubbed her face with it fuck the makeup she didn't want it fuck it not now when she went to the plastic surgeon in New York the lousy fuck looking at her this way and that way the pictures the diagrams five thousand dollars he said then the hinting around looking at her legs four thousand if she puts out a few times it's painless he said with a laugh anyway you'll be like new I promise especially the nose you've got to get the nose fixed it looks bad I'll do my best with the scar tissue but it depends on how well you take the grafts maybe I could have a look at the body now check things out ordinary physical okay. Fuck you, she said. He looked at her, What? I said fuck you, stick a thumb up your ass and tickle your brains. And she walked out left the office crying inside on pigfucking Park Avenue made up her mind to do nothing live with it the new me this is Linda Rodriguez Puerto Rican Jewish cunt with a broken nose scars the face wrecked oh fuck him fuck all of them where the hell would she get the money anyway?

Then Patti came out with one of the big towels wrapped around her body, What are you doing? Wiping my face, that's what I'm doing? You can have the shower now. First we fuck, then I'll have the shower. Patti giggled, dropped the towel. Horny, baby?

She giggled again as Linda pulled her onto the bed, opened her legs went down on her no preliminaries no stroking no nothing just the mouth down there smelling it the fresh soap smell licking outside and inside Patti groaning now lifting her knees Linda feeding at her this blonde lover she had her face buried in it feeling the tension again the tension still there these days she was always so restless when she wasn't working maybe she ought to suck pussy with her camera in one hand click click lap the clit click click then her fingers in there under her chin Patti tossing around groaning heaving her ass to take it Linda's excitement now she always loved it when Patti went off the noise she made like fireworks sucking the clit again between her lips between her teeth in the alley that time the one with the knife said he'd slice up her cunt if she didn't open her ass to him showing her the point of the blade near her belly near her pussy the way he giggled as he pushed his cock up her ass now Patti crying out telling her she was coming hands over her head legs up in the air wide open her lips and tongue and nose rubbing in it to give her another one.

AFFINITIES

She slept. The blinds were drawn, the room in shadows, her body turning on the sheet. She never slept with Patti, she always slept alone, her own bed. She thought the presence of another body in the bed somehow brought on the nightmares or made it easier for them to happen or whatever, she didn't want it she wanted to be alone with it alone with her dreaming the chaos the shaking the screaming sometimes.

She slept. She was in the alley again, running toward the darkness. There were times when it was only one of them behind her then two then three sometimes more than that but why more when there were only three that time she couldn't explain it if it had an explanation three bodies six hands after her the giggling the mad giggling as they cornered her near an overflowing garbage can. She dreamt her head was in the garbage but that was something that happened only in the dream, in actuality she'd fallen down hit her head against the garbage can stunned like that on the ground and then the hands on her arms dragging her up hitting her throwing her against the wall. But in the dream her head was in the garbage and they had her turned upside down her panties ripped off her legs pulled apart fucking her one after the other while she hung upside down with her head buried in the stinking garbage rotten fruit rotten meat covered with maggots someone doing something to her ass then the maggots on her face crawling over her face and that's the point at which she always woke up screaming.

Like now. She opened her eyes found herself screaming shaking in the dimly lit room alone in the bed the other bed empty Patti? Where's Patti? A panic in her throat as she looked listened for Patti then understood she was all alone in the room Patti gone somewhere the sweat now on her face as she remembered the dream again.

Get up get dressed, she thought. Then she felt cold the air conditioner on full blast so fucking cold and this was Acapulco.

In the elevator there were two men riding down with her two lardasses from the States their eyes on her wondering who this dog was the broad with the beat up face wild eyes tight slacks she ignored them walked out of the elevator into the lobby turned to find the bar past the two palm trees the fountain spitting pink water oh shit why the hell did we come here anyway? here she was running after Patti like a jealous dyke the one thing she didn't want to be was a pushy dyke she hated them hated the way they looked the hard look in the eyes then music from the open door to the cocktail lounge some Mexican crying over his guitar and there was Patti at the bar blonde Patti in a white dress with an older couple two Mexicans maybe in their forties rich looking the guy polished the woman wearing black with lots of jewelry the black dress showing her shoulders and tits the woman's eyes on Linda as she walked over now Patti turned looked smiled at Linda, Hi Linda, introductions my friend we're down here together introducing Carlos and Tina Corona from Mexico City have a drink Linda blah blah the woman's eyes on her wondering in the eyes Patti giggling at something Carlos said then the woman turning away a decision made like a sudden aversion in the eyes now turning to Patti smiling at Patti the two of them obviously interested in Patti their tongues out for Patti's blonde cunt Linda telling herself they do dope you can see it the way they handle themselves a pair of rich dopers rich everything they wanted her they wanted Patti a sudden fear in her belly then relief as the Coronas smiled nodded said good-bye walked off to leave the bar.

Patti came up to the room with her riding up in the elevator talking about what a nice hotel it was feeling the big piña colada she'd had kissing Linda's neck when they were inside the room the door closed, They want me to party with them, Patti said, I get a thousand for it that's great isn't it that pays for half the trip I'm changing my clothes and meeting them downstairs.

Linda felt the knot explode in her stomach choke her throat like a pair of hands in the alley when they slammed her against the brick wall her face slammed against the wall her nose smashed her face torn lacerated by the rough brick.

You can't, Linda said. Linda don't be silly it's a thousand dollars. She suddenly hated all lesbians hated herself hated Patti hated that fucking Mexican bitch and her husband. She screamed at Patti screamed at her never knowing what the words were any word just to scream at her the spit gathering at the corners of her lips as she screamed as she looked at her ravaged face in the mirror as she watched Patti dressing in a hurry putting on a black garter belt in order to be sexy for the bitch and her husband screaming at Patti thinking of New York what she had in New York what New York had done to her done to her face the Bronx the heat on the streets the smell of garbage the smell of piss in the subways Patti slipping into a pair of sling-back heels looking mad wiggling her ass as she hurried out to meet the Corona Coronas the fucking lez bitch and her husband Patti's legs the legs so pretty the door slamming nothing now nothing but her fucked up face in an Acapulco mirror with the faint sound of a mariachi band drifting up from the party of pig-fuckers around the blue pool. She took the two-ounce bottle of tequila from the bar opened it poured it into a glass drank some of it choked on it drank some more be tough, she thought, if you're not tough you'll get fucked over and fried come on Linda be tough baby the fucking blonde bitch who was she anyway some girl from Iowa come to New York to be a hooker be tough Linda go out get out somewhere you can't stay in this fucking room alone no she couldn't go out where could she go in Acapulco? Go to a bar somewhere wiggle her ass instead she opened another double shot bottle of tequila put the glass on the nightstand lay down on the bed to cry her fucked-up face in the pillow her throat clogged her chest heaving the tears coming out in a flood for Linda Rodriguez ten years old yes that's what she remembered Linda Rodriguez ten years old in a pink dress in P.S. 94 in the Bronx the teacher looking at her and telling her, You're so pretty Linda, she felt so good inside all filled with love for everyone the school her teacher the kids her mother her father her brother the world that little girl dead gone nonexistent now it was now Linda Rodriguez thirty-four-year-old dyke in Acapulco crying because her blonde pussycat was out partying with a rich Mexican and his wife the wife an apparent lez who gave her such a look of disdain your face looks like shit darling where do you come off to have a pussycat like this blonde does she feel sorry for you? Even at the job in New York the way they looked at her the photographer the one with the fucked-up face no one ever asking I mean what do they think do they think you get born with a broken nose and switchblade scars fuck them she wanted to sleep the tequila was good anyway no doubt rotting her guts out if only she wasn't alone go on dream baby dream you're not alone dream Patti is here with you blonde Patti cuddling right there the smooth skin all over you the little kisses how seductive she could be when she wanted to saving it all for Linda telling her the johns were such a bore such assholes all she did was think of Linda while she was with them fuck the johns do you love me Patti? she had such love for Patti such a great yearning inside her she wanted just the two of them to be against the world just the two of them together was that too much to ask for just her and Patti like they were when they sometimes walked down Park Avenue to make fun of the rich bimbos climbing into their limos with their hard little asses sticking out like that when they bent over the way Patti always laughed when she told her about Hector and what Hector said about the pig-fuckers on Wall Street she wondered what Hector would say now if he ever got a look at her face he'd say hey baby who cut you up some pig-fucker on Times Square are you peddling it now oh shit she wasn't peddling it only Patti was peddling it a thousand dollars she said a thousand dollars to party with them how can I turn it down she said it's a thousand bucks it's like five tricks in New York or a whole weekend on some asshole's estate on Long Island jumping naked into the swimming pool putting on a show with another girl taking the johns one after the other to a bedroom the host had set aside for the evening's entertainment the bed viewed through a one-way mirror (Patti said she could always tell when they were looking at her like that she felt it on her skin) So what? Did it mean anything? What did it mean as long as she had Patti with her this was Mexico wasn't it this was Acapulco come on let's have a good time baby the way they were at each other in such a hot fuck as soon as they were inside the room it couldn't be any better with anyone else it was always the best with Patti she couldn't live in New York without Patti she would die in New York without Patti she needed Patti she was thirty-four years old and she needed someone yes she did she knew she couldn't be alone not ever not alone she went crazy when she was alone she had to be with someone she was always afraid she'd get hooked on dope if she got really desperate the end of her the end of her life she might as well move up to the barrio walk the streets to make her next dime bag oh Shit don't even think about it baby it's not you it never was you you're not one of them you've got a fucking college degree don't you so what? Shit what does she do with it she does nothing with it does she? It's bullshit just nothing what did she have she had the cameras and she had her clothes and maybe a dozen books in the apartment she cared about and the memory of a rape that's what she had she had the memory of a rape on 14th Street in daylight with her head slammed against a brick wall and one cock after the other pumping in her cunt and ass she'd never figured out how many times in which hole or how many times all together or how many times her face had been slammed against the brick wall or how many times they'd cut her face with the knife after they were finished for no reason at all or how many of them had actually pissed on her when they were through with her was it one or two or three tick-tock the mouse ran up the clock what time was it now Linda baby what time is it now? Patti putting on that black garter belt for the two Mexicans for who the man or the woman or both one thousand dollars rolled up and deposited right up her blonde snatch here you go lovely they bought her like you buy a pound of chopped beef in a market I'll take a pound

AFFINITIES

of blonde pussy how much a thousand American well that's cheap isn't it if she's any good at the you know what the woman what's her name Tina having a go at the chopped meat while the husband looks on smoking one of his perfectos are they really from Mexico City maybe they're from California she goes out at night on the strip another pushy dyke in a leather bar oh shit she was dizzy she felt the tequila in her head now each time she moved her head on the pillow the fuckers the lousy pig-fuckers what difference did it make Manhattan or Mexico City they were still pig-fuckers Hector's pig-fuckers la Corona Coronas the motherfucker and his shitass wife having a lark with a blonde pussycat from Nuevo Yorko shit yes she ought to find them and take pictures of them the two of them just as a keepsake or maybe find a way to do something to the woman fuck her up the ass with a cucumber while she rims Patti the rotten bitch lez Mexican whore Linda baby who's the whore Patti's the whore Patti the pussycat hooker my true love my one and only Alan would giggle wouldn't he and what about the asshole Gwertz he'd say it doesn't serve any purpose to pass from one set of problems to another you've allowed circumstances to inflate a normal latent homosexuality stick it up yours doctor and take pictures yes why not pictures of the alley this is where I got raped and sliced up make some slides to show on the wall at Christmas parties and this is my new lez hairdo which at first I wanted because I thought it went with my face then I found out it was me Linda the butch dyke so I can walk into a bar in the Village and not get stared at it's me Linda the butch dyke what do you expect baby? She didn't know what do you want she didn't know she never did know did she? Patti wiggling her ass somewhere for the amusement of the Mexican couple I didn't want that did I? Not that I didn't want that Patti was hers Patti would always be hers it hurts motherfucker it hurts me it hurts little Linda Rodriguez in the pink dress, You look so pretty Linda, well this is what I am the little girl in the pink dress is dead this is what I am what do you think this is what I am and I'm nobody else but what I am now.

In the morning she went out on the beach and she stood there watching the sea as the sun came up behind her, and after a while when she turned she saw Patti coming across the empty sand holding her shoes in her hands. Blonde Patti crossing the white sand. Patti came up to her smiled slipped an arm around her waist and she slipped an arm around Patti's waist and they leaned their heads one against the other kissed each other and said hello.

MARCY

She tells me her name is Gail. It's a leather bash at Chicky's and I'm standing at the bar with my second beer and a taco chip. She tells me her name is Gail, and then she says, "You have such lovely hair."

She's very thin, tall, wasted looking, too much dark hair. She says she runs a clothes boutique on Oak Street, but I don't know whether I should believe her. Oak Street is swank, chichi, one long block of phoniness, and maybe I should not believe her. But why would anyone come to Chicky's and tell a lie like that? No, it must be the truth. I think I've seen her other places, too, but I'm not certain. I ask her whether she owns the shop and she says yes, she owns it and she runs it. "It's all mine," she says. "Believe me, it gets boring."

What she does for excitement is cruise the bars

looking for cunt. Yes, that's how it is; I can see it clearly. She's looking for it; she's looking at me. The only leather I'm wearing is my watchband. I look at her boots. I look at her vest. Well, it's enough, isn't it? That's enough black leather to make the point without equivocation. As if to be certain I understand things, she pulls back one side of the vest to uncover a silver chain dangling from one pocket. I get a rush as I stare at it. It looks like real silver, a dangling silver chain. Why am I hesitating? I have no job and almost no money. My life since Teresa threw me out has been completely stupid. And now Gail is here. She has money; she wears leather; she has that poisoned look in her eyes.

Outside Chicky's she waves down a taxi, and once we're inside it, she puts her hand on my knee and squeezes it. It's a possession; she already possesses my knee.

She takes me to a high-rise on the Gold Coast, a building with a uniformed doorman and vases filled with roses in the lobby. "I walk to work," Gail says. "I adore living here."

The apartment is filled with streamlined Italian furniture, leather and chrome and furs on the chairs. It's more luxury than I've seen in a long time. Teresa doesn't have as much as this. Gail tells me to make myself a drink and leaves me. I don't want to drink anything; my hands are shaking too much. Instead I stand at the window and look down at the water and the beach.

When Gail comes back, she's wearing the vest and the boots and nothing else. The silver chain is gone, but in one hand she's carrying a riding crop.

Her cunt hair is dark, trimmed to a perfect black triangle. Ignoring me, she walks to the bar and pours something from one of the bottles into a glass. "I always use a word," she says. "When it gets to be too much for you, say 'Claudia'."

Why Claudia? Who is Claudia? She says, "Aren't you drinking anything?" I tell her no. I watch her as she adds two cubes of ice to the drink. She sips the drink, then she turns to look at me. "Come on, get naked," she says.

There's not a hint of warmth in her voice. Maybe the warmth will come later. Sometimes I get it and sometimes I don't. Usually I don't care, not at the beginning. Right now I'm not here for the warmth, I'm here for something else. My legs are trembling because I know she intends to use that riding crop. I avoid her eyes as I peel off my clothes. I take everything off, get myself completely naked, my bare toes curling into the thick rug.

She looks at me. She can't hide the interest in her eyes. She puts her drink down, then walks toward me with her eyes on my belly. When she's close enough, she surprises me by sliding her free arm around my waist and kissing my mouth hard. I feel the leather vest pressing against my breasts, her hand sliding down from my waist to my ass. Then she finishes the kiss, pulls away from me, and says, "First, let's find out what you can take. Why don't you bend over the back of that chair?"

I look at the easy chair. It has a low roll back and no arms. I walk over to it, stand behind it, and then lean forward to double my body over the roll. My head is hanging down, my legs apart, my feet on the rug, my hands trembling as I grip the upholstery to steady myself.

She comes to the front first, and then she taps the riding crop against my face, against my mouth.

I kiss it. I kiss the source of imminent pain. She pulls the riding crop away and moves behind me. I keep my eyes closed, waiting, feeling the blood in my head, feeling my heart pound.

I hear the stroke before I feel it, a hissing sound, then a burning slash across my buttocks.

She does it again. And again. And the fire begins in my cunt as I wait for the next stroke.

I don't like the pain that much. If I have a choice between pain and other forms of punishment, I usually choose the other forms. But pain is often necessary because many of the tops like inflicting it. They like watching you get it. I've never met a top who seemed bored while inflicting real pain. They get bored only if they have a need to inflict real pain, but the opportunity isn't there. Sometimes the opportunity isn't there because they can't admit to themselves how much they want it. That's the best kind of top. She's always irritated by you, and she finds ways to make your life a constant torment. She never ignores you, because whenever you're there, you remind her of the inner conflict she feels.

My goal in life is to find the perfect top; someone who will never ignore me, never mark me permanently, inflict only minimum pain and have enough money to pamper me.

I do need to be pampered.

But now I'm not being pampered, I'm being whipped. And I'm moaning. Gail hears me moaning, but the whipping continues. I lose count of the strokes, but finally Gail stops whipping me. I can't move. My ass is on fire, and my body is covered with a film of sweat.

I moan again. And Gail says, "Shut up, will you? I've stopped." Then I feel her hands on my ass, her fingertips running over the welts. Her touch makes me wince, but I do my best not to moan; if I moan now, she might whip me again and make the hurt even worse.

She starts probing. I knew it would happen, and I'm ready for it. When I feel her fingers in my cunt, I whimper to show my pleasure. I'm wet, of course; the whipping has brought the juices out, and her fingers have no difficulty penetrating me deeply. Then I feel another finger pushing at my anus. Maybe it's her thumb. Yes, it must be; I can feel the thickness of the second knuckle. She pushes her thumb deep inside my ass while she holds the other fingers in my cunt. She starts fucking me. She takes me completely, hard, fast, no dalliance at all. I start coming almost immediately, and now I'm squealing with happiness as she makes me her complete slave.

Then suddenly the fingers are gone, my two holes empty. "Don't move," she says. She backs away and leaves me. I hear her go to the bar. I hear the ice dropping into the glass. My cunt is tingling, the aftereffects of the strong orgasm not yet dissipated. When I close my thighs, I can feel the wetness.

Gail returns. She knows I want her fingers again, but instead I get the riding crop. I cry out at the first blow. She does it harder this time and the pain quickly becomes excruciating. I'm afraid to use the code word for fear she'll find me unworthy, find me too quick to end the physical punishment, too unsuitable to keep at her beck and call. I don't want to be unsuitable. I sob. I beg her to stop. But of course she pays no attention, and she goes on with it.

Finally it's too much. My soul at the edge of destruction, I gasp the word she gave me: "Claudia!"

She has me on her bed on my belly as she soothes me with tenderness and dabs of Lanacaine on the welts.

"Poor little girl," she says. She kisses my shoulder. She tells me the skin isn't broken anywhere. "Is it still bad?"

"No, it's better."

"I'll get you some aspirin if you like."

"No, I'm fine. Really I am." She strokes my head and kisses my shoulder again. Then she leaves me and walks around to the other side of the bed to lie down beside me. I turn my head to look at her. She's naked now, her nipples like tiny dark turrets at the tips of her small breasts. As she lies on her side, she sees me looking at her breasts and smiles and maneuvers her body to get one of her nipples between my lips.

She toys with my hair as I suck her breast. Then she murmurs something, her hand pushing at my head, the meaning clear. I turn my body and move over her, slide my face over her belly and down to the perfect dark triangle. With a sigh, she raises her knees, then lifts her legs over my shoulders as I burrow into the wet trough.

At first it's the wetness; the flowing stream is all I experience. The whipping caused her faucet to flow, and the cunt syrup is everywhere. I lick slowly, gathering the nectar, avoiding her clitoris except for an occasional rub with the tip of my nose. My mouth and chin quickly become inundated with her warm juices. Now my tongue probes more deeply, my mouth pressing against the opening as I hold the long lips to each side with my fingers. She starts rocking her knees as my tongue dances in her vagina. Using her hands, she pulls her knees all the way back to her breasts and lifts her legs to point her toes at the ceiling.

No sound penetrates the room from outside. The only sounds in the room are an occasional moan made by Gail's throat and the liquid sounds made by my tongue and lips as I suck at her cunt.

I adore the wetness. The wetness is an affirmation of her interest in me, this wetness caused by her excitement when she hurt me. I scour the hole, cleaning it, sucking at it, still avoiding her clitoris that now protrudes like a tiny animal seeking to be stroked. With a groan, she pushes my head farther down, and immediately I attack the smaller opening, licking it, applying my lips to it, pushing my tongue inside her ass as once again she rocks her knees in her pleasure.

"Oh, you little bitch," she says. She hooks one leg around my neck to hold my face in place, to keep my mouth sucking at her dark little hole. I lose myself in it, unaware of anything now except her anus, her thighs, the wetness of her cunt against my face. Then I feel one of her hands touching my forehead, and the next moment she begins rubbing her clitoris while I continue sucking her asshole. That's how she comes. She rubs herself off as I work my tongue in a frenzy. Her legs rock, she groans, and still my lips remain fastened to the twitching ring.

Later she says, "Have dinner with me tonight. I know a place on Clark where the Spanish chicken is marvelous." Then she questions me about my life in the city. "Where are you living?"

I give her the name of a women's residence near Lincoln Park. "It's ugly."

"Do you have a job?"

"No."

"But what do you use for money?"

"I scrounge."

"Oh, dear." She goes to her purse and pulls out some money. "Here, take this. Do you have anything to wear this evening? Take taxis, will you?"

She hands me five twenties. The bills are brand new. Everything is so easy when you have money.

I go home to shower and get dressed for dinner. A

girl I know sees me walk into the lobby after leaving the taxi.

"Hey, what happened to you? You get rich?"

"I'll write you a letter."

"All right, I won't ask." She won't ask where I got the money, or she won't ask to borrow some? When I get to my room, I lock the door and strip off my clothes. I feel good. I feel as if something will happen with Gail. A shiver passes up my spine as I remember the whipping. I climb up on the bed and look at my ass in the dresser mirror. The stripes are red and purple, five or six across both cheeks. There's no pain now, nothing at all, and when I run the flat of my hand gently over the stripes, I don't feel any hurt from it.

After a while I put on a robe, grab a towel and some soap, leave my room, hurry down the hall to shower. I hate this place. The halls are dingy and the bathroom stinks. Sometimes the pipes in the bathroom are broken and it's a filthy mess. I heard someone talk about a girl on one of the upper floors who killed herself a month ago.

When I'm finished in the shower, I hurry back to my room to dress. What should I wear? Now I'm sorry I didn't ask Gail whether she wanted me to wear something special. What does she like? I try to imagine what she likes as I pull the clothes out of the closet. There isn't much anyway, but I do my best to throw together an outfit that doesn't look too freaky. I don't think Gail wants me to look too freaky; I think what she wants is an all-American girl type who just happens to be a sick masochist willing to have everything done to her, even the worst of it. I've had the worst of it, and let me tell you: while I'm having it, I love it. It's only afterward that I feel horrible. Afterward I feel like crawling into a dark hole.

"You look lovely," Gail says. The restaurant is cozy,

chic, the lighting dim enough to be like candlelight. Classical guitar music can be heard in the background. Is it Segovia? We both order arroz con pollo. Gail has a bottle of red wine brought to the table, and after the wine is poured, she lifts her glass. "To Marcy and Gail," she says.

When our eyes meet, I remember how I was bent over that chair in her living room with my ass under the riding crop. I remember the taste of her flooded cunt, the warm juices sliding over my teeth. I listen now as she talks about her business affairs, the fashion shows in New York, her travels in Europe. What I want to know is who was her last slave, but I'm afraid to ask. Instead I sip the red wine, think about her, hope that she's thinking about me and what she'd like us to do later on.

Then she wants to know when I came out. "In college?"

"Yes."

"College is always a great transition for people."

"Yes."

"You're lovely." Does she mean I'm lovely as a slave or lovely period? Is she remembering things? Her eyes tell me nothing; I want so much to know everything, but her eyes tell me nothing.

When we leave the restaurant and stand on the sidewalk waiting for a taxi, she takes my hand in hers and holds it. I suppose anyone looking at us would think I'm her niece. It's amusing, isn't it?

"Can you stay?" She says this the moment we enter her apartment. It's now nearly eleven o'clock, and I've already planned to stay the night, packed the necessities in my purse because I'm desperate to stay here. The idea of going back to that dreary hole I've been living in puts a knot in my chest.

When I tell her I can stay, she smiles and takes me in her arms. She says, "I wouldn't let you go anyway. I was just asking."

Then she kisses me and, as she presses her mouth against mine, I'm feeling the red wine. My legs are unsteady. She pushes her tongue between my lips and gives it to me in and out, in and out, her wet tongue sliding like a living thing while she puts her hands on my ass.

When she pulls her mouth away, she says, "Does it still hurt?"

"No, I'm fine." She takes me to the living room and she makes me stand in the center while she undresses me. When she has uncovered my breasts, she takes my nipples with both hands and says, "Let's try this." She starts pinching. She pinches hard. The sudden pain is too much, and I cry out like a wounded animal. She laughs and releases me. "All right, finish undressing yourself."

She leaves me. She goes to the bar to pour some brandy into two glasses. By the time she returns to me, I'm naked, and when she hands me one of the brandy glasses, I want it in order to fortify myself. Tonight it will be bad with her. I sense that. I can see in her eyes that everything will be bad. We sip the brandy awhile without saying anything, and then she takes my glass and puts it down on one of the small tables and puts her glass down beside it. Then she turns to me and takes my breasts in her hands again, but this time she's gentle, fondling them, lifting them, then bending her head to take a nipple in her mouth and bite it gently with her teeth. Then she wants to look at my ass and I have to turn my back to her so she can see the marks on my buttocks.

"Much better," she says. She makes me turn

around again to face her. She laughs and says, "The marks turn me on."

She sits down and has me stand in front of her. Then she wants one of my legs raised to make it easier to see my cunt. So I do that; I put my left foot on the edge of the sofa beside her and swing my knee to the side to expose myself.

She touches me. She separates my labia with her fingers to look at my clitoris. She looks at me a long time, tugging here and there, touching me in various places, the examination more clinical than casual, and of course, before long, my syrup is flowing in abundance, and that amuses her. She toys with me, stroking me with her fingers, a light feathery stroking designed to make me want more. I moan and move my hips as her fingertips graze around my clitoris. Then she pushes two fingers inside me. She curls her fingers and lifts her hand, the fingers acting as a hook to pull me forward.

She looks up at me. "Hello, darling." My knees tremble. "Hello."

"Move your ass some more. Yes, that's better." Then suddenly she pulls her fingers out and says, "Turn around."

I do that, and in a moment I feel her hand gliding over my thighs and then between them to find my cunt. Without her asking for it, I move my legs apart and bend forward a bit. She slides her fingers inside me again and tells me to move my hips as she begins fucking me. "That's it. Go on, come if you want."

It's like a dam breaking open. I hear the grunting in my throat, feel her fingers thrusting in and out of my wet hole as my body shakes from head to toe.

After that she takes me to her bedroom. She undresses while I lie on the bed and watch her. Is she wet? I imagine her cunt dripping on the insides of her thighs, and I want to sniff it and lick each drop with my tongue.

Before long she's on the bed. Naked, she straddles me with her knees under my shoulders, her hands gripping the headboard, her cunt grinding against my face.

"Yes, like that," she says. She pushes down, the hairy mouth possessing me, swallowing me, her syrup gushing. She rocks back and forth. She moans. I hold her buttocks in my hands as I drink from the fountain.

Afterward she says, "There's a spare bedroom down the hall. You don't mind, do you? I never like sleeping with anyone."

I don't care one way or the other. After all the wine and brandy, and then her juices flowing in my mouth, I'm drunk with happiness. The spare bedroom is really a maid's room, but it's better than the hole I live in at that women's residence. In the morning Gail has breakfast with me, but then it's clear she's had enough of me and wants me out. The hundred is sufficient, isn't it? I tell myself the hundred she gave me is fine, so why complain? When I walk out on Lake Shore Drive, it's a new morning, and I can pretend I actually live here. What I decide at this moment is that I'm not taking any more punishment. Am I lying to myself? I'm not sure one way or the other.

MARGOT

Margot was at an age when she thought it useful to tolerate the foibles of other people. It was no longer worth the effort to be critical, even in silence. Maturity, after all, meant an acceptance of varieties of behavior. In any case, the minor weaknesses of the people in her life produced only insignificant difficulties for her. Her husband, Robert, played too much golf. The two boys, now both at Princeton, seemed uninterested in anything serious. She could do nothing about Robert's fanatic devotion to golf, but she hoped the boys would soon outgrow their vapid attitudes. She was now forty-eight, increasingly conscious of the approach of her fiftieth year and surprised at how untroubled she was about it. Was she content? She had no idea one way or the other; the question always struck her as absurd. One could be content today and not content tomorrow. Was it possible for anyone to be in a constant state of contentment? She had her life—the trappings, as one of her friends liked to call the comforts of her class. The two boys were now young men, and rather than feel the loss that everyone had said she would feel, instead Margot felt as though a minor burden had been lifted from her shoulders. Well, that was done, wasn't it? If nothing else, she had raised two children without any bad luck and without much in the way of chaos. The difficulty was that the more she thought about these things, the more she realized the accomplishments—if they were that at all—left her unsatisfied. There could be more, couldn't there? This question arose now and then, drifting to the surface, posing itself, then slowly sinking into the deep again.

One day in the city, Margot noticed a girl in a dress shop. The girl was a salesgirl in one of those expensive little boutiques with Italian names. The shop was located on a street noted for such places, a short upper-class street often crowded with attractive sports cars. Margot liked the street because it reminded her there were people in the world who cared as much for beautiful things as she did. The girl had dark eyes, the most captivating dark eyes Margot had ever seen. Margot told herself that. She looked at the girl, and then she looked again, and then she deliberately turned away in order to avoid being caught staring. Staring was rude, and Margot hated being rude. But the next time Margot looked, the salesgirl caught her at it and came forward immediately. "Can I help you?"

Their eyes met, those lovely dark eyes fixed on Margot's. "I'm not sure," Margot said. "I'm just browsing, really."

"We've a batch of new blouses from Milan. Would you like to see them?"

AFFINITIES

And so Margot looked at the batch of new blouses from Milan, finally bought two of them, knowing she might never wear them. The girl took her credit card, wrote up the sale and, before long, Margot left the shop with a package in her hand. But she did not want the package, she wanted the girl. She realized that as she stepped out onto the sidewalk, and the force of the realization hit her so abruptly that she thought she might lose her balance and fall down.

Many years ago, twenty-eight years ago, to be exact, Margot and another girl had surrendered to each other in a night of frenetic lovemaking in a college dormitory room. Margot had always thought of it as her banal dark secret, an inelegant transgression produced by the passions of youth. Everyone had them, didn't they? She could barely remember the girl now, and it certainly had not been a love affair. They'd been together only that once, all night long, but only that once. The girl had been experienced enough to know exactly what to do and to do it well. She taught Margot how to reciprocate, and Margot had been stunned by how much she liked it, by how much she enjoyed doing things to another girl like that, secret things, forbidden things, using her fingers and mouth with an animal lust she'd never thought herself capable of exhibiting. The girl had never approached Margot again, and Margot had been too upset by the experience to think of repeating it. She told herself that wasn't the sort of thing she wanted in life and, when shortly afterward, Robert suggested they become officially engaged, she quickly accepted. Robert was what she wanted, Robert and a family and a settled life of discreet comfort. So she married Robert, and she had the two boys and the settled life of comfort she thought she wanted. Occasionally, during the years, she remembered the incident at college and wondered what her life might have been like had she followed the instincts aroused so violently during that one night. Did she yearn for it? She was never certain, and the uncertainty was itself an embarrassment, a dark footnote to the dark secret that seemed to grow more and more insignificant because twenty-eight years, after all, was a very long time.

Now, suddenly, the secret was no longer insignificant. Why now? Why had the girl in the boutique upset her so? Margot had no idea. She thought of it constantly for a week, but she could find no answer at all. Was it something working inside her without her awareness? Why this particular girl? The salesgirl was attractive, but certainly not startling. Margot knew girls who were more beautiful, women who were more alluring. She'd even been approached by women on occasion, once in Paris and once in a hotel in St. Louis of all places, but she had never yielded, never accepted the approach. Why this girl? Why did she suddenly want this girl? And then, after a week came the second realization, and with almost as much force as the first: the girl in the boutique bore a striking resemblance to the girl Margot had known in college. The dark eyes were the same, the same dark eyes and the same heart-shaped face, the same rosebud lips. Margot shuddered now as she realized it, as she realized she had to see the girl again; she had to see if indeed the resemblance was as strong as she thought it was.

The girl's name was Elena. Margot learned that a few moments after she stepped into the shop, for the girl came to her immediately, said she remembered her, and asked if she might help her again. "My name's Elena," the girl said.

AFFINITIES

This time she showed Margot some skirts, but Margot saw nothing she liked, and she bought nothing this time. They chatted anyway. Yes, Elena did bear a striking resemblance to that girl Margot had known in college. Margot felt more at ease as she talked to Elena, but more captivated by the girl than ever. In order to avoid the appearance of being too forward, she deliberately cut short her stay in the shop with the excuse that she had to meet someone. "I'll come back another time," Margot said with a smile. "You're usually here, aren't you?"

Elena nodded, her dark eyes unwavering. "Every day until six."

But when Margot returned three days later, Elena was out, not working that day. Margot felt a sharp disappointment, passed an irritable day shopping at the larger stores, and then an irritable evening at home coping with Robert's boring talk about his business friends. You're becoming obsessed, Margot thought. Was she? Yes, she thought, she was. Late the next morning, she drove into the city and visited the boutique again.

This time Elena was there. The girl showed Margot some blouses that had just arrived. Margot bought three French blouses, and when she asked Elena whether she cared to have lunch with her, Elena seemed unsurprised and accepted immediately. "I'm off in a few minutes," Elena said. Margot said she would wait outside in her car.

She sat there behind the wheel of the car, trembling as she waited for Elena. She hadn't thought it would happen so fast, hadn't thought the girl would actually agree to have lunch with her.

Twenty minutes later, she sat with Elena in a chic little restaurant with enormous menus in French and English. It was understood, of course, that Margot would pay for it. Elena, no doubt, would need to work an entire day to pay for her share. Elena agreed to have white wine, and then allowed Margot to choose a filet of salmon almondine for her. They talked easily during the meal, Elena telling Margot about her vague plans to return to college someday. She was only twenty-two years old, but nothing seemed to interest her. Toward the end of the meal, while they were having their coffee, Elena said, "If you want to go to bed with me, I have the afternoon off, and my roommate's out of town."

Margot almost crashed the Mercedes coupe driving to Elena's apartment. She was afraid to talk, afraid to ask how Elena had known everything, afraid that somehow the spell would be broken and she'd lose the moment. Once inside Elena's dull and cluttered apartment, Margot immediately felt awkward, out of place, in foreign surroundings. Elena seemed to sense it, and she smiled. "It's a mess, isn't it?"

"No, it's quite nice."

"There's wine, if you want it."

"No, not really." It was obvious that Elena was waiting for her. Trembling again, Margot stepped forward and took Elena in her arms and kissed her. A light kiss. Then a stronger kiss. Then a third kiss that was more feverish, more to the point. She was thrilled by the girl's soft, wet mouth. She wondered how often Elena did this sort of thing, how often she fell into the arms of middle-aged women who shopped in the boutique. She moved her hands over Elena's body, stroking the girl's back and hips. Elena remained passive as Margot undressed her, pulled at the zippers, undid the buttons, slid the clothes off Elena's slender body until the girl was naked, sleek, her skin like silk under Margot's fingertips.

Laughing, Elena pulled away from Margot. "Let's go to my room. I like doing it on a bed better than on a sofa."

Her eyes on the perfect firm buttocks, Margot followed the naked girl into one of the small bedrooms, a room even more untidy than the living room, the bed unmade, the shades already drawn, a faint smell of cologne and sweat in the air.

Elena slid onto the bed on her back. Without coyness, she opened her legs to show herself. Margot understood what Elena wanted, what Elena expected her to do. For an instant, Margot wanted to balk. Did she really want this? There was no love here, no affection emanating from Elena. Do I want this? Margot thought. Yes, she did want it. The hunger for it was already so great, she felt consumed by it.

She looked at Elena's sex. The girl had an abundance of hair down there, the dark hair hiding everything, a dense thicket that grew wild on the insides of her thighs and gave her sex an animallike appearance.

With a deliberate attempt to tease, Elena slid a hand down to her crotch and slowly opened the long lips with her fingers. "Don't you want to?"

Margot looked at the dark sex a long moment. Then she groaned and threw herself at it.

It was like the other time, that time when she was in college. A frenzy of passion overcame Margot as she pushed her face between Elena's welcoming thighs. Elena groaned and spread her thighs even wider when she felt Margot's breath on her sex. "Come on," Elena said.

Margot opened the flower. She pulled the lips apart and trembled as she gazed at the girl's aggressive clitoris. Margot guessed it was larger than her own; certainly the shaft looked longer. How absurd it was that so many years had passed since she'd looked at another woman like this, had her face this close to it, so close that the scent of the sex was enough to drive her mad with excitement. Oh, you fool! Margot thought. And then she bent her head to kiss the flower, and she stopped thinking about anything but what she had under her mouth. Now she was blind, and she had to discover everything with only her lips and tongue. She licked in the groove along one side of Elena's clitoris and then down the other side. She felt as though she had an entire continent to explore; mountains and valleys and rifts, and down there the deep well of Elena's opening that was now exuding a thick delicious syrup. Margot sucked at the opening and quivered with happiness when she found her nose pressing against the flap of Elena's clitoris. This, too, was like the first time, that time so many years ago. Margot remembered it. She rubbed her nose from side to side against Elena's clitoris as she sucked the warm fluid out of Elena's opening. Elena put her hands on Margot's head as she began moving her pelvis in circles. Sounds came out of Elena's throat, a jumble of words, and Margot strained to hear them as she continued sucking at the wet flower. The bed creaking, her body shaking up and down, Elena finally finished coming. "Oh, wow!" Elena said, her eyes closed, her voice suddenly fatigued.

Margot needed to wipe her face. Rather than use what she expected was a horrible bathroom, she left the room to find her purse and a handkerchief. In the living room she discovered that her hands were shaking, and it bothered her immensely. Oh, dear, she thought. What a poor soul you are. She dried her face, replaced the handkerchief in her purse, and returned to the bedroom. Elena was lying on her side now. Her eyes were open, and when she saw Margot, she smiled and slowly lifted one leg to expose her sex. "I could make it again if you want it."

Margot felt suddenly faint. "No, I don't think so. I really have to go now."

"Are you sure?"

"Yes."

Elena sat up and shrugged. She left the bed and she came to Margot, smiled and leaned forward to lightly kiss Margot's lips. Then Elena turned and she walked in front of Margot to the other end of the apartment where the front door was located. "I loved it," Elena said.

A few minutes later, Margot was on the street, wondering which direction would make it easier to find a taxi.

The event burned in Margot's thoughts for days. Her mind was filled with images of Elena naked, Elena on the bed, Elena's sex unfurled and waiting for Margot's mouth. First she resolved not to see the girl ever again. The she realized that her resolve was ridiculous because she'd never adhere to it. After a week, she understood she could not possibly avoid seeing Elena again. At the end of the second week, in a state of quiet desperation, she returned to the shop where Elena worked. But the girl was not there, and when Margot made an inquiry, she was dismayed to learn that Elena was no longer one of the employees. "She quit," the manager said with a curious look at Margot. "I was about to let her go anyway."

"Is there any way I can reach her?" But the woman who managed the shop was already walking away, obviously uninterested, not at all interested in Margot who was certainly not a regular customer, not anyone who could be counted on for a significant sale.

Snooty, Margot thought. She hated it when salespeople were snooty to her. She turned and walked out hurriedly, wondering why she hadn't been clever enough to get Elena's telephone number while they were together. And now what would she do? Could she find her anywhere? She walked up the street, past one shop after the other, all of them appearing copies of each other, the mannequins in the windows all appearing in the same poses. She peered through each window with the hope that she might see Elena, but of course in never happened, Elena was gone; Elena had vanished; the experience with Elena would become a cold memory.

Well, I'm better off, Margot thought. That girl was too disruptive, disorganizing her life, confusing her. She wanted an orderly life, and a silly obsession with a girl young enough to be her daughter meant not order, but disorder. She would not think of Elena any longer; all that was finished for good.

But oh, those lovely eyes she had, those lovely dark eyes!

MEREDITH

Meredith's premiere occurred on a night it rained so hard that the raindrops sounded like hail. She was home alone when her neighbor Helen came calling, the visit of the older woman surprising Meredith. This was Helen's first time in Meredith's small house, and after she entered, she seemed apologetic about not telephoning first. "I saw the lights on, so I thought you'd be in. My God, what a rotten night this is! You don't mind, do you?"

Meredith assured Helen she didn't mind at all, she was happy to have her company this evening.

Helen was about fifty, a large woman with short blonde hair and a puckered little mouth now painted with red lipstick. She had square shoulders, and under her plaid shirt, her breasts seemed enormous, like two mountains of flesh covered by flannel.

Meredith was much younger, single and shy, a

slender brunette with a sleek body and a quiet way of dealing with life. Did it really do any good to rush and shout at everyone? She preferred to be quiet and passive. She was feminine, with a liking for frills, polka-dot dresses, and homemade bread. She was unattached, unsure of herself, and admittedly lonely. But what she was lonely for she had no idea. What did she want? She could never think beyond the longing for someone to share the bread she baked.

Helen was married, with grown children who were also married; but as far as Meredith could tell, Helen had no liking for her husband of so many years. "So many years of it," Helen said. "It's a wonder I've been able to stand it." The blonde chattered easily about her marital problems, her boredom, her husband's lack of consideration. She called him a lout and hinted that he was sexually inattentive. Helen made a point of saying that even if she was a lusty woman, she never enjoyed men that much anyway. She liked women better, liked their company, liked talking to them. Which left Meredith curious because she had no idea what it all meant. Meredith was curious and interested, always ready to learn something about life, aware very much of her own sexual unhappiness, the desperate loneliness she often felt. She hated it. She hated feeling lonely because it made her feel hopeless.

Meredith brought a pot of tea out of the kitchen, and they sat on the sofa sipping tea and nibbling at some cookies she'd baked. They sipped tea while the rain pelted and shook the windows.

"My God, what a night," Helen said for the fourth time.

"Yes, it's awful."

"You don't get out much, do you, dear? You ought to get out more, you know. Get more pleasure out of life. Have fun, if you know what I mean. A girl your age ought to be adventurous and try new things."

Meredith humored Helen, wondering what she was getting at. She said she thought she was just as adventurous as anyone else. "I love new adventures."

"Do you really?"

"Yes, I think so."

"You're certainly pretty enough to have all the men you want."

Meredith blushed. "Thank you, I'm doing fine." But Meredith actually had no strong interest in men, had never had any as far as she could remember. She had decided long ago that if the problem was sexual tension, she would rather masturbate than have sex with a man. She would rather pleasure herself with her fingers. Was it so wrong? She was aware now of Helen's eyes on her legs and thighs. She had pretty legs, and the robe she wore was rather short and above her knees. Under the robe she wore nothing, and suddenly she was conscious of her nakedness and felt that maybe she ought to be dressed for Helen's visit. But it was too late now, so instead she did her best to keep her robe closed. In any case, Helen diverted Meredith's attention from herself because Meredith was fascinated by Helen's square shoulders and large breasts. Meredith thought that Helen's breasts must look like heavy beach balls when she was naked. She guessed that Helen must be very strong. Yes, her hands did look strong. Meredith was amused by Helen's apparent strength because Helen's husband was a small man. Wasn't it true that opposites attracted each other? Meredith found it difficult to imagine them together.

Helen talked about how difficult life was for women these days. She sighed and said, "Most women don't know what they want from life."

Meredith agreed. She said that if she had her choice, she'd rather live with a woman than a man anytime. That brought a happy smile to Helen's face, and she moved closer to Meredith on the sofa. Now the older woman's voice was softer as they continued talking, her breasts jiggling under her shirt and obviously unfettered. Meredith was fascinated by the billowing movements of Helen's bosom.

Helen took hold of Meredith's hands. "They're beautiful. You have such beautiful hands."

Meredith's fingernails were highly polished but unpainted. As Helen stroked her fingers, it occurred to Meredith that she was young enough to be Helen's daughter. She found the adoration in Helen's eyes embarrassing.

"I'm not beautiful," Meredith said. "Don't be silly, you certainly are beautiful. I've thought that ever since I first laid eyes on you."

Helen touched Meredith's face with her fingertips, a gentle but definite caress. A moment later, Meredith was shocked as the older woman suddenly slid to the floor to press herself against Meredith's knees. What's happening? Meredith thought.

"Helen, what are you doing?"

"Nothing, darling, I just want to be closer to you."

Meredith quivered as she looked down at Helen's blonde head, at the carefully cut bangs on Helen's forehead. Helen was chattering again, bubbling with enthusiasm about Meredith's pretty bare legs, her hands stroking Meredith's ankles above Meredith's slippers. Meredith shuddered with pleasure as she felt the warm hands sliding over her smooth, shaved legs.

Fondling Meredith's ankles again, Helen said, "You have such pretty feet." She stroked Meredith's calves as she kissed Meredith's knees. As she felt

Helen's warm palms on her skin, Meredith wondered whether she ought to stop it. Helen's hands were now under the robe on the outer sides of her thighs. The mood was suddenly and definitely sexual, and it made Meredith afraid. Where was it going? She wanted desperately to stop it. Then she wondered why she was so afraid. Afraid of what? Oh, everything was too uncertain, Helen too mysterious. The rain splattering on the window sounding more and more like stones. But before Meredith had a chance to stop what was happening, Helen rose from her crouched position, her wide shoulders looming even wider and, without warning, leaned forward to kiss Meredith's mouth.

The unexpected kiss shocked Meredith. But the kiss was sweet and tender, and she liked the taste of Helen's lipstick. Yes, she liked it. The kiss was feminine and lovely. As the kiss continued, Helen's hands slid under Meredith's robe with increasing determination. Meredith shivered as Helen caressed her naked thighs, the older woman's fingers rubbing up and down, her palms stroking Meredith's smooth skin. Meredith became aware of a growing excitement as Helen caressed her and soothed her with murmured endearments. The belt of Meredith's robe came loose and, with heavy breathing, Helen parted the robe to reveal Meredith's nakedness underneath, the bush of dark hair at the joining of Meredith's thighs, her white belly, her small fruitlike breasts and tiny brown nipples that were now stiff with excitement.

Helen's strong hands covered Meredith's breasts. "Oh, how lovely," Helen said, her strong fingers gripping the two breasts, lifting them, teasing the nipples, holding the breasts like ripe fruit. She pushed the breasts together, mewling with pleasure as she gazed down at them. Then she lifted Meredith's robe to completely uncover Meredith's smooth white thighs.

Meredith protested. "Helen, please!"

But Meredith's complaining accomplished nothing. She was afraid again, afraid of Helen, fearful of this strong blonde woman who now showed a film of sweat on her forehead, whose hands felt more masculine than feminine as they roamed over her body. And then, an instant later, Helen again covered Meredith's mouth with kisses, her wet mouth against Meredith's, the taste of Helen's lipstick making Meredith very much aware this was a woman kissing her and not a man. Helen's tongue was active, aggressive, searching everywhere inside Meredith's open mouth. At the same time, Meredith's breasts were unequivocally responding to Helen's caresses. Meredith's skin was hot, her nipples burgeoning, tingling under Helen's possessive hands. She was in turmoil. She tried to pull Helen's hands away from her body, but that proved impossible because Helen was too strong. Now Helen used her strength to pull Meredith's body forward, sliding her forward and then forcing her legs open, her knees wide apart. Meredith groaned and again attempted to resist and close her legs. But, in a moment, Helen had herself wedged between Meredith's spread thighs, the lower half of Meredith's body exposed and available, Meredith's belly and dark-haired cunt revealed, her sex ripe and ready below the mound with its neatly clipped triangle that Meredith cared for religiously with scissors and hand mirror. Meredith felt ashamed because she thought herself ugly down there, thick lipped, too much ripe flesh, her sex like a hungry mouth, obscene, the dark lips protruding like wattles. She was embarrassed now as Helen gazed at her, another woman looking at her most intimate secrets.

But there was no sign of derision in Helen. Instead, her eyes were heavy with lust as she gazed at Meredith's cunt, making Meredith groan and cry out.

"Please, I don't want this!"

Helen pleaded, "Give it a chance, darling. Let me show you what I can do."

They struggled together, Meredith desperate, rejecting her excitement, pushing at Helen to get her away; Helen feverish to get on with it, to finish what she'd started, her breasts wobbling beneath her shirt like two mountains of jelly. But Helen was too relentless, too strong. Bending forward again, her face flushed, she sucked one of Meredith's nipples, pursed her lips around the nipple and pulled at it, then a deep sucking of Meredith's breast, the flesh taken, her mouth filled.

Meredith watched it, fascinated by the way Helen sucked her breast like a hungry infant. She seemed so hungry for it, her lips pulling at the nipple with such force. Meredith felt both nipples tingling, her breasts swelling.

She finally yielded to the delightful sensation, the fire in her belly too intense. She relaxed, sighed, threw her head back in a gesture of surrender, aware of what she was now permitting, but unable to prevent herself from permitting it. She was yielding her body to another woman, and what an awful sin that was. Well, wasn't it? She fought a duel in her mind even as the pleasure overwhelmed her. The spreading feeling of ecstasy was irresistible. She was lost, a great warmth enveloping her belly. She wanted everything now.

Helen continued sucking Meredith's breast, squeezing the nipple with her lips, nibbling at it, pulling it outward, the bud extended to a maximum. Helen's hands were now underneath's Meredith's body and on her buttocks, the hands exploring everything in reach, her strong fingers squeezing the firm flesh.

Meredith felt a keen pleasure being handled like that. She instinctively moved her body forward against Helen, her ass sliding on the sofa. But now Helen's mouth suddenly left Meredith's breasts, and her wet lips slid down over Meredith's belly to Meredith's sex, to the hairy mouth already partly open with expectation.

Helen sniffed at it, and Meredith blushed. Meredith's mind was in turmoil as she confronted Helen's lust. She realized that Helen was about to lick her there, use her tongue in there to do God knows what to her sanity. She'll make me crazy, Meredith thought. She found herself unable to close her legs. Did she want to? Her fascination struggled with her need to push Helen's head away. Did she or didn't she want it?

"Helen, please ...," Meredith begged.

But Helen ignored her pleading. "Relax, honey. You just relax and let me show you how good it is."

Then Meredith surrendered as she felt the first touch of Helen's tongue around her clitoris, the tongue tickling, licking along the shaft at random but still rubbing against that one spot that always brought Meredith the greatest pleasure. Her clit felt enlarged, her sex so available. She heaved her body, groaning, desperate to get free again, whimpering. But she succeeded only in bringing her clitoris into stronger contact with Helen's insistent tongue, the sudden full contact producing a hot flame in Meredith's sex and making her realize her defeat, the pleasure too keen to give up. She wanted it. She relaxed, and Helen immediately recognized her victory and began sucking with more determination.

The older woman pulled out Meredith's juices with her mouth. Now she used her fingers to open Meredith's cunt, spreading the dark flaps and holding them apart with her fingers. She massaged Meredith's swollen clit with her tongue, around and around the fat pod, then down to the vaginal opening where the white cream had gathered. Helen's tongue snaked inside, scouring the tunnel.

Meredith squirmed and heaved as Helen sucked noisily at her flowing sex, and then—finally—she yielded completely. Now she responded to every movement of Helen's lips and tongue. She had never had so much pleasure. She pulled her knees back and opened them wide, craning her neck to look down at Helen, at the blonde head, the nose rubbing her clitoris. She was lost, completely lost now, unwilling to stop for anything.

Helen felt joyous, sucking furiously as she now unbuttoned her own shirt to free her huge breasts while she kept her mouth clamped against Meredith's wet cunt. Her breasts were indeed like beach balls, the nipples fat and extended, but Meredith had only a momentary glimpse of them, and then her head was back and her eyes closed and she saw nothing. Her clit felt so huge and hot, she wanted the sucking never to stop. She rocked her knees back and forth as Helen fed on her drenched cunt, on her drippings.

Helen's caress now became more adventurous as she lifted Meredith's knees. She held Meredith's ass up, fingers clutching her buttocks as she moved her mouth down beyond Meredith's vagina to the groove between her globes. The blonde's tongue fluttered over the tight ring of Meredith's anus. After a careful lapping of the opening, which drove Meredith wild, Helen pushed her tongue inside the tight orifice to possess it completely.

Meredith groaned. Helen's tongue remained where it was a long moment as her fingers rubbed Meredith's clitoris. The sensations were now too much for Meredith, and she had a sudden and violent orgasm, her body shaking, her knees jerking in the air out of control.

Finally Helen pulled her mouth away from Meredith's ass and she sat up, grasped her own melonlike right breast with its enlarged nipple, and brought the tip to Meredith's cunt.

Her eyes open now, Meredith realized for the first time that Helen was half-naked. Meredith stared at the huge breasts. She was both shocked and fascinated as she watched Helen maneuver her nipple against her clitoris. The long nipple rubbed against Meredith's swollen clit as Helen started to massage it with her huge breast. In a few moments, Helen's breast glistened with Meredith's juices, and the older woman groaned. "Oh, honey, look at it. Look at the way you're coming on me!"

Meredith had been highly excited by Helen's tongue in her ass, the absolute lewdness of the caress, but this madness with Helen's huge breast turned her off. She was aware that Helen was masturbating herself as she rubbed her nipple over Meredith's clitoris. The act fascinated Meredith, but it left her cold. However, she was content to watch until Helen finally reached a groaning climax and then dropped down to press her face against Meredith's belly.

She's a cow, Meredith thought, and that idea suddenly caused her excitement to return. Helen's huge breasts did indeed excite her, especially the fat nipples that made her mouth water.

After a few moments, Meredith pushed Helen away gently and closed her robe. "I think that's enough for now."

Helen's eyes were glazed as she looked at Meredith. "Did you come, darling?"

"Yes, of course. I think you'd better dress now."

Nothing more was said until Helen was at the door ready to leave. "Can I come to see you again?"

Standing close to Helen, Meredith gazed at the older woman's huge breasts, now hidden by her shirt. She placed her palm over one of the breasts, where she thought the nipple would be, and smiled softly. "I'll call you."

"Will you?"

Meredith took the nipple between her thumb and forefinger and pinched it gently. "Maybe tomorrow."

STEVIE

(from the novel *Illusions*, to be published by
Spectrum Press)

After Stevie opened her eyes, it took a full minute of reconstruction before she remembered that it was Monday. This was Monday morning, and she was home again, back in her bed, back to the routine of daily living. She rolled over onto her left side, expecting to find Mandy there; but the other half of the bed was unoccupied, empty, desolate. Stevie yawned, stretched her right arm, and turned over onto her back. She stared at the white ceiling to look for an omen, a crack in the plaster, a fly, anything to get her out of the womb of the bed and into the real world. Last night on the flight from Los Angeles she had definitely had too much to drink, and now she told herself what a stupid thing it was to drink like that on an airplane. She knew all about the absorption of alcohol in a pressurized cabin, but the flight had been too boring, the alcohol her only recourse, and afterward, her mind in a bourbon fog, she'd arrived home late and hadn't done more than kiss Mandy's cheek before dropping into bed exhausted.

Now Stevie stretched her body again, and then finally she groaned and she rolled out of bed and walked into the bathroom.

She studied her face in the mirror, grimaced at her bleary eyes. She ruffled her short hair and flexed her arms. Monday morning, she thought, oh, damn! The mirror showed a lean body, long and sleek, small breasts and narrow hips, and a full patch of dark hair at the triangle. With a smirk at her image, she grabbed her cunt with her hand as if to make certain it was still there and said oh, damn again. You're crazy, she thought. But how could she be anything but crazy after three days in Los Angeles? Anyway, in a few hours, she'd be something else in a gray suit, wouldn't she? In a few hours, she'd be in a gray suit and a white blouse and a black string tie, and all the pieces would be in place again.

When she was finished in the bathroom, she came out and she looked around for something to wear. She chose a pair of blue running shorts and a white T-shirt, slipped them on, and then padded barefooted into the kitchen.

Mandy was at the kitchen counter making coffee. When she heard Stevie, she turned and smiled. "Morning, love."

Stevie groaned and sat down at the small table. "Was I carrying a book when I came in last night?"

"Yes, you were."

"I couldn't remember, and I was afraid maybe I lost it."

Mandy giggled. "You weren't that soused."

"I was soused enough to go to the wrong rack for

my luggage. God, I hate airplanes! Come over here and kiss me."

Mandy was twenty-six, but she looked much younger. She had a heart-shaped face and sweet rosebud lips that were now painted a light pink. She wore a fluffy white knee-length robe, and she had her hair tied up with a red silk ribbon that emphasized the blonde cutie look. Barefooted like Stevie, she sidled over to where Stevie was sitting at the table and bent forward to kiss Stevie's lips.

"Breakfast?" Mandy asked. When she straightened up, she remained where she was, her legs pressing against Stevie's thigh a she swayed from side to side.

Stevie ran a hand along the outside of Mandy's hip. "Sure, why not? I'm not due at the office until this afternoon." Then Stevie dropped her hand, and this time she slid it under the hem of Mandy's robe to stroke the back of one of Mandy's thighs. She stroked all the way up to the beginning of Mandy's round ass, but only enough to allow her knuckles to touch the curve of one buttock. "I haven't seen you in three whole days," Stevie said.

"Three and a half."

"Miss me?" Mandy quivered as Stevie continued stroking her thigh.

"What do *you* think?"

"All right, let's make up for lost time."

"Before breakfast?"

"*After* breakfast. We'll just think about it while we eat."

Mandy made a happy sound in her throat. "I'll be right back."

Stevie watched her leave. She wanted her coffee now, but she decided to let Mandy pour it. She wondered what she ought to have for breakfast. She'd have a simple breakfast, and after that she'd have Mandy. Yes, she did like the arrangement. After living with Mandy for three months, she liked the arrangement more and more. That's how you get hooked, Stevie thought. That was how thirty-five-year-old butch dykes got themselves hooked into domesticity. Was that what she wanted? She wasn't sure anymore what she wanted. All she knew was that Mandy was too lovely to give up, a pliant and lovely femme who at times could be irresistible. Maybe the best thing about Mandy was that she never talked about anything permanent. She seemed satisfied with what they had; either that or she knew Stevie would be annoyed if she pushed too hard. Of course Stevie would be more than annoyed, she'd hate it. She hated being pushed. She had told Mandy about that at the beginning, and Mandy had agreed to accept Stevie's terms.

"I just want to live with you," Mandy had said. She'd wanted to continue dancing at Rego's, but Stevie would have none of that; no wife of hers dancing half-naked in front of other women, especially at a sewer like Rego's. Stevie would take care of her. She enjoyed doing things for Mandy, enjoyed looking after her, enjoyed having Mandy as a wife, enjoyed that to the very hilt and down to the last knuckle when it made Mandy groan so much that it put a fire in Stevie's belly. She underscores your existence, Stevie thought. Yes, it was true.

Now Mandy returned wearing the same fluffy white robe, but no longer barefooted. On her feet she had high-heeled tan leather mules, a deliberate enticement for Stevie, who had a fetish, an adoration for femmes in high heels and stockings and garter belts. Mandy knew all about it, and she was always eager to do anything to make Stevie want her. The blonde smiled at Stevie and then pranced over to the counter to finish preparing the coffee.

"What would you like for breakfast?" Mandy said.

"I don't know."

"Flakes and strawberries?"

"Sounds good."

"God, I missed you! I always hate it when you're not here."

Stevie watched her working at the counter, watched those lovely long legs in the high-heeled mules.

"Take the robe off," Stevie said.

Mandy made a sound of protest. "I'm not wearing anything under it."

"So what? No one can see anything. Take it off and let me look at you."

Mandy did what Stevie wanted. She untied the belt of the robe, then slipped the robe off her body and tossed it onto an empty chair. Now she looked coyly at Stevie as she swayed her hips from side to side. "Better?"

"Much better." Stevie feasted her eyes on Mandy's pear-shaped breasts, on the full pink nipples that were already extended, on the smooth hairless mound. She watched Mandy as Mandy turned back to the counter again. The blonde's buttocks were delicious to look at, two firm ovals above her long thighs, the four-inch heels firming up the muscles in her calves.

Without turning around, Mandy said, "Am I getting fat?"

Stevie chuckled. "Not at all."

"I think I'm getting fat."

"Where?"

"In my hips."

"Honey, your ass is perfect."

"I don't get as much exercise as I used to because I'm not dancing anymore."

"I don't want you dancing."

"You won't like me when I'm fat."

"You don't need to dance to get exercise. Maybe we'll start running together."

"Yes, I'd like that."

"Bend forward just a little."

Mandy giggled. "You're peeking at me."

"Yes, I'm peeking at you. Bend forward a little and show me something to peek at."

The blonde arched her back and pushed her ass out. "How's this?"

"I can't see anything unless you move your legs apart."

"What about now?"

"That's better." Stevie's blood raced as she gazed at the hairless pouting cunt, still closed but incredibly enticing. "That's beautiful," Stevie said.

"I can't pour the coffee unless we stop this."

"Maybe I'll make you stay like that all day."

Mandy giggled and straightened her body. "You're kinky."

"Yes, and you love it."

"Making me wear heels at nine o'clock in the morning."

"Am I making you do that?"

"No, I'm making myself."

"Coffee, pet." When Mandy brought the coffee to the table, Stevie pulled her closer and ran a hand over Mandy's high, full ass. "You're turning me on, blondie."

"Well, I hope so." Mandy's bald pubis looked freshly powdered, plump and sweet.

When they'd met, she'd had only a sparse tuft, and when Stevie had suggested that it be shaved, Mandy had done that without delay, blushing the first time she'd presented it to Stevie, who now ran a fingertip over the bald mound where the very top of Mandy's slit was visible as a deep indentation in the plump flesh.

Stevie said, "Okay, let's have our breakfast." Mandy seemed disappointed that Stevie did no more with her finger, but she said nothing and she returned to the stove to get the eggs going.

When she finally brought their breakfast to the table, the blonde sat down and said: "Tell me about Los Angeles."

Stevie shrugged. "I told you it was boring, a boring meeting with nothing but boring attorneys."

"Nothing interesting?"

Stevie chuckled. "What you mean is did I meet anyone interesting, and if I did, how far did it go."

"Something like that."

"No one interesting and nothing to go anywhere. All I thought about was getting back to you and giving it to you sixteen different ways."

Mandy giggled. "You're just saying that."

"Ah, but it's true." And, as if to emphasize what she said, Stevie reached across the small breakfast table to lift one of Mandy's fruitlike breasts, holding the breast up, her thumb sliding from side to side over the nipple. "And what about you?" Stevie said. "Did you meet anyone interesting?"

"I didn't go anywhere."

"Was Gilda here?"

"No, not at all."

"Promise?"

"You know I wouldn't lie."

"I hope not." Reluctantly, Stevie pulled her hand away from the tempting breast and returned to breakfast. "Let's finish here and get down to basics."

Mandy quivered. "You always get me so heated up I can't think straight."

Stevie gave her a quiet smile and said nothing. Stevie thought now about what to do, arousing herself by planning what she would do with Mandy later on, how she would have her.

When breakfast was finished and Mandy rose to clear the dishes from the table, Stevie rose also and stopped her. "Leave it," Stevie said.

Mandy blushed as she turned into Stevie's arms. "Oh, Stevie, I love you!"

"I hope you do."

"You know it's true."

"Come on, let's get to the bedroom." They walked down the short hall together, and when they arrived in the bedroom, Stevie told Mandy to kneel on the bed. "Keep the shoes on," Stevie said. But there was no need to say that because Mandy already knew how Stevie liked to fuck her with her shoes on. The blonde knelt with her shoes clearing the edge of the bed, her knees wide apart, her head down on her forearms and her ass elevated in a glorious display of luscious womanhood. The hairless lips of her cunt were open, parted enough to show the delicate pink flaps, the bald fig of her sex pointing upward to the tight pink constriction of her anus.

Stevie's eyes took in everything. No, she couldn't blame Gilda for wanting Mandy. How could she blame anyone for that? But she'd be damned if that sadist Gilda would have Mandy. Put a girl like Mandy in Gilda's hands, and the girl got turned into a shivering wreck. Stevie had seen it happen and she thought Mandy was too sweet for it.

Now she moved behind Mandy and started stroking the ivory buttocks, using both hands, leaning into the raised ass, her eyes on Mandy's smooth back and the mass of blonde curls at her neck; and then, after a while, sliding her fingers between Mandy's thighs to lightly graze the puffed lips of her cunt.

Mandy groaned. "Oh, Stevie ..."

Stevie's fingers gradually became more insistent. She found the flap of Mandy's clitoris and pinched it gently, then eased two fingers inside the wet opening and began the slow, thrusting movement that she knew Mandy adored. The blonde moaned and churned her hips, pleading for more, whimpering with delight as Stevie added a third finger to the drizzling cunt, her fingers stretching the opening, sliding in and out with a more vigorous movement of her wrist. Her voice husky, Stevie said, "Come on, give it to me, baby. Come on my fingers."

As if this command was all she needed, Mandy cried out and began a violent shaking of her ass. Stevie kept on with it, her fingers stroking in and out of the wet cunt, her hand now covered with the blonde's juices. She kept her fingers moving until Mandy finished coming, and then she pulled her fingers out and used both hands to hold the blonde's hips as she started humping her pelvis against the raised ass. Stevie was now primed and ready, and before long the relentless slamming and grinding of her mound against Mandy's buttocks was enough to make her clit explode in a fabulous wrenching orgasm as Mandy churned and urged her on.

Afterward Stevie crouched down to plant a tender kiss on her lover's cunt and taste her running nectar.

"I love you," Mandy said.

Sipping at the sweet flow, Stevie replied, "And I love you too."

When she had all the sipping she wanted, Stevie straightened up, dropped her running shorts, and stepped out of them. She tapped Mandy's ass, and

Mandy immediately turned and slid down to get her face into Stevie's dark bush.

"All for you," Stevie said. And then she moved her legs apart and hunched forward to fuck the blonde's open mouth.

After Stevie left for the office, Mandy considered the options she had for the afternoon and decided she just had to get out today, get out somewhere, out of the apartment after nearly four days of isolation. She hadn't budged out of the apartment while Stevie was gone because she'd been afraid to meet Gilda somewhere. When Stevie was close Mandy could resist Gilda; but with Stevie in California, Mandy had been afraid that Gilda would be too much. The last thing in the world she wanted now was trouble with Gilda, or trouble between herself and Stevie. No, not now. She certainly did not want that. But Stevie was back now, and maybe she could get out of the apartment this afternoon. She told herself that everyone deserved a break now and then. She'd get out of the apartment and get her head clear, or whatever. See the world, little girl. She loved everything she had with Stevie, but she did need to see other people once in a while.

She went to the mirror to primp, ruffled her hair, looked at herself, checked the shape of her breasts in the new T-shirt with an abstract design on the front and back in red and green and black. Well, it was different anyway. Her breasts still looked fine even if they'd started to hang a bit. She had an idea that Stevie would like them standing straight out. Well, those days were gone forever. Anyway, they still looked fine. She could tell that by the eyes on them when she walked into one of the bars, the dykes stealing glances at her, the honey-blonde femme, the eyes always giving her the shivers, making her so hot when they looked at her like that as if they were ready to jump her. And the way Stevie looked at her sometimes, the way Stevie had looked at her this morning because she was so horny after three days in Los Angeles. Stevie was always hot for it on Monday morning, anyway; hot to look at her naked in the kitchen like that, always hot to look at her wearing something sexy, taking her any which way she wanted but usually kneeling with her ass in the air. She remembered Stevie's fingers tickling her open before she got her fingers inside to make her wild.

Thinking about this morning—the full pleasure of it—made Mandy restless, and with a quiver of delight, she pulled the T-shirt over her head and tossed it away. She slid her panties down her thighs and off her legs, then shook her shoulders from side to side to watch her breasts jiggle. The fact was, she wanted to dance again. She loved dancing, showing herself on a stage, having them cheer when she did a sexy grind that showed her boobs and ass to advantage. Go-go-go, little girl.

Now she grabbed the T-shirt and panties and walked naked down the hall to the bedroom. She tossed them into the laundry basket in the bedroom closet, and then walked into the bathroom and turned on the shower. She wanted a hot shower to make her feel fresh and clean. She covered her head with a shower cap and had ten minutes of soap and hot water before coming out to dry herself with one of the big white towels Stevie liked having in the bathroom. Stevie, her lover. Stevie, whom she loved so much it made her tremble sometimes. Oh, yes, I do love her, Mandy thought. She loved everything about Stevie, especially the way Stevie knew how to give it to her, the way Stevie knew how to give her what she needed. The trouble with so many dykes was they'd never learned how to fuck. They never knew what a girl needed. They wanted soul bonding and the acting out of some personal dopey little dyke drama with their playing the leading role, their name on the marquee as the big attraction; come watch the tragedy of my life. Mandy rubbed her cunt with the flat of her hand a full minute as she thought about all of this, a slow rubbing designed to be a compromise between the need to get dry and the need to get the pleasure of the rubbing. Then, finally, she said the hell with it and stopped the rubbing and turned to get her hair fluffed out.

In the bedroom, she closed the bathroom door in order to look in the full-length mirror and see everything. She fluffed her hair again with both hands, watching the lifting of her breasts, turning her body to the side to see the shape of her breasts and her belly and her ass. She thought of Stevie again and what they had done that morning, what they had almost done before breakfast because Stevie was always so hot for it on Monday morning. Stevie feeling her up like that while she was standing near the table. Mandy remembered someone who said the evidence of a hot love affair was having sex after you were out of bed but before breakfast. She stood in front of the full-length mirror, remembering the morning, and now she moved her legs apart. She slid a hand between her thighs to tickle herself just enough to get the lips opening. Then she pulled her hand away and used both hands to hold her breasts up, her thumbs and forefingers tugging at her nipples the way she liked to do on the stage, watching everything in the mirror with her hips slowly swaying from side to side as if she were dancing in some Arabian Nights palace like a harem girl.

Well, that's what she was, wasn't she? She was a harem girl—Stevie's harem girl—only she wished that Stevie would pay more attention to her, take her out more, do more things with her, treat her with more consideration. What she needed was a butch who cared more. Not that Stevie didn't care, but sometimes she wasn't that certain about Stevie; not that certain about what Stevie wanted or what Stevie didn't want, especially when Stevie got that quiet look as if she was thinking about something complicated with her forehead wrinkled and her lips pursed. Of course Stevie was a lawyer, and that meant she had a brain, which was also something that attracted Mandy; but she thought it ought to be possible for Stevie to have a brain and still not shut her out like she sometimes did. Stevie looked so faraway when she did that.

She had her own brain too, didn't she? Her eyes on the full-length mirror, she fingered herself, slipped the tips of two fingers inside the hole as the heel of her palm pressed and rubbed against the hard little tip of her clit, rubbing around and around as the two fingers probed in the wetness. Her eyes fixed on her swaying body. Her breasts now looked swollen. Her belly weaved from side to side, the muscles in her thighs and legs tightened by the pleasure that streamed up from her cunt in one hot wave after the other. It was wonderful. It was always wonderful when she did it like this alone in front of a mirror with only herself and her body and her eyes and her hands and her wet cunt begging for it. At moments like this she needed no one—not Stevie, not anyone. Groaning, her ass pumping forward and backward, she jiggled her hand more rapidly until the searing pleasure caused her knees to weaken and her eyes to close.

"Mandy, you look great," one of the girls said. Mandy had just walked into the coffee shop on Halsted, and now she recognized the two girls—or at least she recognized one of them; a girl named Terri she'd known at Rego's.

"Where have you been hiding?" Terri said. "This is Sal. Do you know Sal?"

Mandy sat with them and ordered a double cappuccino. She liked sitting with them because they were both attractive enough so that everyone in the place stared at them, the two attractive butches and the honey blonde.

"I'm not dancing anymore," Mandy said.

"Why not?"

"I'm living with someone, and she doesn't like it."

Terri made a face and nudged Sal. "You should see her go at it—she's marvelous." Then Terri said to Mandy, "Sal is from Denver—she's just moved here."

"Oh." Sal gave her a sultry smile, a casual look down at her breasts and then up at her face again. "You're pretty," Sal said.

"Thank you."

"How would you like to play with us?" Terri said, smiling as she fixed her eyes on Mandy.

"What do you mean?"

"Come on, Mandy, you know what I mean."

"Listen, I just got here."

"To do what? Drink cappuccinos? It's starting to rain outside, and it's a boring fucking day. The only thing I like to do when it rains is ball. Isn't that right, Sal?"

"Sure," Sal said.

Mandy pouted. "I told you I'm living with someone."

"For keeps?"

"I don't know yet."

Terri rolled her eyes. "I wanted Sal to watch you dance."

"I told you I don't dance anymore."

"Then why don't you just watch us? How about that, Mandy? Wouldn't you like that? Me and Sal?"

The coaxing went on for another twenty minutes before Mandy finally agreed to it. What harm would it do to watch them? What else could she do when it was raining like this and the afternoon was so gray now that it depressed her? She wondered what they would look like anyway, the two girls. She'd seen Terri go at it at some party or other, but it was so long ago that she couldn't remember anything. They looked so much alike, Terri and Sal, two butch girls with short dark hair greased up to a shine and bright red lipstick. Stevie wouldn't be home for another four hours, and Mandy hated the idea of returning to the apartment.

"Okay, come on," Mandy said. She walked out of the coffee shop with them, and on the sidewalk she moved between them and giggled as she took an arm in each hand. The rain had stopped, and she felt good. "I feel great," she said.

Yes, she did; she felt happy.

VERNA

Early one evening I'm sitting alone at the bar in Jorjet's wondering if I ought to leave this place because tonight it's like a graveyard, when the street door opens and a tall woman dressed in black walks in and looks around for a place to sit. She can sit anywhere, since there aren't more than six customers in the room, and except for me the bar stools are empty. She turns and looks at me. She's about forty, with a long neck and an oval face, dark eyes and dark brown hair drawn back in a tight chignon. She finally pulls her eyes away and she walks past me to sit at the bar only two stools down. I look her up and down, at the sleek hairdo and the sheer black hose. I watch her order white wine, and then, when the bartender brings the wine, I watch the woman's long fingers as she lifts the wineglass to her lips. Maybe she's closer to forty-five than forty, a stately brunette with small clip earrings. She could be a bank executive because she's so efficient looking, some kind of businesswoman, no rings on her fingers and obviously on the prowl walking into a girl bar like this one. She's not here by accident. She gives me a glance again, and her sultry eyes look interested. And I'm interested, too, and wondering now who will make the first move.

For a while I pretend to ignore her, sipping my draft beer and not turning to look at her. Then I decide it's too much; either we connect or I leave, because what I don't want is another wasted evening. I turn and I stare at her until she turns her head to look at me with those dark eyes.

And I say, "Hi, I'm Verna. Can I sit with you?" Now comes the terrible moment of a possible rejection. But she gives me a quiet smile, and she nods. Relief. I move over, dragging my beer along the bar, settling onto the stool beside her, smelling her perfume for the first time, and I say, "I don't have any money to buy you a drink."

Does she mind? She smiles. "I was going to invite you to sit with me, so I'll buy. What would you like?"

"I'll have what you're having." The bartender brings me a glass of white wine, which I like much better than beer anyway.

The woman says, "My name is Bernita." She has red lipstick on a wide mouth, and when she smiles, she merely stretches her lips without showing her teeth. "You're very attractive," she says, the eyes sultry again. "You look very sexy. Are you sexy?"

Is she teasing me? I look directly at her. "I'm always sexy."

She smiles. "That sounds interesting."

"I like the way you dress. Black is my favorite color."

"Is it?"

"Are you a banker?"

She laughs. "No, I'm not a banker. Why?"

"I don't know. I thought you look like a banker. Or at least an executive of some kind."

"Well, I *am* an executive. I run a small advertising agency."

"That must be interesting."

She smiles again. "Right now I'm more interested in you. You're very pretty."

"Oh, I'm not that pretty."

"Yes, you are. And I bet you're even prettier when you have your clothes off. Would you like to come home with me?"

Her eyes are steady, boring into mine. No more games. Five minutes later, we're out of there and into a taxi, the evening fixed for me.

She takes me to a swank apartment on East Chestnut, a rug about a foot deep, huge rooms, a magnificent view of the Gold Coast, the lake, the high-rises like a wall running north. She sends the maid away and mixes us a pitcher of martinis.

Bernita says, "I like martinis more than I ought to."

"I'll pass out."

"No, I won't let you."

"I won't do more than sip mine."

She looks at me, a hard look, estimating me. "Do you think I'm an old dyke?"

"You're not old."

She smiles. "Some people would say I'm a dirty old dyke."

"Well, you don't look it."

"I'm just an ordinary dyke who likes lovely things, lovely girls like you. Especially with their clothes off." She hesitates, looking at me directly. "Would you?"

She hasn't even touched me yet, but I'm imagining it. "I don't mind."

"I'll give you some money later. Will a hundred dollars be all right?"

"That's fine."

"Why don't you undress and lie on the carpet over there while I change into something more comfortable."

She walks out, and all I'm thinking about now is the hundred dollars and what I can do with it. So I'm hustling, but so what? Isn't everyone hustling in one way or another? I suppose she expects me to earn the money before the evening is over. But she turns me on anyway, so I don't mind doing whatever she wants. The idea sends shivers up my back. Maybe I can get even more than a hundred out of her. I'm greedy. I drop my clothes, strip naked, and lie on the rug near the one of the wide windows. If anyone is looking in here with a telescope, they might see something interesting. The rug is soft and delicious under me. I lie there looking at the high ceiling and the chandelier with a zillion little bulbs, wondering what the apartment cost her.

Finally she returns wearing a long black-and-white embroidered caftan. She stands near me and smiles down at me as she looks at my body. "I just want to look at you awhile."

I say nothing. She goes to an easy chair a few feet away and sits down and sips her martini. She has a blissful little smile on her face, as if it's perfectly ordinary for her to be sitting there like that near the window overlooking the city with a naked girl lying on her rug. Should I show more of my pussy? I lift one knee casually to make my crotch more visible. Then I slowly roll onto my side and lie facing her as I try my best to appear cool. Does she approve? I'm nervous because she still hasn't touched me. That's a bit weird, isn't it?

And now she says, "You're really lovely to look at."

"Thank you." She sits there so chic and composed, her eyes rattling me as they take me apart. The way she looks at me makes me hot, the way she moves her eyes back and forth between my breasts and my pussy. I'm tingling down there; if she's trying to make me crazy, the attempt is a success.

A long time passes during which she says nothing. There is only silence in the room, and an occasional soft sound as she sips her martini. I watch her mouth, her red lips.

Then she asks me how long I've been out. "Is it a long time?"

"Only a few years."

"Does your family know?"

"No." She crosses her legs under the caftan. What the hell difference does it make whether or not my family knows? I stare at her feet in their gold slippers.

And then she looks amused. She says, "Do you enjoy it with dykes like me? Or is it just the money?"

I feel myself blushing. "I really enjoy it." That seems to make her happy. It's true anyway.

"I believe you," she says. I slide a hand down and casually stroke my bush with my fingers. "I hope so."

"I hate phony little girls," she says. "I hate young lesbians who lie about themselves. I hate girls who fake it."

And while she's talking like that, I wonder how many girls she's had. I tell her I never fake anything, and that's true, too.

Then she says I can have a shower if I want. "I'll wait for you. There's a guest bathroom down the hall you can use."

She wants me clean. So I get up from the rug, and I leave her. I walk out, aware of her eyes on me, her dark eyes on my ass that I wiggle just enough to call attention to it in case she hadn't noticed. But of course she's noticed everything, and there's really no need for it.

I find the bathroom down the hall and I have a shower. Lots of soap everywhere, especially between my legs. I don't mind it, because maybe it means she intends to go down on me. I don't blame her for wanting me clean. I'm not gamy, but I could be, couldn't I? She needs to be careful picking up strange girls and bringing them home. It's dangerous. I shower, dry off with a large towel, and then I return to her fresh and clean.

She smiles at me. Now she's happy. "Come close to me." Barefooted, I walk across the rug to where she sits on the sofa. When I'm close to her, she reaches out to touch my legs, her long fingers moving up my thigh, stroking me, sliding up to stroke my ass, her fingers petting one buttock as her dark eyes look up at me.

And she says, "All right, let's go to the bedroom now." Which makes me happy because lying on the rug is too awkward.

She rises from the sofa, and I follow her out of the living room and down a short hall to a huge bedroom with a view of the lake, an enormous bed, mirrors on every wall, two vases filled with flowers.

Bernita says, "Lie down, won't you. On your back." She knows what she wants. I climb onto the huge comfortable bed and roll over onto my back. I like the luxury, the smell of money. Bernita turns and watches me. She stands at the foot of the bed looking at my body as she unzips the caftan. Her eyes are on my pussy. "Open your legs a little more," she says.

I do it. The way she looks at me excites me. I like to be looked at. I like it when an old dyke like her looks at me as though she's about to devour me. I pull my knees back to show more of my pussy. I open it with my fingers. Maybe I ought to shave it, show the lips more, but I like the hair. I like the dykes who pull the hair with their teeth.

Bernita's eyes are bright as she gazes at my pussy. Can she see my clitoris?

"You're lovely," she says. Of course she means my cunt is lovely. "I'm going to enjoy doing you," she says.

I wish she would do it now. She makes me quiver, the way she stares at my naked pussy with those horny dark eyes. I can see both of us in the mirrors. Two women, me naked on the bed, spread out on this huge bed in a posh high-rise, spread like a hooker, my dark bush dripping no doubt, and Bernita just slipping out of the caftan. She has a long white body, a round little belly, long breasts and extended dark nipples. Suckable breasts. And a wild-looking dark bush, thick and untrimmed, delicious. She rolls her nipples with her fingers as she looks at my cunt.

Her eyes rattle me. She has fire in her eyes. I wish I could see her ass. I have a sudden desire to see her bending over with that hairy pussy staring back at me, see if the flaps are visible and whether the hair grows into the groove between her buttocks. Imagining her like that excites me tremendously. Then I look past her at the mirror behind her and I do see her ass, but she's not bent over the way I'd imagined her. She's not bad for her age, the ass still firm looking and no loose flesh on her body.

She comes around to the side of the bed. She walks like a dancer, a smooth, gliding movement, her long breasts jiggling, the long brown nipples exciting to look at. Now her bush is so close that the wild hair seems to be everywhere.

"Open your legs wider," she says. And I do that. Her eyes are on my belly as I show myself to her. I pull my knees back to my breasts and raise my ass a little to show her everything, make all of my cunt visible.

I quiver with anticipation, wondering what will happen next, my eyes on that wild bush she has. I wish I could see her clit. I wonder whether she's wet, turned on, the juice flowing in there.

Now she climbs onto the bed, her long legs everywhere, her breasts hanging, the nipples stiffening. Her eyes are on my pussy as I hold my knees back to show myself. I feel a great excitement now because I know in a moment she'll be down on me. I did not expect it in the beginning—not earlier this evening—but now I know her better.

Suddenly her head drops down and her face is right in there, in the wet. I gasp. At last. Her head is jammed between my thighs, only the top of her head visible, her chignon, as I hold my knees back and wide open. I feel her hot breath on my naked pussy. Delicious. I feel her slick tongue gently lapping me, getting to know me, all around my clitoris, teasing me, making me moan as I feel the powerful waves of pleasure rise up from my belly. With marvelous skill, she beats my clitoris back and forth with her tongue. I rock my knees and groan as my syrup flows. I love it. I always love it when they do it this way, a hot mouth licking my wet slit as I hold my knees back to my breasts, her mouth and lips and tongue eating me up, lapping steadily on the shaft of my clit, again and again the strong waves of pleasure melting my insides, my cunt tingling.

How delicious it is! I forget everything. All I want

is to have my clit licked and tongued, an expert dyke giving me her tongue. Now she laps harder, faster, aiming to bring me to a climax, beating my sensitive little clitoris, hitting the flap repeatedly as I moan and feel my pussy creaming. At this moment, I'm nothing but a huge hole down there, hot sticky juice flowing with her steady lapping. As I cry out, Bernita presses her mouth more firmly against my clitoris, sucking my flesh, pulling at it as I hunch upward against her face. I give it to her, give her everything, out of control now, getting my own, a molten flood of cream gushing out to wet her face. Go on, suck it! She stays with it, her head moving, her mouth slurping, my knees rocking back and forth. I bounce my ass up and down, and no doubt she loves that, too. It's what she wants. I hear the gurgling and snorting noises down there, Bernita losing herself as she gobbles my trough, tasting my juices, my cunt thick in her mouth, sucking everything inside, pulling at the lips as I come again like crazy, crying out, heaving, crying out again.

When I open my eyes, I see Bernita sitting up and smiling at me. Her face is flushed. She dabs at her chin with a tissue, then at her wet lips. "Did you like that?" she says.

I nod. What does she think? Doesn't she know? "Yes, very much."

Then she asks me how old I am, how many women do I go with in a week, which I try not to answer because that's too personal. That's no one's business, is it? I don't have that many women, anyway. If she wants to wonder about it, she's free to do so. Then she dips her head to take me again. I'm ready for her, raising my legs immediately, pulling my knees back to make my cunt available to her mouth. Quivering with anticipation, I watch her face as she moves in to nuzzle my pussy. Her hair tickles the insides of my thighs, and I feel one of her earrings scraping against my skin. I feel her hot breath on my pussy, on my swollen lips that are now completely unfurled, open and wet. She smiles up at me, teasing me, then sticking her tongue out long and pink, her tongue pushing between my labia, fluttering between them, turning me on, getting me shaking again. I'm wide open, the cream pouring out of me as she tickles me with her long snaky tongue.

She pulls back and licks her lips. "You're a lovely girl." She smiles as I open my legs farther, begging for it. She dips her head again, but this time she moves her tongue directly to my vagina, and she scours the opening. My knees are back again as I make myself available, her tongue sliding around and around, tickling me, then pushing deep inside, pushing inside my vagina. I fold my legs all the way back, my ass turned up as her serpent's tongue slides in and out. I try to grip it, contracting my vaginal muscles to grip her thrusting tongue, arching my body upward to get more of it. She tongues me faster and faster, in and out, the juices gushing out of me, a waterfall all over her face, her mouth and chin again wet and sloppy as I have another orgasm. This one is even better than the first and I'm coming like crazy, still coming as she continues to tongue-fuck me and suck me at the same time.

Finally she stops. "Do you like it?"

I groan. "I love it!"

She makes me keep my knees back to show everything, her eyes on my pussy now wet and swollen. "You have a good taste," she says, licking her lips, touching me again, her fingers in my slit, her fingers tickling along the outer lips, pulling one lip, then tickling down around my anus, her fingertip grazing up and down the groove between my buttocks.

Her face dips again, like a bird, but this time her tongue slides down to my anus. The first touch of it makes me gasp. Her tongue tickles me, touching all over the crack, wet and warm, making me shake with pleasure. I love it. I melt as she moves her tongue around and around my anus. And, then, finally, she pushes her tongue inside, and I gasp and hold my breath as I feel it wiggling in there, sliding around inside me, making me crazy as it explores my second opening. Her thumb is now on my clitoris, the bud stiff and swollen, her thumb vibrating my clit as her tongue thoroughly probes my anus. She's an expert, and within moments I'm coming, heaving upward, grunting like a pig because I like it so much.

Finally she pulls her face away, and she gives an exhausted sigh. This time she lies down beside me on her back, our two sweaty bodies side by side on the wide bed.

What does she want now? I'll do anything she wants, just anything. I sit up and look at her, at her brown nipples and wild dark bush. She smiles at me as she puts her hands on her breasts.

"Happy?"

I nod, staring at her white belly. "Do you want me to eat you?"

But Bernita shakes her head. "No, I don't want that. Just use your hand, if you want. I'd like that better. Make me come with your hand."

I kiss her breasts first, running my lips over the velvety white skin around her nipples. I take each long nipple in my mouth and suck it briefly. Then I sit up again and I put my hand on her wild bush. I watch her face as I feel the full lips under my fingers. I watch her pleasure as she closes her eyes. Her red lips are wet with my juices. Now my fingers are between her flaps, spreading them, opening her cunt until she groans and draws her knees apart.

I look at it. Her pussy is dark and wet. She has a strong clit, a thick shaft, and when I take it between two fingers and squeeze it gently, she groans again. I jerk her clitoris up and down repeatedly. Yes, she likes that. She moans more softly now. She moves her hips around, her ass moving on the bed as I give it to her with my hand, as I rub everything with my palm, her flesh wet and slippery under my fingers. What a juicy pussy she has!

"Should I go inside?"

"No, just the outside." I'm disappointed, but I do what she wants. I rub the outside, rubbing her faster and faster until she comes, her body shaking from head to toe as she lies there with her eyes closed. Her pussy wets my hand, her flesh hot against my palm as I continue rubbing her cunt.

And then I can't resist the urge anymore and I get my mouth on it, sucking her flesh, sucking her juices thick and plentiful, sucking all of her cunt in my mouth as she strokes my head and gives me everything.

Later, casually, she asks me whether I want a job. She says she needs a girl at the reception desk in the office. "I think you'd work out nicely there." Her dark eyes are fixed on me. "Do you want it?"

"Do I get to be with you once in a while?"

She smiles. "Do you want that?"

My two hands covering my pussy, I say yes.

People are talking about:

The Masquerade Erotic Newsletter

◆◆◆◆◆◆◆◆◆◆◆◆◆◆◆◆◆◆

FICTION, ESSAYS, REVIEWS, PHOTOGRAPHY, INTERVIEWS, EXPOSÉS, AND MUCH MORE!

◆◆◆◆◆◆◆◆◆◆◆◆◆◆◆◆◆◆

"I received the new issue of the newsletter; it looks better and better."
—*Michael Perkins*

"I must say that yours is a nice little magazine, literate and intelligent."
—*HH, Great Britain*

"Fun articles on writing porn and about the peep shows, great for those of us who will probably never step onto a strip stage or behind the glass of a booth, but love to hear about it, wicked little voyeurs that we all are, hm? Yes indeed...."
—*MT, California*

"Many thanks for your newsletter with essays on various forms of eroticism. Especially enjoyed your new Masquerade collections of books dealing with gay sex."
—*GF, Maine*

"... a professional, insider's look at the world of erotica ..."
—*SCREW*

"I recently received a copy of **The Masquerade Erotic Newsletter.** I found it to be quite informative and interesting. The intelligent writing and choice of subject matter are refreshing and stimulating. You are to be congratulated for a publication that looks at different forms of eroticism without leering or smirking."
—*DP, Connecticut*

"Thanks for sending the books and the two latest issues of **The Masquerade Erotic Newsletter.** Provocative reading, I must say."
—*RH, Washington*

"Thanks for the latest copy of **The Masquerade Erotic Newsletter.** It is a real stunner."
—*CJS, New York*

Free GIFT

WHEN YOU SUBSCRIBE TO:
The Masquerade Erotic Newsletter

Receive two **MASQUERADE** books of your choice

Please send me **TWO MASQUERADE BOOKS FREE!**

1. _____

2. _____

☐ I've enclosed my payment of $30.00 for a one-year subscription (six issues) to: **THE MASQUERADE EROTIC NEWSLETTER.**

Name _____

Address _____

_____ Apt. # _____

City _____ State _____ Zip _____

Tel. ( ) _____

Payment: ☐ Check ☐ Money Order ☐ Visa ☐ MC

Card No. _____

Exp. Date _____

Please allow 4–6 weeks delivery. No C.O.D. orders. Please make all checks payable to Masquerade Books, 801 Second Avenue, N.Y., N.Y., 10017. Payable in U.S. currency only. Order by phone: 1 800 458-9640 or fax: 212 986-7355.

THE MASQUERADE EROTIC LIBRARY

ROSEBUD BOOKS
$4.95 each

PRIVATE LESSONS *Lindsay Welsh*
A high voltage tale of life at The Whitfield Academy for Young Women—where cruel headmistress Devon Whitfield presides over the in-depth education of only the most talented and delicious of maidens. Elizabeth Dunn arrives at the Academy, where it becomes clear that she has much to learn—to the delight of Devon Whitfield and her randy staff of Mistresses in Residence! **3116-0**

PROVINCETOWN SUMMER *Lindsay Welsh*
This completely original collection is devoted exclusively to white-hot desire between women. From the casual encounters of women on the prowl to the enduring erotic bond between old lovers, the women of *Provincetown Summer* will set your senses on fire! A nationally bestselling title. **3040-7**

MISTRESS MINE *Valentina Cilescu*
Sophia Cranleigh sits in prison, accused of authoring the "obscene" *Mistress Mine*. She is offered salvation—with the condition that she first relate her lurid life story. For Sophia has led no ordinary life, but has slaved and suffered—deliciously—under the hand of the notorious Mistress Malin. Sophia tells her story, never imagining the way in which she'd be repaid for her honesty.... **109-8**

LEATHERWOMEN *edited by Laura Antoniou*
A groundbreaking anthology. These fantasies, from the pens of new or emerging authors, break every rule imposed on women's fantasies, telling stories of the secret extremes so many dream of. The hottest stories from some of today's newest and most outrageous writers make this an unforgettable exploration of the female libido. **3095-4**

BAD HABITS *Lindsay Welsh*
What does one do with a poorly trained slave? Break her of her bad habits, of course! When a respected dominatrix notices the poor behavior displayed by her slave, she decides to open a school: one where submissives will learn the finer points of servitude—and learn them properly. "If you like hot, lesbian erotica, run—don't walk ... and pick up a copy of *Bad Habits* ..." —Karen Bullock-Jordan, *Lambda Book Report*. **3068-7**

PASSAGE AND OTHER STORIES *Aarona Griffin*
An S/M romance. Lovely Nina is frightened by her lesbian passions until she finds herself infatuated with a woman she spots at a local café. One night Nina follows her and finds herself enmeshed in an endless maze leading to a mysterious world where women test the edges of sexuality and power. **3057-1**

DISTANT LOVE & OTHER STORIES *A.L. Reine*
In the title story, Leah Michaels and her lover Ranelle have had four years of blissful, smoldering passion together. One night, when Ranelle is out of town, Leah records an audio "Valentine," a cassette filled with erotic reminiscences of their life together in vivid, pulsating detail. **3056-3**

EROTIC *PLAYGIRL* ROMANCES
$4.95 each

WOMEN AT WORK *Charlotte Rose*
Hot, uninhibited stories devoted to the working woman! From a lonesome cowgirl to a supercharged public relations exec, these uncontrollable women know how to let off steam after a tough day on the job. Career pursuits pale beside their devotion to less professional pleasures, as each proves that "moonlighting" is often the best job of all! **3088-1**

LOVE & SURRENDER *Marlene Darcy*
"Madeline saw Harry looking at her legs and she blushed as she remembered what he wanted to do.... She casually pulled the skirt of her dress back to uncover her knees and the lower part of her thighs. What did he want now? Did he want more? She tugged at her skirt again, pulled it back far enough so almost all of her thighs were exposed...." **3082-2**

THE COMPLETE *PLAYGIRL* FANTASIES
The very best—and very hottest—women's fantasies are collected here, fresh from the pages of *Playgirl*. These knockouts from the infamous "Reader's Fantasy Forum" prove, once again, that truth can indeed be hotter, wilder, and *better* than fiction. **3075-X**

DREAM CRUISE *Gwenyth James*
Angelia has it all—a brilliant career and a beautiful face to match. But she longs to kick up her high heels and have some fun, so she takes an island vacation and vows to leave her sexual inhibitions behind. From the moment her plane takes off, she finds herself in one hot and steamy encounter after another, and her horny holiday doesn't end on Monday morning! Rest and relaxation were never so rewarding. **3045-0**

RHINO*CEROS* BOOKS
$6.95 each

THE REPENTENCE OF LORRAINE *Andrei Codrescu*
An aspiring writer, a professor's wife, a secretary, gold anklets, Maoists, Roman harlots—and more—swirl through this spicy tale of a harried quest for a mythic artifact. Written when the author was a young man, this lusty yarn was inspired by the heady—and hot—days and nights of the Sixties. A rare title from this perenially popular and acclaimed author, finally back in print. **124-1**

THE WET FOREVER *David Aaron Clark*
The story Janus and Madchen—a small-time hood and a beautiful sex worker—*The Wet Forever* examines themes of loyalty, sacrifice, redemption and obsession amidst Manhattan's sex parlors and underground S/M clubs.. Its combination of sex and suspense makes *The Wet Forever* singular, uncompromising, and strangely arousing. **117-9**

ORF *David Meltzer*
He is the ultimate musician-hero—the idol of thousands, the fevered dream of many more. And like many musicians before him, he is misunderstood, misused—and totally out of control. From agony to lust, every last drop of feeling is squeezed from a modern-day troubadour and his lady love on their relentless descent into hell. Long out of print, Meltzer's frank, poetic look at the dark side of the Sixties returns. A masterpiece—and a must for every serious erotic library. **110-1**

MANEATER *Sophie Galleymore Bird*
Through a bizarre act of creation, a man attains the "perfect" lover—by all appearances a beautiful, sensuous woman but in reality something far darker. Once brought to life she will accept no mate, seeking instead the prey that will sate her supernatural hunger for vengeance. A biting take on the war of the sexes.
103-9

THE MARKETPLACE *Sara Adamson*
"Merchandise does not come easily to the Marketplace.... They haunt the clubs and the organizations, their need so real and desperate that they exude sensual tension when they glide through the crowds. Some of them are so ripe that they intimidate the poseurs, the weekend sadists and the furtive dilettantes who are so endemic to that world. And they never stop asking where we may be found...." A compelling tale of the ultimate training academy, where only the finest are accepted—and trained for service beyond their wildest dreams.
3096-2

VENUS IN FURS *Leopold von Sacher-Masoch*
This classic 19th century novel is the first uncompromising exploration of the dominant/submissive relationship in literature. The alliance of Severin and Wanda epitomizes Sacher-Masoch's dark obsession with a cruel, controlling goddess and the urges that drive the man held in her thrall. Also included in this volume are the letters exchanged between Sacher-Masoch and Emilie Mataja—an aspiring writer he sought as the avatar of his forbidden desires.
3089-X

ALICE JOANOU

TOURNIQUET **3067-9**
A brand new collection of stories and effusions from the pen of one our most dazzling young writers. By turns lush and austere, Joanou's intoxicating command of language and image makes *Tourniquet* a sumptuous feast for all the senses.

CANNIBAL FLOWER **72-6**
"She is waiting in her darkened bedroom, as she has waited throughout history, to seduce and ultimately destroy the men who are foolish enough to be blinded by her irresistible charms. She is Salome, Lucrezia Borgia, Delilah—endlessly alluring, the fulfillment of your every desire.... She is the goddess of sexuality, and *Cannibal Flower* is her haunting siren song."
—Michael Perkins

MICHAEL PERKINS

EVIL COMPANIONS **3067-9**
A handsome edition of this cult classic that includes a new preface by Samuel R. Delany. Set in New York City during the tumultuous waning years of the 60s, *Evil Companions* has been hailed as "a frightening classic." A young couple explore the nether reaches of the erotic unconscious in a shocking confrontation with the extremes of passion

THE SECRET RECORD: Modern Erotic Literature **3039-3**
Perkins, a renowned author and critic of sexually explicit fiction, surveys the field with authority and unique insight. Updated and revised to include the latest trends, tastes, and developments in this much-misunderstood and maligned genre.

SENSATIONS *Tuppy Owens*
A piece of porn history. Tuppy Owens tells the unexpurgated story of the making of *Sensations*—the first big-budget sex flick. Originally commissioned to appear in book form after the release of the film in 1975, *Sensations* is finally released under Masquerade's stylish Rhinoceros imprint. A document from a more reckless, bygone time!
3081-4

MY DARLING DOMINATRIX *Grant Antrews*
When a man and a woman fall in love it's supposed to be simple, uncomplicated, easy—unless that woman happens to be a dominatrix. Devoid of sleaze and shame, this honest and unpretentious love story captures the richness and depth of this very special kind of love. Rare and undeniably unique.
3055-5

ILLUSIONS *Daniel Vian*
Two disturbing tales of danger and desire on the eve of WWII. From private homes to lurid cafés to decaying streets, passion is explored, exposed, and placed in stark contrast to the brutal violence of the time. *Illusions* peels the frightened mask from the face of desire, and studies its changing features under the dim lights of a lonely Berlin evening. Two unforgettable and evocative stories.
3074-1

LOVE IN WARTIME *Liesel Kulig*
Madeleine knew that the handsome SS officer was a dangerous man. But she was just a cabaret singer in Nazi-occupied Paris, trying to survive in a perilous time. When Josef fell in love with her, he discovered that a beautiful, intelligent, and amoral woman can sometimes be even more dangerous than the fiercest warrior.
3044-X

MASQUERADE BOOKS
$4.95 each

ODD WOMEN *Rachel Perez*
These women are lots of things: sexy, smart, innocent, tough—some even say odd. But who cares, when their combined ass-ettes are so sweet! There's not a moral in sight as an assortment of Sapphic sirens proves once and for all that comely ladies come best in pairs.
123-3

AFFINITIES *Rachel Perez*
"Kelsy had a liking for cool upper-class blondes, the long-legged girls from Lake Forest and Winnetka who came into the city to cruise the lesbian bars on Halsted, looking for breathless ecstasies. Kelsy thought of them as icebergs that needed melting, these girls with a quiet demeanor and so much under the surface...."
3113-6

JENNIFER *Anonymous*
From the bedroom of an internationally famous—and notoriously insatiable—dancer to an uninhibited ashram, *Jennifer* traces the exploits of one thoroughly modern woman. Moving beyond mere sexual experimentation, Jennifer slowly comes to a new realization of herself—as a passionate woman whose hungers are as boundless as they are diverse. Nothing stops the insatiable Jennifer!
107-1

HELLFIRE *Charles G. Wood*
A vicious murderer is running amok in New York's sexual underground—and Nick O'Shay, a virile detective with the NYPD, plunges deep into the case. He soon becomes embroiled in an elusive world of fleshly extremes, hunting a madman seeking to purge America with fire and blood sacrifices. But the rules are different here, as O'Shay soon discovers on his journey through every sexual extreme.
3085-7

ROSEMARY LANE *J.D. Hall*
The ups, downs, ins and outs of Rosemary Lane, an 18th century maiden named after the street in which she was abandoned as a child. Raised as the ward of Lord and Lady D'Arcy, after coming of age she discovers that her guardians' generosity is truly boundless—as they contribute heartily to her carnal education.
3078-4

HELOISE *Sarah Jackson*
A panoply of sensual tales harkening back to the golden age of Victorian erotica. Desire is examined in all its intricacy, as fantasies are explored and urges explode. Innocence meets experience time and again in these passionate stories dedicated to the pleasures of the body. Sweetly torrid tales of erotic awakening! 3073-3

MASTER OF TIMBERLAND *Sara H. French*
"Welcome to Timberland Resort," he began. "We are delighted that you have come to serve us. And you may all be assured that we will require service of you in the strictest sense. Our discipline is the most demanding in the world. You will be trained here by the best. And now your new Masters will make their choices." Luscious slaves serve in the ultimate vacation paradise. 3059-8

GARDEN OF DELIGHT *Sydney St. James*
A vivid account of sexual awakening that follows an innocent but insatiably curious young woman's journey from the furtive, forbidden joys of dormitory life to the unabashed carnality of the wild world. Pretty Pauline blossoms with each new experiment in the sensual arts. 3058-X

STASI SLUT *Anthony Bobarzynski*
Adina lives in East Germany, far from the sexually liberated, uninhibited debauchery of the West. She meets a group of ruthless and corrupt STASI agents who use her as a pawn in their political chess game as well as for their own gratification—until she uses her undeniable talents and attractions in a final bid for total freedom in the revolutionary climax of this *Red*-hot thriller! 3052-0

BLUE TANGO *Hilary Manning*
Ripe and tempting Julie is haunted by the sounds of extraordinary passion beyond her bedroom wall. Alone, she fantasizes about taking part in the amorous dramas of her hosts, Claire and Edward. When she finds a way to watch the nightly debauch, her curiosity turns to full-blown lust and the uncontrollable Julie goes wild with desire! 3037-7

THE CATALYST *Sara Adamson*
After viewing a controversial, explicitly kinky film full of images of bondage and submission, several audience members find themselves deeply moved by the erotic suggestions they've seen on the screen. Each inspired coupling explores their every imagined extreme, as long-denied urges explode with new intensity. 3015-6

LUST *Palmiro Vicarion*
A wealthy and powerful man of leisure recounts his rise up the corporate ladder and his corresponding descent into debauchery. Adventure and political intrigue provide a stimulating backdrop for this tale of a classic scoundrel with an uncurbed appetite for sexual power! 82-3

WAYWARD *Peter Jason*
A mysterious countess hires a tour bus for an unusual vacation. Traveling through Europe's most notorious cities, she picks up friends, lovers, and acquaintances from every walk of life in pursuit of unbridled sensual pleasure. Each guest brings unique sexual tastes and talents to the group, climaxing in countless orgies, outrageous acts, endless deviation—and a trip none would forget! 3004-0

ASK ISADORA *Isadora Alman*
Six years of collected columns on sex and relationships. Syndicated columnist Alman has been called a hip Dr. Ruth and a sexy Dear Abby. Her advice is sharp, funny, and pertinent to anyone experiencing the delights and dilemmas of being a sexual creature in today's perplexing world. 61-0

LOUISE BELHAVEL

FORBIDDEN DELIGHTS
Clara and Iris make their sexual debut in this chronicle of the forbidden. Sexual taboos are what turn this pair on, as they travel the globe in search of the next erotic threshold. The effect they have on their fellow world travelers is definitely contagious! **81-5**

FRAGRANT ABUSES
The saga of Clara and Iris continues as the now-experienced girls enjoy themselves with a new circle of worldy friends whose imaginations definitely match their own. Polymorphous perversity follows the lusty ladies around the globe! **88-2**

DEPRAVED ANGELS
The final installment in the incredible adventures of Clara and Iris. Together with their friends, lovers, and worldly acquaintances, Clara and Iris explore the frontiers of depravity at home and abroad. **92-0**

TITIAN BERESFORD

A TITIAN BERESFORD READER
A captivating collection! Beresford's fanciful settings and outrageous fetishism have established his reputation as one of modern erotica's most imaginative and spirited writers. Wildly cruel dominatrixes, deliciously perverse masochists, and mesmerizing detail are the hallmarks of the Beresford tale—the best of which are collected here for the first time. **3114-4**

CINDERELLA
Titian Beresford triumphs again with castle dungeons and tightly corseted ladies-in-waiting, naughty viscounts and impossibly cruel masturbatrixes—nearly every conceivable method of erotic torture is explored and described in lush, vivid detail. **3024-5**

JUDITH BOSTON
Young Edward would have been lucky to get the stodgy old companion he thought his parents had hired for him. Instead, an exqusite woman arrives at his door, and Edward finds his compulsively lewd behavior never goes unpunished by the unflinchingly severe Judith Boston! **87-4**

CHINA BLUE

KUNG FU NUNS
"When I could stand the pleasure no longer, she lifted me out of the chair and sat me down on top of the table. She then lifted her skirt. The sight of her perfect legs clad in white stockings and a petite garter belt further mesmerized me. I lean particularly towards white garter belts." **3031-8**

SECRETS OF THE CITY
China Blue, the infamous Madame of Saigon, a black belt enchantress in the martial arts of love, is out for revenge. Her search brings her to Manhattan, where she intends to call upon her secret sexual arts to kill her enemies at the height of ecstasy. **03-3**

HARRIET DAIMLER

DARLING • INNOCENCE
In *Darling*, a virgin is raped by a mugger. Driven by her urge for revenge, she searches New York for him in a furious sexual hunt that leads to rape and murder. In *Innocence*, a young invalid determines to experience sex through her voluptuous nurse. Two critically acclaimed novels in one extraordinary volume. **3047-4**

THE PLEASURE THIEVES
They are the Pleasure Thieves, whose sexually preoccupied targets are set up by luscious Carol Stoddard. She forms an ultra-hot sexual threesome with them, trying every combination from two-on-ones to daisy chains—but always on the sly, because pleasures are even sweeter when they're stolen! **036-X**

AKBAR DEL PIOMBO

SKIRTS
Randy Mr. Edward Champdick enters high society—and a whole lot more—in his quest for ultimate satisfaction. For it seems that once Mr. Champdick rises to the occasion, almost nothing can bring him down. Nothing, that is, except continual, indiscriminate sexual gratification under the nearest skirt. **3115-2**

DUKE COSIMO
A kinky, lighthearted romp of non-stop action is played out against the boudoirs, bathrooms and ballrooms of the European nobility, who seem to do nothing all day except each other. **3052-0**

A CRUMBLING FAÇADE
The return of that incorrigible rogue, Henry Pike, who continues his pursuit of sex, fair or otherwise, in the most elegant homes of the most irreproachable and debauched aristocrats. **3043-1**

PAULA
"How bad do you want me?" she asked, her voice husky, breathy. I shrank back, for my desire for her was swelling to unspeakable proportions. "Turn around," she said, and I obeyed, willing to do as she asked. **3036-9**

ROBERT DESMOND

PROFESSIONAL CHARMER
A gigolo lives a parasitical life of luxury by providing his sexual services to the rich and bored. Traveling in the most exclusive circles, this gun-for-hire will gratify the lewdest and most vulgar sexual cravings. Every exploit he performs is described in lurid, throbbing detail in this story of a prostitute's progress! **3003-2**

THE SWEETEST FRUIT
Connie is determined to seduce and destroy Father Chadcrof. She corrupts the priest into forsaking all that he holds sacred, destroys his peaceful parish, and slyly manipulates him with her smoldering looks and hypnotic sexual aura. **95-5**

MICHAEL DRAX

SILK AND STEEL
"He stood tall and strong in the shadows of her room … Akemi knew what he was there for. He let his robe fall to the floor. She could offer no resistance as the shadowy figure knelt before her, gazing down upon her. Why would she resist? This was what she wanted all along.…" **3032-6**

OBSESSIONS
Victoria is determined to become a model by sexually ensnaring the powerful people who control the fashion industry: a voyeur who enjoys photographing Victoria as much as she enjoys teasing him; Paige, who finds herself compelled to watch Victoria's conquests; Pietro and Alex, who take turns and then join in for a sizzling threesome. Anything—and everything—goes! **3012-1**

LIZBETH DUSSEAU

CAROLINE'S CONTRACT
After a long life of repression, Caroline goes out on a limb. On the advice of a friend, she meets with the dark and alluring Max Burton—a man more than willing to indulge her deepest fantasies of domination and discipline. Caroline soon learns to love the ministrations of Max—and agrees to a very *special* arrangement.... **122-5**

MEMBER OF THE CLUB
"I wondered what would excite me ... And deep down inside, I had the most submissive thoughts: I imagined myself ... under the grip of men I hardly knew. If there were a club to join, it could take my deepest dreams and make them real. My only question was how far I'd really go?" A young woman faces the ultimate temptation. **3079-2**

THE APPLICANT
"Adventuresome young woman who enjoys being submissive sought by married couple in early forties. Expect no limits." Hilary answers an ad, hoping to find someone who can meet her special needs. The beautiful Liza turns out to be a flawless mistress, and together with her husband Oliver, she trains Hilary to be the perfect servant. **3038-5**

JOCELYN JOYCE

CAROUSEL
A young American woman leaves her husband when she discovers he is having an affair with their maid. She then becomes the sexual plaything of various Parisian voluptuaries. Wild sex, low morals, and ultimate decadence in the flamboyant years before the European collapse. **3051-2**

SABINE
One of the most unforgettable seductresses ever. There is no one who can refuse her once she casts her spell; no lover can do anything less than give up his whole life for her. Great men and empires fall at her feet; but she is haughty, distracted, impervious. It is the eve of WW II, and Sabine must find a new lover equal to her talents and her tastes. **3046-6**

THREE WOMEN
A knot of sexual dependence ties three women to each other and the men who love them. Dr. Helen Webber finds that her natural authority thrills and excites her lover Aaron. Jan, is involved in an affair with a married man whose wife eases her loneliness by slumming at the local bar with the working guys. A torrid, tempestuous triangle reaches the boiling point! **3025-3**

THE WILD HEART
A luxury hotel is the setting for this artful web of sex, desire, and love. A newlywed sees sex as a duty, while her hungry husband tries to awaken her. A Parisian entertains the wealthy guests for the love of money. Each episode provides a delicious variation in this libidinal Grand Hotel! **3007-5**

DEMON HEAT
An ancient vampire stalks the unsuspecting in the form of a beautiful woman. Unlike the legendary Dracula, this fiend doesn't drink blood; she craves a different kind of potion. When her insatiable appetite has drained every last drop of juice from her victims, they hunger for more! **79-3**

HAREM SONG
Young, sensuous Amber flees her cruel uncle and provincial village in search of a better life, but finds she is no match for the glittering light of London. Soon Amber becomes a call girl and is sold into a lusty Sultan's harem—a vocation for which she possesses more than average talent! **73-4**

JADE EAST

Laura, passive and passionate, follows her domineering husband Emilio to Hong Kong. He gives her to Wu Li, a Chinese connoisseur of sexual perversions, who passes her on to Madeleine, a flamboyant lesbian. Madeleine's friends make Laura the centerpiece in Hong Kong's underground orgies—where she watches Emilio recruit another lovely young woman. A journey into sexual slavery! **60-2**

RAWHIDE LUST

Diana Beaumont, the young wife of a U.S. Marshal, is kidnapped as an act of vengeance against her husband. Jack Beaumont sets out on a long journey to get his wife back, but finally catches up with her trail only to learn that she's been sold into white slavery in Mexico. **55-6**

THE JAZZ AGE

The time is the Roaring Twenties; A young attorney becomes suspicious of his mistress while his wife has an interlude with a lesbian lover. *The Jazz Age* is a romp of erotic realism from the heyday of the flapper and the speakeasy. **48-3**

ALIZARIN LAKE

AN ALIZARIN LAKE READER

A selection of wicked musings from the pen of Masquerade's perennially popular author. It's all here: *Business as Usual, The Erotic Adventures of Harry Temple, Festival of Venus,* the mysterious *Instruments of the Passion,* the devilish *Miss High Heels*—and more. Each unforgettable moment of lust makes this a deliciously prurient page-turner! **106-3**

SEX ON DOCTOR'S ORDERS

A chronicle of selfless devotion to mankind! Beth, a nubile young nurse, uses her considerable skills to further medical science by offering incomparable and insatiable assistance in the gathering of important specimens. No man leaves Nurse Beth's station without surrendering exactly what she needs! A guaranteed cure for all types of fever. **3092-X**

MISS HIGH HEELS

It was a delightful punishment few men dared to dream of. Who could have predicted how far it would go? Forced by his wicked sisters to dress and behave like a proper lady, Dennis Beryl finds he enjoys life as Denise much more! **3066-0**

THE INSTRUMENTS OF THE PASSION

All that remains is the diary of a young initiate, detailing the twisted rituals of a mysterious cult institution known only as "Rossiter." Behind sinister walls, a beautiful young woman performs an unending drama of pain and humiliation. What is the impulse that justifies her, night after night, in consenting to this strange ceremony? And to what lengths will her aberrant passion drive her? **3010-5**

CLARA

The mysterious death of a beautiful, aristocratic woman leads her old boyfriend on a harrowing journey of discovery. His search uncovers a woman on a quest for deeper and more unusual sensations, each more shocking then the one before. **80-7**

FESTIVAL OF VENUS

Brigeen Mooney fled her home in the west of Ireland to avoid being forced into a nunnery. But her refuge in Dublin turned out to be dedicated to a different religion. The women she met there belonged to the Old Religion, devoted to sex and sacrifices. Lusty ladies debased by the sex ceremonies of pagan gods! **37-8**

PAUL LITTLE

THE DISCIPLINE OF ODETTE
Odette's family was harsh, but not even public humiliation could keep her from Jacques. She was sure marriage to him would rescue her from her family's "corrections." To her horror, she discovers that Jacques, too, has been raised on discipline. An explosive and shocking erotic coupling. **3033-4**

ALL THE WAY
Two excruciating novels from Paul Little in one hot volume! *Going All the Way* features an unhappy man who tries to purge himself of the memory of his lover with a series of quirky and uninhibited women. *Pushover* tells the story of a serial spanker and his celebrated exploits in California. **3023-7**

SLAVES OF CAMEROON
This sordid tale is about the women who were used by German officers for salacious profit. These women were forced to become whores for the German army in this African colony. The most perverse forms of erotic gratification are depicted in this unsavory tale! **3026-1**

THE PRISONER
Judge Black has built a secret room below a women's penitentiary, where he sentences the prisoners to hours of exhibition and torment while his friends watch from their luxurious box seats. Judge Black's House of Corrections is equipped with one purpose in mind: to administer his own brand of rough justice—and sizzling punishments—to the tenderest skin of his pleading captives! **3011-3**

CAPTIVE MAIDENS
Three beautiful young women find themselves powerless against the wealthy, debauched landowners of 1824 England. Their masters force them to do their bidding beneath the bite of the whip. For resisting, they are sentenced to imprisonment in a sexual slave colony where they are corrupted into eager participation in every imaginable perversion. Innocent maidens corrupted beyond belief! **3014-8**

SLAVE ISLAND
Lord Henry Philbrock, a sadistic genius, has built a hidden paradise where captive females are forced into slavery. They are trained to accommodate the most bizarre sexual cravings of the rich, the famous, the pampered and the perverted. Once in Philbrock's power, these women are pushed beyond all civilized boundaries! **3006-7**

THE AUTOBIOGRAPHY OF A FLEA III
That incorrigible voyeur, the Flea, returns for yet another tale of outrageous acts and indecent behavior. This time Flea returns to Provence to spy on the younger generation, now just coming into their own ripe, juicy maturity. With the same wry wit and eye for lurid detail, the Flea's secret observations won't fail to titillate yet again! **94-7**

END OF INNOCENCE
The early days of Women's Emancipation are the setting for this story of some very independent ladies. These girls were willing to go to any lengths to fight for their sexual freedom, and willing to endure any punishment in their desire for total liberation. **77-7**

RED DOG SALOON
Arabella Denburg took a vow to avenge her cousin, who was kidnapped d by Quantrill's Raiders. Bella intended to get herself accepted as a camp follower of Quantrill, find the men responsible, and kill them. Her pursuit led her through whorehouses, rapes, and terrible violence until at last she held each of the guilty ones, unsuspecting, between her legs. **68-8**

CHINESE JUSTICE & OTHER STORIES
Li Woo, the Magistrate of Hanchow, swore to destroy all foreign devils. Then he would subject their women to sexual sports, hanging them upside down from pulleys while his two lesbian torturers applied kisses to their tender, naked flesh. Afterwards, they would perform fellatio on his guests, while enduring the sting of the lash. This is what lay in store for every foreign woman in Hanchow! **57-2**

PASSION IN RIO
For four days and nights during the great Carnival, when all sexual inhibitions are temporarily cast aside, Rio de Janiero goes mad. For lesbian designer Kay Arnold, it begins when the lovely junior designer returns her kiss. For the Porters, the carnival begins when they learn how to satisfy each other. The world's most frenzied sexual fiesta! **54-8**

THE DELICIOUS DAUGHTER
Lonely widower Arthur Hadley learns the importance of a firm hand from Eleanor Stanfield and her daughter Betty. "Whenever Betty disobeys me or does something I consider entirely out of character, she is punished for it. And I don't mean Dr. Spock's hogwash! I'm not a modern mother!" **53-X**

LUST OF THE COSSACKS
The countess enjoys watching beautiful peasant girls submit to her perverse lesbian manias. She tutors her only male lover in the joys of erotic torture and in return he lures a beautiful ballerina to her estate, where he intends to present her to the countess as a plaything. Painful pleasures abound when innocence encounters corruption! **41-6**

TURKISH DELIGHTS
"With a roar of triumph, Kemil gripped the girl's breasts and forced her back upon the thick rug on the floor.... He went at her like a bull, buffeting her mercilessly, and she groaned ... to her own amazement, with ecstasy!" Perverse desires indulged! **40-8**

POOR DARLINGS
Here are the impressions and feelings, the excitement and lust, that young women feel when they submit to desire. Not just with male partners—but with women too. Desperate, gasping, scandalous sex! **33-5**

THE LUSTFUL TURK
In 1814, Emily Bartow's ship was captured by Tunisian pirates. The innocent young bride, just entering the bloom of womanhood, was picked to be held for ransom—but held in the harem of the Dey of Tunis where she was sexually broken in by crazed eunuchs, corrupted by lesbian slave girls and then given to the queen as a sexual toy. Turkish lust unleashed! **28-9**

MARY LOVE

THE BEST OF MARY LOVE
The very hottest excerpts of this popular writer. Well-known for her outrageous scenes of unbridled sexual indulgence, Mary Love leaves no coupling untried and no extreme unexplored in these selections from *Mastering Mary Sue, Ecstasy on Fire, Vice Park Place, Wanda,* and *Naughtier at Night.* There's more than a little satisfying something for everyone in this explosive collection of Mary Love's greatest moments! **3099-0**

ECSTASY ON FIRE
An inexperienced young man is initiated by the worldy Melissa Staunton, a well-qualified teacher of the sensual arts. Soon he's in a position—or two—to give lessons of his own! Innocence and experience in an erotic explosion that rocks Monte Carlo society from haughty top to naughty bottom! **3080-6**

NAUGHTIER AT NIGHT
"He wanted to seize her. Her buttocks under the tight suede material were absolutely succulent—carved and molded. What on earth had he done to deserve a morsel of a girl like this?" **3030-X**

VICE PARK PLACE
Rich, lonely divorcée Penelope Luckner drinks alone every night, fending off the advances of sexual suitors that she secretly craves. Then she meets Robbie, a much younger man with a virgin's aching appetites, and together they embark on an affair that breaks all their fantasies wide open! **3008-3**

MASTERING MARY SUE
Mary Sue is a rich nymphomaniac whose husband is determined to pervert her, declare her mentally incompetent, and gain control of her fortune. He brings her to a castle in Europe, where, to Mary Sue's delight, they have stumbled on an unimaginably depraved sex cult! **3005-9**

ANGELA
Angela's game is "look but don't touch," and she drives everyone mad with desire, dancing for their viewing pleasure but never allowing a single caress. Soon her sensual spell is cast, and she's the only one who can break it! **76-9**

ALEXANDER TROCCHI

HELEN AND DESIRE
Helen Seferis' flight from the oppressive village of her birth became a sexual tour of a harsh world. From brothels in Sydney, to opium dens in Singapore, to sheik's harems in Algiers, Helen chronicles her adventures fully in her diary. Each thrilling encounter is examined in the diary of the sensitive and sensual Helen! **3093-8**

THE CARNAL DAYS OF HELEN SEFERIS
P.I. Anthony Harvest is assigned to save Helen Seferis, a beautiful Australian who has been abducted. Following clues in Helen's explicit diary of sexual adventures, he descends into the depths of white slavery. Through slave markets and harems he pursues Helen, the ultimate sexual prize. **3086-5**

WHITE THIGHS
A dark fantasy of obsession from a modern erotic master. This is the story of young Saul and his sexual fixation on the beautiful, tormented Anna of the white thighs. Their scorching and dangerous passion leads to murder and madness every time they submit. Saul must possess Anna again and again, no matter what or who stands in his way. A disturbing masterpiece! **3009-1**

SCHOOL FOR SIN
When Peggy leaves her country home behind for the bright lights of Dublin, her sensuous nature leads to her seduction by a stranger. He recruits her into a training school where no one knows what awaits them at graduation, but each student is sure to be well schooled in sex! **89-0**

MY LIFE AND LOVES (THE 'LOST' VOL.)
What happens when you try to fake a sequel to the most scandalous autobiography of the 20th century? If the "forgers" are two of the most important figures in modern erotica, you get a masterpiece, and THIS IS IT! **52-1**

MARCUS VAN HELLER

ADAM & EVE
Adam and Eve long to escape their dull lives by achieving stardom—she in the theater, and he in the art world. Eve soon finds herself acting cozy on the casting couch, while Adam must join a bizarre sex cult to further his artistic career. Everyone has their price in this electrifying tale of ambition and desire! **93-9**

KIDNAP
P.I. Harding is called in to investigate a mysterious kidnapping case involving the rich and powerful. Along the way he has the pleasure of "interrogating" an exotic dancer named Jeanne and a beautiful English reporter, as he finds himself further enmeshed in the sleazy international crime underworld. **90-4**

LUSCIDIA WALLACE

FOR SALE BY OWNER
Susie was overwhelmed by the lavishness of the yacht, the glamour of the guests. But she didn't know the plans they had for her. How many sweet young women were taught the pleasures of service in this floating prison? How many had suffered the same exquisite punishments? And how many gave as much delight as the newly-wicked Susie? **3064-4**

THE ICE MAIDEN
Edward Canton has ruthlessly seized everything he wants in life, with one exception: Rebecca Esterbrook. Frustrated by his inability to seduce her with money, he kidnaps her and whisks her away to his remote island compound, where she learns to shed her inhibitions and accept caresses from both men and women. **3001-6**

KATY'S AWAKENING
Katy thinks she's been rescued after a terrible car wreck. Little does she suspect that she's been ensnared by a ring of swingers whose tastes run to domination and unimaginably depraved sex parties. With no means of escape, Katy becomes the newest initiate into this private club—and is soon welcomed personally by each demanding and perverse member! **74-2**

DON WINSLOW

CLAIRE'S GIRLS
You knew when she walked by that there was something special about that woman. She was one of Claire's girls, a woman carefully dressed and groomed to fill a special role, to capture a look, to fit an image meticulously crafted by the sophisticated proprietess of an exclusive escort agency. **108-X**

GLORIA'S INDISCRETION
"He looked up at her. Gloria stood passively, her hands loosely at her sides, her eyes still closed, a dreamy expression on her face ... She sensed his hungry eyes on her, could almost feel his burning gaze on her body, and she was aware of the answering lusty need in her loins...." **3094-6**

MASQUERADE READERS

THE COMPLETE EROTIC READER
The very best in erotic writing—from the scandalous to the sublime—come together in a wicked collection sure to stimulate even the most jaded and "sophisticated" palates. All inhibitions are surrendered, and no desire is left unflaunted in these steamy celebrations of the body erotic. **3063-6**

THE VELVET TONGUE
An orgy of oral gratification! *The Velvet Tongue* celebrates the most mouth-watering, lip-smacking, tongue-twisting action. A feast of fellatio and succulent *soixante-neuf* awaits at this steamy suck-fest. **3029-6**

A MASQUERADE READER
Infamously strict lessons are learned at the hand of *The English Governess* and *Nina Foxton*, where the notorious Nina proves herself a very harsh taskmistress. Scandalous confessions are to be found in *The Diary of an Angel*, and the harrowing story of a woman whose desires drove her to the ultimate sacrifice in *Thongs* completes this collection. **84-X**

INTIMATE PLEASURES

Try a tempting morsel of the forbidden liaisons in *The Prodigal Virgin* and *Eveline*, or the bizarre public displays of carnality in *The Gilded* and *The Story of Monique*, or the insatiable cravings in *The Misfortunes of Mary* and *Darling/Innocence*. **38-6**

LAVENDER ROSE

A classic collection of lesbian erotica: from the writings of Sappho, the queen of the women-lovers of ancient Greece, whose debaucheries on her island have remained infamous for all time, to the turn-of-the-century *Black Book of Lesbianism*; from *Tips to Maidens* to *Crimson Hairs*, a recent lesbian saga. **30-0**

EASTERN EROTICA

DEVA DASI

Dedicated to the cult of the Dasis, the sacred women of India who devoted their lives to the fulfillment of the senses, this book reveals the secret sexual rites of Shiva. **29-7**

HOUSES OF JOY

A masterpiece of China's splendid erotic literature. This book is based on the *Ching P'ing Mei*, banned many times. Despite its frequent suppression, it has somehow managed to survive—read it and see why! **51-3**

KAMA HOURI

Ann Pemberton, daughter of a British commander in India, runs away with her servant. Forced to live in a harem, she accepts her position and offers herself to any warrior who wishes to mount her. **39-4**

THE CLASSIC COLLECTION

INITIATION RITES

Every naughty detail of a young woman's breaking in! Under the thorough tutelage of the perverse Miss Clara Birchem, Julia learns her wicked lessons well. During the course of her amorous studies, the resourceful young lady is joined by an assortment of characters—each hellbent on a lifetime of excess! **120-9**

TABLEAUX VIVANTS

Fifteen breathtaking tales of erotic passion. Upstanding ladies and gents soon adopt more comfortable positions, as wicked thoughts explode into sinfully scrumptious acts and ingenious variations. Carnal extremes and explorations abound in this tribute to the spirit of Eros—the lustiest common denominator! **121-7**

LADY F.

A wild and uncensored tale of Victorian passions and penalties. Master Kidrodstock suffers deliciously at the hands of the stunningly cruel and sensuous Lady Flayskin—the only woman capable of taming his wayward impulses. Pleasures are paid for dearly in this scorching diary of submission and delectable penalties. **102-0**

MAN WITH A MAID

The adventures of Jack and Alice have delighted readers for eight decades! A classic of its genre, *Man with a Maid* tells an outrageous tale of desire, revenge, and submission that is bound to keep yet another generation breathless. **3065-2**

MAN WITH A MAID II

Jack's back! With the assistance of the perverse Alice, he embarks again on a trip through every erotic extreme. Jack leaves no one unsatisfied—least of all, himself, and Alice is always certain to outdo herself in her capacity to corrupt and control. An incendiary sequel. **3071-7**

MAN WITH A MAID: The Conclusion

The final chapter in the epic saga of lust that has thrilled readers for decades. The adulterous woman who is corrected with enthusiasm and the clumsy maid who receives grueling guidance are just two who benefit from these lessons! **3013-X**

THE YELLOW ROOM

Two legendary erotic stories. The "yellow room" holds the secrets of lust, lechery, and the lash. There, bare-bottomed, spread-eagled, and open to the world, demure Alice Darvell soon learns to love her lickings. Even more exciting is the second torrid tale of hot heiress Rosa Coote and her adventures in punishment and pleasure with her two sexy, sadistic servants, Jane and Jemima. Feverishly erotic! **96-3**

THE ENGLISH GOVERNESS

When Lord Lovell's son was expelled from his prep school for masturbation, his father hired a very proper governess to tutor the boy—giving her strict instructions not to spare the rod to break him of his bad habits. But governess Harriet Marwood was addicted to domination. The downward path to perversion! **43-2**

PLEASURES AND FOLLIES

The exploits of a libertine: "Ashamed by excesses provoked by my reading, I compiled a well-seasoned Erotikon and it excited me to such a degree that I ... well, pick up my book and see whether it has a similar effect upon you." A shocking volume chronicling each lurid excess of a man for whom there are no sexual limits! **26-2**

STUDENTS OF PASSION

When she arrives at the prestigious Academy, Francine is young, innocent, and eager to learn what she needs to get by in life. Her teachers and schoolmates enroll her in a course devoted to passion, anatomy, and lust ... and Francine embarks on a course of study sure to leave her breathless—and at the head of her class! **22-X**

SACRED PASSIONS

Young Augustus comes into the heavenly sanctuary seeking protection from the enemies of his debt-ridden father. Within these walls he learns lessons he could never have imagined and soon concludes that the joys of the body far surpass those of the spirit. **21-1**

THE NUNNERY TALES

The Abbess forces her rites of sexual initiation on any maiden who falls into her hands. After exposure to the Mother Superior and her lustful nuns, sweet Emilie, Louise, and the other novices are sexual novices no longer. Each devotes her nubile body to the pursuit of distinctly worldly pleasures. Cloistered concubinage! **20-3**

CLASSIC EROTIC BIOGRAPHIES

THE ROMANCES OF BLANCHE LA MARE

When Blanche loses her husband, it becomes clear she'll need a job. She sets her sights on the stage—and soon encounters a cast of lecherous characters intent on making her path to sucksess as hot and hard as possible! Blanche stops at nothing—and stoops to everything—in her quest to make it *big*. **101-2**

MAUDE RIVERS

Under the tutelage of Charles, Maude learns to abandon the restraints of her strict upbringing and embrace the rewards of unbridled sexual indulgence. The lustful Charles leads his lovely charge on an erotic journey of breathtaking variety, and introduces her to a cast of insatiable accomplices. **3087-3**

KATE PERCIVAL

Kate, "the Belle of Delaware," divulges the secrets of her scandalous life, from her earliest sexual experiments to the deviations she learns to love. Nothing is secret, and no holes are barred in this titillating tell-all that reveals the hidden lives of turn-of-the-century lads and ladies. **3072-5**

THE STORY OF MONIQUE

Between the lesbians who came to Sonia's parties, and the convent where nuns and monks fell upon each other in orgiastic madness, Monique soon discovered within herself an endless appetite for sex! **42-4**

THE FURTHER ADVENTURES OF MADELEINE

"What mortal pen can describe these driven orgasmic transports?" writes Madeleine as she explores Paris' sexual underground. She discovers that the finest clothes may cover the most twisted personalities of all.! **04-1**

THE AMERICAN COLLECTION

LOVE'S ILLUSION

Elizabeth Renard yearned for the body of Dan Harrington. Then she discovers Harrington's secret weakness: a need to be humiliated and punished. She makes him her slave, and together they commence a journey into depravity that leaves nothing to the imagination—*nothing!* **100-4**

THE RELUCTANT CAPTIVE

Sarah is kidnapped by ruthless outlaws who kill her husband and burn their prosperous ranch. Her journey takes her from the bordellos of the Wild West to the bedrooms of Boston, until she is bought at last by a mysterious stranger from her past. **3022-9**

LUSTY LESSONS

David Elston had everything except the ability to fulfill the unrelenting demands of his passion. His efforts end in failure until he meets a voluptuous stranger who takes him to a forbidden land of pleasure. **31-9**

DANCE HALL GIRLS

The dance hall studio in Modesto was ruthless trap for men and women of all ages. They learned to dance under the tutelage of sexual professionals. So grateful were they for the attention, they opened their hearts and their wallets. Scandalous sexual slavery! **44-0**

TICKLED PINK

From her spyroom, Emily sees Lady Lovesport tongue-whip her maid into a frenzy as Mr. Everard enters from behind. Emily is joined in her spying by young Harry, who practices the positions he observes. They become active participants in group sex! An erotic vacation! **58-0**

THE GILDED LILY

Lily knows what she wants—pleasure, passion, and new experiences. But more than that, she wants the big break that will launch her career in the movies. She looks for it at Hollywood's most private party, where nothing is forbidden and the only rule is sexual excess! **25-4**

THE PRODIGAL VIRGIN

Not all of America was depressed in the 1930s. In a summer colony on the shores of Lake Michigan, the waters came to a boil. Man explored woman; a young wife and her husband formed a threesome; and the wealthy and socially prominent were seduced into an orgiastic world of ecstasies. **23-8**

MAUDE RIVERS

ANONYMOUS

THE MASQUERADE LIBRARY

Title	Code	Price
ADAM & EVE	93-9	$4.95
AFFINITIES	3113-6	$4.95
ALL THE WAY	3023-7	$4.95
ALL-STUD	3104-7	$4.95
AN ALIZARIN LAKE READER	3106-3	$4.95
ANGELA	76-9	$4.95
APPLICANT, THE	3038-5	$4.95
ARENA, THE	3083-0	$4.95
ASK ISADORA	61-1	$4.95
AUTOBIOGRAPHY OF A FLEA III	94-7	$4.95
B.M.O.C.	3077-6	$4.95
BAD HABITS	3068-7	$4.95
BADBOY FANTASIES	3049-0	$4.95
BAYOU BOY	3084-9	$4.95
BEAST OF BURDEN	3105-5	$6.95
BEST OF MARY LOVE, THE	3099-7	$4.95
BIG SHOTS	3112-8	$4.95
BOUDOIR, THE	85-8	$4.95
CANNIBAL FLOWER	72-6	$4.95
CAPTIVE MAIDENS	3014-8	$4.95
CARNAL DAYS OF HELEN SEFERIS, THE	3086-5	$4.95
CAROLINE'S CONTRACT	3122-5	$4.95
CAROUSEL	3051-2	$4.95
CATALYST, THE	3015-6	$4.95
CHINESE JUSTICE & OTHER STORIES	57-2	$4.95
CINDERELLA	3024-5	$4.95
CLAIRE'S GIRLS	3108-X	$4.95
CLARA	80-7	$4.95
COMPLETE EROTIC READER , THE	3063-6	$4.95
COMPLETE PLAYGIRL FANTASIES, THE	3075-X	$4.95
CRUMBLING FAÇADE	3043-1	$4.95
DANCE HALL GIRLS	44-0	$4.95
DARLING • INNOCENCE	3047-4	$4.95
DEADLY LIES	3076-8	$4.95
DELICIOUS DAUGHTER, THE	53-X	$4.95
DEMON HEAT	79-3	$4.95
DEPRAVED ANGELS	92-0	$4.95
DEVA-DASI	29-7	$4.95
DISCIPLINE OF ODETTE, THE	3033-4	$4.95
DISTANT LOVE	3056-3	$4.95
DREAM CRUISE	3045-8	$4.95
DUKE COSIMO	3052-0	$4.95
ECSTASY ON FIRE	3080-6	$4.95
END OF INNOCENCE	77-7	$4.95
ENGLISH GOVERNESS, THE	43-2	$4.95
EVIL COMPANIONS	3067-9	$4.95
EXPOSED	3126-8	$4.95
FESTIVAL OF VENUS	37-8	$4.95
FOR SALE BY OWNER	3064-4	$4.95
FORBIDDEN DELIGHTS	81-5	$4.95
FRAGRANT ABUSES	88-2	$4.95
FURTHER ADVENTURES OF MADELEINE, THE	04-1	$4.95
GARDEN OF DELIGHT	3058-X	$4.95
GILDED LILY, THE	25-4	$4.95
GLORIA'S INDISCRETION	3094-6	$4.95
GOLDEN YEARS	3069-5	$4.95
HAREM SONG	73-4	$4.95
HEIR • THE KING, THE	3048-2	$4.95
HELEN AND DESIRE	3093-8	$4.95
HELLFIRE	3085-7	$4.95
HELOISE	3073-3	$4.95

my darling dominatrix

- DEVOID OF SLEAZE AND SHAME
- A VERY POWERFUL BOOK ...
  —MISTRESS BRIGIT

GRANT ANTREWS

$6.95 (CANADA $7.95) • RHINOCEROS BOOKS

Title	Code	Price
ICE MAIDEN, THE	3001-6	$4.95
ILLUSIONS	3074-1	$4.95
IMRE	3019-9	$4.95
INITIATION RITES	3120-9	$4.95
INSTRUMENTS OF THE PASSION, THE	3010-5	$4.95
INTIMATE PLEASURES	38-6	$4.95
JADE EAST	60-2	$4.95
JAZZ AGE, THE	48-3	$4.95
JENNIFER	3107-1	$4.95
JUDITH BOSTON	87-4	$4.95
KAMA HOURI	39-4	$4.95
KATE PERCIVAL	3072-5	$4.95
KATY'S AWAKENING	74-2	$4.95
KIDNAP	90-4	$4.95
KUNG FU NUNS	3031-8	$4.95
LADY F.	3102-0	$4.95
LAVENDER ROSE	30-0	$4.95
LEATHERWOMEN	3095-4	$4.95
LETHAL SILENCE	3125-X	$4.95
LEWD CONDUCT	3091-1	$4.95
LOVE AND SURRENDER	3082-2	$4.95
LOVE IN WARTIME	3044-X	$4.95
LOVE'S ILLUSION	3100-4	$4.95
LUST	82-3	$4.95
LUST OF THE COSSACKS	41-6	$4.95
LUSTFUL TURK, THE	28-9	$4.95
LUSTY LESSONS	31-9	$4.95
MAN WITH A MAID	3065-2	$4.95
MAN WITH A MAID II	3071-7	$4.95
MAN WITH A MAID: THE CONCLUSION	3013-X	$4.95
MANEATER	3103-9	$6.95
MARKETPLACE, THE	3096-2	$6.95
MASQUERADE READER, A	84-X	$4.95
MASTER OF TIMBERLAND	3059-8	$4.95
MASTERING MARY SUE	3005-9	$4.95
MAUDE CAMERON	3087-3	$4.95
MEMBER OF THE CLUB	3079-2	$4.95
MEN AT WORK	3027-X	$4.95
MIKE AND ME	3035-0	$4.95
MILES DIAMOND	3116-7	$4.95
MISS HIGH HEELS	3066-0	$4.95
MISTRESS MINE	3109-8	$4.95
MR. BENSON	3041-5	$4.95
MUSCLE BOUND	3028-8	$4.95
MY DARLING DOMINATRIX	3055-5	$4.95
MY LIFE AND LOVES (THE 'LOST' VOLUME)	52-1	$4.95
NAUGHTIER AT NIGHT	3030-X	$4.95
NUNNERY TALES, THE	20-3	$4.95
OBSESSIONS	3012-1	$4.95
ODD WOMEN	3123-3	$4.95
ORF	3110-1	$6.95
PASSAGE & OTHER STORIES	3057-1	$4.95
PASSION IN RIO	54-8	$4.95
PAULA	3036-9	$4.95
PLEASURE THIEVES, THE	36-X	$4.95
PLEASURES & FOLLIES	26-2	$4.95
PLEASURES AND FOLLIES	26-2	$4.95
POOR DARLINGS	33-5	$4.95
PORTABLE TITIAN BERESFORD, THE	3114-4	$4.95
PRISONER, THE	3011-3	$4.95
PRIVATE LESSONS	3116-0	$4.95
PRODIGAL VIRGIN	23-8	$4.95

Title	Code	Price
PROFESSIONAL CHARMER	3003-2	$4.95
PROVINCETOWN SUMMER	3040-7	$4.95
RAWHIDE LUST	55-6	$4.95
RED DOG SALOON	68-8	$4.95
RELUCTANT CAPTIVE, THE	3022-9	$4.95
REPENTANCE OF LORRAINE, THE	3124-1	$6.95
REUNION IN FLORENCE	3070-9	$4.95
ROMANCES OF BLANCHE LE MARE, THE	3101-2	$4.95
ROSEMARY LANE	3078-4	$4.95
SABINE	3046-6	$4.95
SACRED PASSIONS	21-1	$4.95
SCHOOL FOR SIN	89-0	$4.95
SCORPIOUS EQUATION, THE	3119-5	$4.95
SECRET DANGER	3111-X	$4.95
SECRET LIFE, A	3017-2	$4.95
SECRET RECORD, THE	3039-3	$4.95
SECRETS OF THE CITY	03-3	$4.95
SENSATIONS	3081-4	$6.95
SEX ON DOCTORS ORDERS	3092-X	$4.95
SEXPERT, THE	3034-2	$4.95
SEXUAL ADVENTURES OF SHERLOCK HOLMES, THE	3097-0	$4.95
SILK AND STEEL	3032-6	$4.95
SINS OF THE CITIES OF THE PLAIN	3016-4	$4.95
SKIRTS	3115-2	$4.95
SLAVE ISLAND	3006-7	$4.95
SLAVES OF CAMEROON	3026-1	$4.95
SLAVES OF THE EMPIRE	3054-7	$4.95
SLOW BURN	3042-3	$4.95
SORRY I ASKED	3090-3	$4.95
STASI SLUT	3050-4	$4.95
STOLEN MOMENTS	3098-9	$4.95
STORY OF MONIQUE, THE	42-4	$4.95
STUDENTS OF PASSION	22-X	$4.95
SWEET DREAMS	3062-8	$4.95
SWEETEST FRUIT, THE	95-5	$4.95
SWITCH, THE	3061-X	$4.95
TABLEAUX VIVANTS	3121-7	$4.95
TALES FROM THE DARK LORD	3053-9	$4.95
TELENY	3020-2	$4.95
THREE WOMEN	3025-3	$4.95
TICKELD PINK	58-0	$4.95
TOURNIQUET	3060-1	$4.95
TURKISH DELIGHTS	40-8	$4.95
VELVET TONGUE, THE	3029-6	$4.95
VENUS IN FURS	3089-X	$6.95
VICE PARK PLACE	3008-3	$4.95
WAYWARD	3004-0	$4.95
WET FOREVER, THE	3117-9	$6.95
WHITE THIGHS	3009-1	$4.95
WILD HEART	3007-5	$4.95
WOMEN AT WORK	3088-1	$4.95
YELLOW ROOM, THE	96-3	$4.95
YOUTHFUL DAYS	3018-0	$4.95

STASI SLUT

ANONYMOUS

ORDERING IS EASY!

MC/VISA orders can be placed by calling our toll-free number

PHONE 800-458-9640 / FAX 212 986-7355

or mail the coupon below to:

Masquerade Books 801 Second Avenue New York, New York. 10017

BUY ANY FOUR BOOKS AND CHOOSE ONE ADDITIONAL BOOK AS YOUR FREE GIFT.

QTY.	TITLE	A 113-6	NO.	PRICE
		SUBTOTAL		
		POSTAGE & HANDLING		
		TOTAL		

Add $1.00 Postage and Handling for tthe first book and 50¢ for each additional book. Outside the U.S. add $2.00 for the first book, $1.00 for each additional book. New York state residents add 8-1/4% sales tax.

NAME _____

ADDRESS _____ **APT. #** _____

CITY _____ **STATE** _____ **ZIP** _____

TEL. (____ **)** _____

PAYMENT: ☐ CHECK   ☐ MONEY ORDER   ☐ VISA   ☐ MC

CARD NO. _____ **EXP. DATE** _____

PLEASE ALLOW 4-6 WEEKS DELIVERY. NO C.O.D. ORDERS. PLEASE MAKE ALL CHECKS PAYABLE TO MASQUERADE BOOKS. PAYABLE IN U.S. CURRENCY ONLY

ANONYMOUS

Garden of Delight